OTHERS AVAILABLE BY DK HOLMBERG

The Dark Ability

The Dark Ability
The Heartstone Blade
The Tower of Venass
Blood of the Watcher

The Cloud Warrior Saga

Chased by Fire
Bound by Fire
Changed by Fire
Fortress of Fire
Forged in Fire
Serpent of Fire
Servant of Fire

The Painter Mage

Shifted Agony
Arcane Mark
Painter for Hire
Stolen Compass

The Lost Garden

Keeper of the Forest
The Desolate Bond
Keeper of Light

THE DARK ABILITY

THE DARK ABILITY
BOOK 1

ASH Publishing
dkholmberg.com

The Dark Ability

ISBN-13: 978-1523228508
ISBN-10: 1523228504

ASH Publishing
dkholmberg.com

THE DARK ABILITY

THE DARK ABILITY
BOOK 1

CHAPTER 1

Rsiran crouched atop the rocky outcropping, looking down upon Elaeavn. Clouds swirled distantly above the city, and a wind he hadn't felt below pulled at his shirt. As usual, when he sat atop the flat-topped Krali Rock, he stared down at the Floating Palace, wondering what it would be like to live within the high white walls. At least here, standing atop Krali, he could pretend he was someone different, and not the son of a smith the Great Watcher had cursed.

From here, the daylight was prolonged. Already down in the palace, pale blue lights glowed in a few windows, the soft light so different than anywhere else in the city. Elvraeth light. Around the rest of the city, simple candles flickered for light. Smoke drifted lazily from chimneys before catching the wind and rising high into the sky to join the clouds.

Rsiran knew he should return to his parents' home, but he felt at peace high above Elaeavn. Once back in the city, the ever-present knot at the pit of his stomach would return, gnawing painfully. Unlike everyone else with a real ability, that knot would probably never leave.

Another gust of wind blew across the rock, a mixture of smoke and the distant sea. The vague scent of lorcith from the mines in the north drifted with the wind, bitter and sharp and so familiar from years spent at the smith with his father.

He sighed. Staying here would do nothing but further irritate his father. Closing his eyes, he Slid, stepping from atop the rock and back to his house in the middle of the city. The Slide took him to the alley outside the house, careful to conceal his return. Rsiran considered simply Sliding into his room, but that opened him to more questions than he wanted. As far as his father was concerned, his ability should never be used. Only those cursed by the Great Watcher had the ability to Slide, and—as his father saw it—it was an ability meant for little more than thieving and killing. That Rsiran knew of no others with his ability meant his father was probably right.

His sister sat as if waiting for him as he opened the door. "You should not have returned," Alyse said.

Rsiran let the door close silently behind him and looked over at his sister's oval face and deep green eyes, sleek black hair tied over her shoulder, and frowned. "Where else would I have gone?"

She shrugged. "Tonight will not be a good night for you."

He swallowed. Few nights were good for him anymore. Ever since their father had learned of his ability, Rsiran had feared returning, sneaking into the house as late as possible to avoid him. Better than sleeping in the street. "Is he here?"

She looked down the hall and nodded. "A bottle deep."

"Of?"

"Ale. You know the shop isn't doing well."

She didn't need to tell him that. As his father's apprentice, he saw how little work they had. Even the journeyman Thenis knew something was off.

Rsiran sighed. It was bad enough when his father was angry with him about his ability. It was worse when he was drunk. That was how he'd learned he was a Slider in the first place.

"Can you not use it?" Alyse asked.

He glared at her. "Can't all have your gifts."

He pushed his mental barrier back into place. Years of living with her had trained him to be careful around Alyse. She was Sighted and a Reader. Almost as blessed as the Elvraeth themselves. But all in Elaeavn had learned to protect themselves from Readers, learning early in life how to build mental barriers.

She returned his stare defiantly. Though he was taller and stronger, she did not fear him, using the two years she had on him to her advantage. "I will not apologize for the fact that the Great Watcher gifted me with my abilities."

Rsiran pushed past her. "You were doubly blessed while I was cursed," he muttered. "At least that's how *they* view it."

"Rsiran!" she hissed.

He took another step before stopping and turning back to her. Worry marked her face, twisting the corners of her eyes. One slender hand clutched the small necklace hanging from the lorcith chain their father had made, a Shaer gift given when her abilities had manifested, a gift so rare for any but the Elvraeth to possess. He would receive no such gift from his father.

"Maybe you should…"

"Should what?" he whispered. "Not return? Stay out on the street? Give up my 'ship?"

To her credit, Alyse did not look away. "Yes."

His heart dropped. Even Alyse abandoned him. "Where would I go?"

She shook her head but did not answer.

Rsiran glared at her for another moment before turning away and sulking down the narrow hall toward his room. He could simply Slide into his room, but if his father discovered that he did *that*, there would be no return. At least this way, he could pretend the ability did not exist.

As he grabbed the handle to the door, he smelled his father's approach. The stink of ale weighed heavily in the air, burning at Rsiran's nostrils.

"'S late," his father rumbled.

Rsiran froze, uncertain if an assault would follow.

"Ya get the shop cleaned?" his father asked.

He turned and faced his father. Nearly the same height but twice as wide, his father loomed over him. His eyes were reddened and his face ruddy. Soot still smeared his cheeks and clothes from the forge. The fumes from the ale mixed with the soot.

"The shop is clean," Rsiran answered, straightening his back.

"Took ya that long, did it?"

Rsiran blinked. Again, he considered Sliding away. That he would think such a thing only reinforced how badly his father treated him, but doing so would only make everything worse. He considered his next words carefully. "I worked at the forge a bit," he admitted. His father would see the results of his work regardless.

Reddened eyes narrowed. "Did I say ya could work the forge?"

Rsiran took a steadying breath. If his father became unwilling to sponsor his apprenticeship, he truly would be lost. Working at the forge was the only thing he enjoyed. "Sir?"

His father stumbled, catching himself on the wall near Rsiran's head with a beefy hand. Rsiran flinched, unable to help himself. A dark look flittered across his father's pale green eyes, the mark of their people.

"You think you already know enough?" he asked. "Think yourself ready to be a journeyman?"

"I'm nearly of age, and I have apprenticed now for three years."

His father pushed off from the wall with a grunt. He wobbled briefly as he stared at Rsiran. "Three years and you think you can run my shop?"

"That's not what I—"

"Three years and you can work *my* forge?" he said, raising his voice.

His mother slipped into the hall, wearing a pale yellow robe and slippers. Her face was drawn, and her greying hair pulled severely over her head into a tight roll. Just once, he hoped she would intervene instead of simply watching. Her eyes flared deeper green as she Read his father. As drunk as he was, his barriers were likely down. Not for the first time, Rsiran wished he shared *that* gift, as useless as it often was in Elaeavn.

"You pay attention when I speak to you!" his father shouted.

Rsiran snapped his eyes back to his father. His heart hammered. Get away, back to his room, close the door, and let his father sleep off the ale. Tomorrow he could pretend none of this happened. "Father?"

His father's mouth turned into a sneer. "Do not call me 'Father.' Not while I hold your 'ship."

"Yes, sir," Rsiran said. He tried slipping back a step, but his heel hit the wall.

His father leaned in, his breath hot and stinking of ale. "Did you fire down the forge after you finished your 'work'?"

Rsiran blinked, sudden panic freezing his mind. *Had* he tampered the coals? Leaving the forge blazing could damage it, or worse, the shop.

"I think so," he stammered.

His father leaned back and shifted his weight. In an instant, he drew back and slapped Rsiran across the face with an open palm. The force sent him flying backward and slamming into the wall. "You think?" he roared.

Rsiran clutched his cheek. Heat burned across his face, and he leaned forward, steadying himself from falling. "I will return to the shop and check," he managed to say.

His father tottered backward and leaned against the opposite wall. "You will tell me if you failed to tamper the forge." The rage in his voice seemed to be fading, the effort of striking him stealing some of his anger.

Rsiran stood and nodded.

"Restock the coals while you are there."

Rsiran could only nod again.

His mother would not meet his eyes as he turned. She stood with arms crossed over her chest, her jaw set tightly in a frown. As usual, she said nothing.

Rsiran started toward the front of the house. Alyse stood near the door, her face less severe than their mother's but no more compassion lining it. "I told you that you should not have returned," she whispered.

He looked down at her and shrugged. "Where else would I go?" he asked again.

As he grabbed the handle to the door, his father lumbered out of the hall. "Rsiran."

Rsiran turned, hoping for an apology, a show of emotion, of *something* that would tell him that he was useful. "Sir?"

"What were you forging?"

Rsiran noted the dangerous tone in his voice. "Iron," he lied. He did not dare mention that he used lorcith.

His father sniffed. "And what did you make?"

Rsiran blinked. "Something simple."

His father snorted. "Simple. Don't ya go tarnishing my shop with any dark creations." He coughed and bounced off another wall. "Another mistake, and I'll send you to the mines till you're better prepared for your 'ship." Without waiting for a response, his father turned and weaved back down the hall, his wide back slowly fading into the shadows.

Rsiran stepped out the door and back onto the street. Half of him hoped his mother or sister would come after him; tell him his father was being unreasonable. But they would not. Alyse wouldn't risk angering either of them, and Rsiran could not seem to stop.

Rain now fell from the grey sky. The air had a hint of salty sea spray mixed with the smells from the fishmongers wafting up from the docks. He considered Sliding to the shop but decided against it. Walking might clear his head, and the rain would cool the flame in his cheek where his father had struck him.

Pulling his cloak tight around his neck, he started up the slanted street. Rainwater cascaded down carefully set stones, forming small pools in the wide flat areas between streets. Narrow drains filtered the water through hidden pipes, draining toward the sea far below. The earliest city engineers were artisans in how they designed the city, and from above, the effect appeared like a waterfall.

Few others were out in the streets tonight, the rain keeping doors and shutters closed. Rsiran didn't mind the damp. His cloak kept him warm, and his boots kept his feet dry. After spending all day sweating in the heat of the forge, the rain felt refreshing. As he walked, his hand drifted to the solid metal blade he had forged earlier.

It was made entirely of lorcith mined in the Ilphaesn Mountain to the north. Lorcith had long been coveted for its durability and hardness. Items forged out of the precious metal were highly valued in places like Asador or Yleran, great cities to the east and north, far past the Aisl Forest. Never weapons, though. The Elaeavn smiths would never create weapons out of lorcith; the ruling Elvraeth forbade such craftings, though Rsiran had not yet learned why. Another thing his apprenticeship had not yet taught him.

Rsiran rubbed his finger along the blade, wincing as he felt the sharp edge that had taken hours to hone, hours when he was supposed to be organizing and cleaning his father's shop. His finger slid over the mark he had etched into the base. The chunk of lorcith had almost sung to him, demanding to be shaped into the slender blade.

The rain tapered to little more than a steady mist as he neared the shop. All around were other stores, most closed for the evening. Another smithy was down the street, flickering light filtered through closed shutters. The steady muted clang of hammer on metal rang out.

Not for the first time, he wished his father had apprenticed him with a different smith. Such an arrangement had been done before and would likely benefit them both. Instead, his father chose to torment him. Rather than teaching him to work the forge, his father forced him to clean the shop and keep the coals lit, telling him he would learn first by watching. Rarely, he was allowed to be striker, doing little more than swinging the heavy hammer. To him, those were the good days.

Inside the shop, a soft glow radiated from the forge, heating the room. He hadn't tampered the coals as his father had asked. Rsiran's heart sank. He would have to tell his father. He hoped in the morning, the punishment would be less severe. He considered lying, but never knew how much the journeymen who worked in the shop shared with his father. Getting caught in a lie would be worse than admitting what he'd neglected.

Rsiran sighed and moved to the small lantern set atop one of the workbenches, without Sight, he saw little more than simple shadows in the darkness. He lit the lantern using the coals from the forge, and it bloomed to life.

The shop was simply built out of stone like most of the buildings in Elaeavn. Tools hung on hooks along one wall. A bin beneath them held hunks of unshaped metal. His father's recent works stacked atop a long shelf along the opposite wall. Mostly lanterns, decorative platters, and utensils—all items that sold well. He pulled the slender blade out of his pocket and set it next to work done by his father, spinning it on the table. A waste of lorcith. A forbidden forging. Much like his ability, one given by the Great Watcher to thieves and murderers, it was something he had to hide.

Rsiran sighed. If he could change the ability given to him, he would. Something useful, like Sight or perhaps Listening. Anything but an ability he was compelled to hide.

Returning to the forge, he began to tamp the coals but stopped. More than anything, he needed to clear his head before he returned. Maybe give his father enough time to fall asleep.

The lorcith called to him, a strange and seductive call that he couldn't resist. Though he knew he shouldn't, he took an unshaped piece, fired up the forge, and began heating the metal. He would show his father he could smith items of value. Perhaps then, he would let him do more than simply sweep the floors.

CHAPTER 2

ANIC SET IN AS RSIRAN REALIZED that he'd made another slender blade, a twin of the first. Weapons were forbidden for him to forge, but even more so out of lorcith. How long had he been hammering? Would his father still be awake when he returned home, determined to know if he had put out the coals, or would he wonder what had taken him so long to check the forge?

As he looked at the blade, he still couldn't help but feel proud of what he had created. The shape matched the first perfectly and had a pleasing heft. Not surprisingly, the lorcith folded well and took a sharp edge as he honed it on the grinding wheel. It didn't matter that Rsiran had no use for such blades. The crafting mattered.

Pocketing both blades, he hurriedly put out the coals. After extinguishing the lantern, he left the shop, careful to lock the door behind him. He would not provide his father with another excuse to punish him. The missing lorcith would be reason enough. Hopefully, he wouldn't notice. These days he noticed less and less.

Drizzling rain still misted down. Rsiran rubbed a hand across his face and pulled away a handful of dark soot. He wiped his hands on his cloak, feeling the reassuring weight of the blades hidden in one of the pockets. In spite of himself, he smiled. For some reason, it felt good to have something else that was forbidden besides his ability.

At this hour, the sky was dark, a hint of rolling clouds far overhead and waves crashing along the shore beneath Elaeavn. Somewhere nearby, there came the sound of hushed voices arguing, and he paused to listen, wondering at the source.

"I'll have your money—"

"It's no longer about the money. I have another way for you to repay me."

Rsiran backed into the shadows, suddenly not wanting to be out on the street.

"I don't like the sound of that—"

"Have I ever led you astray? Besides, you wouldn't want your secret discovered, would you?"

A soft laugh drifted out. "Not much of a secret." The voice paused. "What is it you want from me?"

"Tomorrow. Near the docks. I'll show you."

Another laugh. "Dramatic, aren't you? Fine. Tomorrow then."

Rsiran scrambled back, trying to hide, when a shape burst out of the shadows of a nearby alley and crashed into him.

Rsiran fell to the ground in a heap. One of his blades flew from the pocket in his cloak and clattered to the stones. Someone grunted nearby, shuffling on the stone.

He pulled himself to his knees and reached for the blade. Another hand reached it first.

"That's mine." Rsiran tried to keep the terror from his voice and failed. What would happen if this were one of the constables? He couldn't be caught with a lorcith knife. His father wouldn't have to kill him then; he'd be thrown in prison, or worse, sent to the mines to serve penance.

The man standing across from him wore a dark cloak that was not quite black, greying hair slicked back over his head, his sun-weathered face wrinkled at the eyes as he frowned. He spun the knife in his hand. "Yours?" he asked, frowning. "Not a common knife, is it? Not common at all." He spun it in his hand as he looked at the light softly reflecting off the metal. "A knife like this seems like it has a purpose." His voice was as rough as his face. Even in the darkness, Rsiran could tell that his eyes were the palest of greens, a sign of limited ability.

Rsiran nodded. "It's mine," he repeated carefully, praying the man wouldn't recognize what the knife was made from. Violence in this part of Elaeavn was rare, not like in Lower Town. Rsiran had even overheard his father speaking to Seval, one of the other master smiths, about a rebellion, but he found that hard to believe. Still, he couldn't help the nervous flutter he felt in his stomach. He held his hand out but took a step back.

The man held the knife close up to his face. Not Sighted, at least, though as pale as his eyes were, whatever ability he had would be weak. "How would you acquire something of this quality?" the man asked.

Rsiran felt a surge of pride at the compliment. If only his father would pay him such compliments. "I didn't acquire it."

The man frowned again. "Did you steal it?"

Rsiran shook his head. "I…" How to answer? What would this man do? "I made it."

The man turned it over again and looked over at Rsiran. "Made it?" One finger traced the etching near the base of the blade where Rsiran had carved his initials in a flourish, creating a specialized mark. "Are you not a bit young to be a smith?"

Rsiran shrugged. He still had his hand out, and the man final-ly placed the knife into Rsiran's palm. As he pocketed it, it clanged against the other. The man's eyes widened slightly, and the hint of a smile turned the corner of his mouth.

"Not a smith," Rsiran answered. "Still an apprentice." He still couldn't tell which of the two men he'd heard arguing this was. Both had sounded angry, but one of them owed the other money. Would this man rob him of the knives? If he did, what could Rsiran even say?

"Apprentice?" The man laughed, a deep-throated sound that hung in the misty air.

Rsiran shook his head and turned away. His father laughed at him enough; he did not need this stranger to do it too.

"Hey, boy, I didn't mean to offend you."

Rsiran stopped and turned back.

"I'm not used to seeing lorcith blades, at least not anymore. There was a time when our folk made many weapons, knives, and swords of such quality that they were highly prized. Problem was, men killed *for* the blades." He shook his head. "I haven't even seen a blade forged out of lorcith in years and thought that this must be the work of some ancient weapon smith. Most smiths these days don't even mark their work."

Panic settled in his chest, sending his heart racing. Rsiran swal-lowed, trying—and failing—to tamp down his nerves. The etching had felt like a touch of vanity, but he had done it the same, almost drawn to make the marks, as if he had known it was not complete without them.

"Your master must have shown you how to forge such blades." He smiled. "Perhaps the smiths have changed their stance? Work like that…"

He shook his head. "My master," he began, deciding not to men-tion that his father ran the shop—it wouldn't do to get his father in trouble with him, "thinks this blade was a waste of ore."

13

The man frowned. "Waste? Why—because a knife can kill? So can a fork or a platter or whatever else the smiths think is in fashion these days. You hit someone hard enough with lorcith, and they'll die the same as if you cut them."

Rsiran started to turn. The hour was late, and he would have to be up before his father and back in the shop, getting the forge fired up and ready for the day. Lingering in the street would only leave him tired. He didn't want to think what would happen were he to oversleep.

"You thought about selling that knife?" the man asked.

He glanced over his shoulder at the man and shook his head. Other than the smith guild, none were allowed to sell forged lorcith wares. "I already told you I'm only an apprentice," Rsiran said carefully. This man already knew about the lorcith blades. If he wanted, he could report Rsiran to the constables, or worse, to the guild. Then Rsiran would never become a master smith.

The man leaned against a nearby wall, pale eyes holding Rsiran intently. The misting rain didn't seem to bother him, but he ran a hand through his hair, slicking it back. "Because you're an apprentice doesn't mean you can't profit from your work." He smiled. "Knife like that would probably fetch at least three dronr." He shrugged. "Probably quite a bit more outside the city."

"Is that your offer?"

The man leaned forward and his smile broadened. "Didn't say *I* would buy it for three dronr." He laughed and there was darkness in the way that he laughed.

Rsiran started to turn away, ready to run. What was he even doing waiting here? Already he would be home late—probably late enough to anger his father further—that he shouldn't wait any longer.

"Hey, now," the man said, catching his sleeve, "didn't say I would buy it for three dronr, but didn't say I wouldn't buy it at all."

Rsiran reached into his pocket and fingered the knives. He wouldn't have to tell his family where he got the coin and could even use some of the money to buy more lorcith. Then his father wouldn't have any reason to be upset with his forging. "I can't sell it for three dronr," he said. "That would barely pay for the lorcith."

The man narrowed his eyes and took a step forward. A smile stayed fixed on his face and wrinkled the corner of his eyes. Rsiran worried that he might simply take the knife from him again. "Four?" the man asked.

He swallowed. "I would need five dronr."

The man leaned back and looked up at the sky. "Five! And here I thought the Great Watcher finally smiled upon me."

He turned away. Had he pushed his luck too hard? Nothing stopped this man from simply *taking* the knives. Rsiran wouldn't even be able to report the theft.

The man turned back, hand outstretched, five silver dronr cupped in his palm. Rsiran pulled one of the knives out of his pocket and handed it to him, hilt out, taking the dronr and slipping them into a different pocket.

"I probably would have given you more, kid," the man said.

Rsiran let out a nervous laugh. "I probably would have taken three."

The man narrowed his eyes and frowned as he shook his head. Then a deep and hearty laugh erupted from his mouth. "I'm Brusus," he said, extending his hand.

Rsiran hesitated before shaking Brusus's hand, debating whether to share his name. "Rsiran."

"Well, Rsiran, can we get out of the rain? I know a place where we can still get a warm mug of ale."

Thinking of his father, Rsiran shook his head. He needed to get home and to sleep so that he could get up in time to replace the lorcith he'd used. "No ale."

Brusus shrugged, twisting the knife in his hand and glancing to Rsiran's pocket where the other knife remained. "Fine. Come and watch me drink it as I show off your craftsmanship to a few friends. I have a way that you could sell a few more of these."

"I need to get back," he said, starting to pull away. "I have to be in the shop early."

Brusus grabbed him around the shoulders and pulled him down the street, away from home and away from the shop. "What do you mean? It *is* early!"

"I… I can't."

Brusus smiled, and his expression changed as he did, softening and becoming friendlier. "Listen, kid, come along and I won't have to mention anything about your knives. To anyone."

There seemed a hint of a threat, and Rsiran took a step back. Brusus's smile deepened, as if he knew his thoughts. Rsiran fortified his mental barriers, careful to shield his thoughts. What would happen if he *didn't* go with Brusus? Would he find Rsiran's father, and explain how he'd bought the knife? That might be worse than simply going along with the man.

Unable to think of anything different, he let himself be dragged along with Brusus, wishing he'd never made the knives in the first place.

CHAPTER 3

BRUSUS LED RSIRAN to a small tavern near the docks. The stench of the fisheries almost overwhelmed him as they neared Lower Town. Waves crashed steadily along the rocks, giving the streets a sense of rhythm that was missing from Upper Town. Light struggled to filter through the buildings towering overhead, making the shadows appear longer and more twisted than he was accustomed to.

He should not be here. Not down in the dangerous and dirty lower section of the city, awake when he should be sleeping. Dawn would come quickly, and with it, he would have to be up. Each time he had considered pulling away, turning back toward home and his waiting bed, Brusus had grabbed onto his sleeve and pulled him along. Eventually he had come so far that turning back seemed too much work, unless he were to Slide back, but that involved revealing his ability, or at least risking it. That was worse than Brusus knowing that he forged lorcith into knives.

Brusus didn't stop pulling him until they reached a simple stone building. A small etching on one of the stones outside the door provided the only marking that this was a tavern. The door was made of stout oak, heavy and oiled to protect from the spray of sea salt in the air. Brusus swung the door open and pushed Rsiran in first.

Inside was small. A length of counter ran along one wall. A plain hearth angled in the corner where a warm fire flickered. A pair of lanterns hanging on hooks glowed softly with orange light, pushing back whatever shadows the fire missed. Tables made of the same rough oiled oak littered the remaining space. Brusus led him to one where another man sat next to a boy that had to be younger than Rsiran. Both nursed steaming mugs of ale.

"Brusus," the other man said. He was wider than Brusus, and his lined eyes flared green as they approached. A long scar ran from one ear down his check.

Brusus threw himself onto one of the chairs. A smile quirked his mouth. He scanned the room with his pale green eyes before nodding toward the back. "Haern. Quite the night," he said, rubbing his hand through damp hair. "I brought a friend. This is Rsiran."

Haern looked over at Rsiran, eyes flashing a deeper green. "Are you sure you should bring a smith here with what you're—"

Brusus cut him off with a look.

Rsiran wondered how Haern knew, but realized that after a night working at the forge he must be practically covered with dirt and soot. Suddenly, he felt very aware of how dirty he must be, even to these men of Lower Town, and a rising terror about what he was even doing here began to settle in his chest. Would Brusus try to blackmail him into making more knives? Was that the reason he'd brought him here?

Brusus's smile deepened. "Sit," he said, waving toward a tall stool.

Rsiran pulled a chair to the edge of the table. He noticed a small ring with a pale blue stone on Brusus's finger. One of the servers brought over two mugs of ale, setting them in front of Brusus and

Rsiran. Brusus handed him a silver dronr, and the server slipped back toward the counter, leaving them alone.

"How has *your* night gone?" Brusus asked, taking a deep drink from his mug.

Haern looked at Rsiran for a long moment, his eyes a deep green as he watched the newcomer.

"It's okay, Haern."

Haern stared at Rsiran for another moment, before he turned to Brusus. "Thean thinks we should hurry."

Brusus nodded. "And you don't?"

Haern shook his head, his eyes deepening briefly.

Rsiran suddenly understood. Haern was a Seer. The ability was usually confined to the Elvraeth family and probably almost as rare as his ability to Slide, though he knew of none other than him with that dark gift. The weakest Seer could only See moments into the future. Some Saw flashes farther into the future, but they were glimpses only, rarely anything useful. What could Haern See?

"Jessa thinks we should hurry too," Haern said.

Hurry with what? Rsiran wondered.

He worried about what he had fallen into. He'd overheard Brusus arguing about the money, and then he'd bought a knife from him. Now there was whatever Haern referenced. Who were these people?

Brusus shifted his gaze to the other person at the table who had so far been silent. Jessa…so not a boy as he had thought, though her slender face and deep brown hair cut short across the back made her look more like one. A blue flower with wide petals and a spiny stem stuck through her jacket. She watched him with suspicious eyes that were not as dark as Haern's but not nearly as pale as Brusus's. As usual when meeting someone new, Rsiran wondered at her ability. Then he felt the strange sensation of a Reader probing in his mind.

He pushed up the barriers he'd long ago learned to build and turned away from her.

"Why the rush, Jessa?" Brusus asked.

She pursed her lips but said nothing, instead shook her head.

"You think you have something to fear from him?" Brusus asked, tipping his head toward Rsiran.

Jessa looked over at Rsiran. "You're always too trusting, Brusus. How can you be sure you don't?"

Brusus shrugged. "Rsiran here has his own secrets." He reached into his pocket, pulled out the lorcith-forged knife, and set it spinning on the table.

In the pale light of the tavern, the grey metal gleamed dully, as if the lantern light slipped along the surface of the blade. The knife spun along its center before slowly coming to rest with its tip pointed at Rsiran.

Haern set a wide hand atop the knife and held it to the light. "Where did he steal this?" Rsiran noted he said it without any hint of judgment. Haern spun the knife, twirling as if he'd always known it.

Brusus's smile returned with a flash of teeth. Wrinkles at the corners of his eyes deepened and his pale eyes seemed to dance. "Why would he need to steal a blade like that?"

Haern glanced from Brusus to Rsiran. "This is a lorcith blade. I can count on one hand the number of blades I've seen. Can't say I recognize the mark here, though. So—where did he get the knife if he didn't steal it?"

Brusus shook his head. "Haern. Why would a *smith* need to steal a blade like this?"

Haern leaned forward and looked more closely at the knife. "Are you saying he made it?"

Brusus shrugged, taking a long sip of his ale. "That's what he tells me."

Jessa looked from Rsiran to Brusus, green flaring in her eyes.

"How much did you pay for this blade, Brusus?" Haern asked.

Brusus smiled. "You don't believe he made this?"

"How much?" Haern asked.

"Five dronr."

Haern looked at the knife for a long moment before handing it back to Brusus. Then he leaned back in his chair. "You could probably move that for ten, maybe even a talen."

Brusus looked at Rsiran sideways. "I told him I would have given him more."

"After," Haern said.

Brusus laughed, nodding. "After."

"Think he can learn to negotiate?" Haern asked.

Brusus smiled. "He's already got a talent for it. I started at three."

Haern was taking a sip of ale and snorted. Next to him, Jessa smiled as she sipped her own. The smile didn't quite reach her eyes.

"You started at three, and he got you to five?" Haern asked.

"Isn't that what I said?" Brusus said. He leaned back and finished his ale.

Which of them men Rsiran had overhead was Brusus? Did he owe money or was he collecting it? Either way, he had no idea what Brusus did, but the way they talked—and the fact Brusus bought one of his knives—made him think his work might not be approved by the constables. Worse, the way Brusus and Haern spoke made him wonder maybe they weren't a part of the rebellion.

Rsiran realized that he had to say something or they would question him more. The more they said around him, the more he feared being pulled into whatever it was they were a part of. All he wanted was to return to the smith. If not the smith, then at least his bed. He needed to get away from them if he could. So far, Brusus didn't know which smith he worked, there were dozens in the city, so he could get away from whatever they were into and focus on his apprenticeship and forget about the way the lorcith had called him to forge knives.

"I still have plenty to learn," Rsiran said, "I would have taken three."

Haern snorted again and raised a hand, waving the server over to their table to refill the mugs of ale. Brusus pulled a small felt pouch from inside one of his pockets and shook a pile of dice onto the table.

Haern shrugged. "Haven't you already lost enough money tonight?"

"Maybe I can earn some of it back from Rsiran."

Rsiran shook his head and took a hesitant sip of his mug to hide the edge of his nerves, finding the bitter flavor enjoyable. "I don't dice."

"Don't dice?" Brusus asked, sounding disgusted. "What kind man doesn't dice?"

"Or woman," Jessa reminded, setting a small stack of dronr on the table.

"The kind that likes to keep their money," Haern said, picking up the dice. "A dronr?"

Brusus and Jessa both nodded.

"Or one that doesn't have any," Rsiran said softly. At least the talk about the knives, and whatever their plans were, had stopped. Maybe he would be able to slip away, get home with enough time to sleep…

Haern threw the dice and they scattered across the table. "Well, now that you do, watch a few hands and decide if you want to lose it again."

Rsiran hesitated again, glancing to the door that seemed so far away, with Brusus situated in front of it, as if knowing how he blocked him from leaving. Every so often, Brusus glanced to Rsiran's pocket and a knowing look came to his face. What choice did Rsiran have but to sit and dice and try not to hear too much?

As he grabbed the dice, a nagging fear settled into his chest that told him he should risk leaving. Brusus stared at him, almost as if knowing his thoughts, but with his pale eyes, he couldn't be much of a Reader.

He sighed, and tossed the dice, wishing again that he'd never made the knife.

CHAPTER 4

THE MORNING AIR WAS CRISP. Rsiran squinted against the rising sun filtering through thick clouds no longer fat with rain as he walked up the slanted road toward Upper Town. Far below him, waves crashed loudly against the shore in a steady rhythm. The chaotic sounds of the waking city mingled with the waves. There were shouts of fishermen heading out for the day, shops opening, and hammers distantly ringing against metal in the smithies. Everything around was vibrant and awake. Except for him.

Rsiran rubbed sleep from his eyes. He smelled of smoke and ale mixed with sweat from working the forge the night before. His shirt had been stained sometime during the night, leaving a crusty trail of white on one sleeve. Wrinkled pants pulled out of his boots, and he paused to tuck them back in. He carried his cloak over one arm, careful to keep the lorcith knife wrapped inside.

He didn't know when he had fallen asleep at the tavern. Sometime after playing a few rounds of dice and losing three of the five dronr, his belly full with his second mug of ale. Still not the five his father usually managed, but more than he had ever consumed. The table had welcomed his head like a pillow. He had awoken to find the others gone, a stack of the three dronr lost playing dice set near his head.

He didn't know what to make of Brusus and his friends. They welcomed him without questions, but what of the subtle threat he felt from Brusus? And who was Brusus meeting by the docks today?

He pushed away the thought. It was none of his concern… except now it was. Brusus had told him that they'd see him again, looking at him knowingly as if reminding him that they'd find him if he didn't show. Did he want more lorcith knives? Rsiran didn't know that he could sneak anymore than what he had. And when would he see them? He might be able to find the tavern again, but that meant he had to get away from home at night, and risk his father—and sister—discovering.

He sighed. That was a concern for later; he had a greater concern now. First he had to reach the smithy or his father would be even angrier with him than he already was.

Rsiran hurried toward his father's shop, fearful he would be late for the day of work ahead of him. He tried running, but his pounding head kept him from moving too quickly. It was a measure of his headache that he didn't initially try to Slide, though the number of people in the street also had much to do with that decision. Sliding in the daylight was risky, but did he have any other choice?

He licked dry lips as he stepped into the shadows between buildings. Then he took a step forward, Sliding. The sound of air rushed through his ears, and it felt like wind blew across his face, as if he were running instead of taking only a single step. The air smelled musty and dry, and he held his breath to avoid tasting it, remembering well how bitter it felt on his tongue the first time he managed to Slide. When everything stopped, he opened his eyes.

He emerged from the Slide in the small fenced area behind his father's shop. Walls of stone created a courtyard outside the smith, and a place of privacy. An iron pump with its handle starting to rust sat next to him, a small wooden bucket hanging from the end of the spigot. A pile of scrap metal, mostly steel and iron but some small amount of lorcith mixed in, towered in the corner of the fenced area, a long, sloped roof overhead leaving it filled in long shadows and darkness.

Rsiran grabbed the bucket and pumped the handle a few times, filling it quickly. If his father was in the shop, he could at least pretend he had been busy in the back, either stacking the scrap or fetching water. Both were jobs he did several times throughout the day.

He splashed some of the water on his face and rubbed his eyes to clear them. The scent of ale lingered on him, almost like perfume. If he stayed near the forge, the smoke coming off might mask the ale. Chances were good his father wouldn't notice anything anyway.

As he approached the door, momentary concern flickered that it might be locked. Had he slid the bolt into the lock last night? Most of the time it didn't matter—the small fenced area could only be accessed through the shop. If locked, he would either have to admit he was late or Slide through the door. Neither option appealed to him.

Thankfully, it was not.

He pulled the door open a crack and peeked inside. Thenis peered over the long bench on the far wall. Rsiran stepped in and shuffled toward the forge, setting the bucket down to the side.

Thenis turned and looked at him. He had closely shorn brown hair and an angry, healed burn mark along one cheek that left his face in a permanent frown. His eyes were pale though not quite as pale as Brusus's. "Where did you come from?" he asked.

Rsiran nodded toward the back door. "The yard,"

Thenis nodded, flicking his eyes over to the door. "When did you go out there?"

Rsiran shrugged and turned to the forge, grabbing the shovel and piling in coals. Thenis came over and helped him, getting the coals lit and glowing brightly. They both stood back and watched the flames for a moment. Would Thenis tell his father? Had he already noticed the missing lorcith? Either would be grounds for some sort of punishment.

"Is he—" Rsiran started.

Thenis shook his head. "Not here yet."

Rsiran took a deep breath, relief washing over him. Mornings were when his father met with customers, created his work list, but he didn't have meetings every morning.

"What are you working on today?" Rsiran asked.

Thenis was generally pleasant, much nicer than some of the journeymen who had rotated through his father's shop. Some could be nearly as nasty as his father. Though his father was usually professional and reserved while working around the journeymen, he didn't know if the other master smiths treated them the same way.

Thenis glanced at the bench along the far wall, turning his attention to the sheet of paper tacked to the wall that listed the projects and shrugged. "Ten feet of steel chain is next," he said. "Then a lorcith platter and bowl, though that's for the Elvraeth, and your father will probably do that work." He turned and looked out the lone window, looking up the street in the direction of the palace. "Come. You can help with the chain."

Rsiran hid his smile. While his father rarely let him do much more than shop maintenance, Thenis would occasionally include him in projects. A chain might not be very exciting to a journeyman smith, but to Rsiran it was much better than fetching coals or moving scraps of metal.

Thenis directed him toward the iron bars. Rsiran looked up at him, and Thenis shrugged again. "Need steel for the chain. Not enough from the last forging, so we'll have to smelt the iron into steel."

They worked to get the fire blazing hot, turning the iron into molten metal. After they had been working for a while, Thenis took a step back and looked at Rsiran. "Why don't you work on something while I'm getting this ready?"

Rsiran blinked at the offer. "Anything I can do to help?"

Thenis glanced over at the list tacked on the wall. "Probably, but why don't you show me something of your own. Pretend you're a journeyman preparing to move on."

Rsiran understood what he was asking. Each journeyman completed a project for the different master smiths they rotated with before leaving to spend time with another. The projects were useful items, usually decorative, and meant to showcase their skill as a token of thanks. Rsiran's father had never sold any of the projects the journeymen made over the years, keeping them displayed in a side room of the shop.

"Iron?" he asked. Iron was the least expensive metal they had in the shop but limited what he could do.

Thenis smiled. "Whatever draws you."

Rsiran nodded. Such freedom was a luxury he never experienced, and a tingle of nervousness went through him that his father might catch him working and Thenis would claim ignorance. Yet even if he wanted to refuse the opportunity, while his father was gone, Thenis was in charge of the smithy.

Still, whatever drew him posed a risk. The lorcith seemed to *want* him to work with it, as if hoping that he'd forge it into something dark and dangerous. Even if he resisted now, what would happen if Brusus found the smith, and demanded that he make more of the knives?

Rsiran walked over to the bins of metal. Bars of iron stacked high in one, each mined outside the city and carefully formed before it was sold to the smiths. There was copper and grindl as well, each stack smaller and meant primarily for decoration. In a locked cabinet along a back wall his father kept various precious metals: gold, silver, and some platinum he saved for specific requests. Usually jewelry, but Rsiran had seen other decorative work from his father as well. Unfortunately those jobs, while high paying, came fewer and fewer. Rsiran did not remember the last time the cabinet had been unlocked. Yet as always, it was the lorcith that drew him.

Lorcith was different than many of the metals in the shop. As far as he knew, it could not take an alloy, leaving all works of lorcith made from the pure ore. Forging lorcith changed something about it, making it nearly impossible to reshape, so it was delivered in the same lumps pulled from Ilphaesn Mountain by the miners. Many still had hunks of rock still clinging to them, as if the mountain did not want to let go of the lorcith. Mostly it was the Elvraeth who could afford lorcith-forged items.

He stared at the pieces, knowing that he shouldn't use lorcith, but one drew him more than the others. He shouldn't use lorcith. His father would learn, or Thenis would say something, but maybe he could claim this was why the others were missing.

Rsiran reached for it, but pulled his hand back. Iron would be safer, so much better for him, but the lorcith drew him, calling to him.

Knowing better of it, he grabbed the piece.

Thenis watched him from the corner of his eye. His scarred face pulled in a half smile, and he shook his head but didn't say anything. A thick chunk of rock held to this piece, and Rsiran chiseled it off before heating the lorcith until it glowed a soft bluish-orange. Then he began hammering.

For some reason, lorcith seemed to almost speak to him, as if demanding it be shaped. Each time before, he had not known what would come of his shaping until he finished. Most things were simple: bowls or platters, a few candleholders, once a small pot. The knives were new and what did it mean that they had come as much from the metal as from him? What did that make him?

As he began hammering, he felt the strange connection to the lorcith that he had each time before. There was an understanding of where the metal needed to be hammered, how much force to use, when to heat it. He worked, ignoring the sound of Thenis working nearby, grunting occasionally. There was only the sound of his hammer, steady and rhythmic, like the waves slapping the shore down in Lower Town.

It wasn't until he had been working for a while, sweat dripping from his face and slicking his back leaving his shirt clinging to him, that he realized what it was the lorcith directed him to make. And then he nearly stopped.

The blade was long and slender, so different than the knives he had made the times before. This blade folded slowly, the curved back different than anything he had seen. A wide tip narrowed as it worked toward the base of the blade. Curls of color—grey and black from the way the metal had taken shape—swirled along both sides of the blade in a pattern. Somehow, he knew that when it took an edge, it would be an impressive blade.

He had not heard the front door to the shop open or his father approach. Only when his father looked over his shoulder, his breath hot, the stench of the night's ale still clinging to his it, did Rsiran realize his father had returned.

His father said nothing. Instead, grabbing a set of iron tongs, he pulled the blade from Rsiran and threw it into the forge. The flames leapt high, blue and red, sparking and hissing. Then he took a hammer and began reshaping the lorcith with a rage nearly as hot as the coals in the forge.

Rsiran stood frozen, terrified to even speak. He'd made another weapon, and a *sword* this time. How could he have let himself lose control like that?

Thenis glanced at him from where he worked smelting the steel. His face wore a strange look, a mix of apology and disgust, all twisted by his scar. As much as it would help Rsiran, Thenis said nothing.

"You will not touch anything in this shop unless I instruct you to. Is that understood?" his father asked as he worked. His voice was low and soft, simmering with anger.

He pointed at him with the still red-hot tongs, and Rsiran jerked back, afraid of getting burned. He nodded. "I didn't know..." He was unable to finish.

His father stepped closer, the tongs falling to the ground. "Didn't know? You think you can use that as an excuse?" he said, his voice barely above a whisper. "Do you know that lorcith grows so expensive I can almost not afford to stock it? Do you know that the supply from the mines has trickled off? Do you know what you nearly cost me?"

He punctuated each question with a hard strike of the hammer.

"You think I hold you back, that you have watched me or one of the journeymen enough times you can simply pick up a hammer and make whatever comes to mind. You have no control. You are barely strong enough to control iron, let alone work with something as seductive as lorcith."

Rsiran swallowed. "The lorcith told me what to make."

Thenis glanced over, his eyes flaring deeper green for a moment.

"And you are not yet strong enough to ignore it." His father sighed, frustration and sadness heavy in the sound. "You think I do not understand, Rsiran, but I do. I know fully how the lorcith can sing, drawing you to make dark and dangerous weapons, tools that were not meant to come from an Elaeavn smith." He shook his head.

"How?" Rsiran asked.

His father snorted and started to turn away. For a moment, Rsiran thought he would not answer. When he did, the answer surprised him.

"It's in our blood," he said, still hammering on the lorcith. Now it was shaped into a flat sheet. His father's face tensed and contorted as he worked. "There are some that it calls to, demanding a certain shape." He hammered at the metal a few more times. "Lorcith cannot guide you. Such a thing is nearly as dark as…" He trailed off, glancing at Thenis, then shook his head. "As what I was warned you'd become. And here I see it coming true. And with this, you risk not only yourself, but *my* smith as well. All of us could suffer because of your lack of control." His eyes hardened as he looked over at him, the hammer rising and falling as he glared at Rsiran. "A true smith learns to control the lorcith, not the other way around."

Rsiran looked over to the forge and remembered the knives he had made, how the lorcith seemed so eager to take the shape, as if the metal told him where to place the hammer. Even when he made simple items, things like bowls or hooks, the metal seemed to tell him what to do. "I didn't know," he said again.

His father leaned into him. Tightly controlled anger still pulled on his cheeks and lips, his pale eyes almost quivering. "You are an apprentice. There has been no reason *for* you to know." He grunted as he hammered, forcing the shape with the force of his will. "Not all smiths are pulled by lorcith the same way. Some cannot even hear the call of the ore, never hear how it sings. They are skilled, but rarely match the skill of the greatest smiths."

Rsiran glanced over at Thenis. He worked silently over the smelted steel, for all intents focused on his work, but there was a stiffness to his back that told Rsiran that he listened. Rarely had his father spoken so much to him, and never so much about his trade.

"You have proven time and again that you cannot master yourself, let alone have the strength of will to master lorcith." His father took a step back, the heavy tongs dragging across the ground. "I think it is time I stop coddling you or else you will never learn enough to join the guild." He inhaled deeply, and he shook his head. "Next week you will report to the mines in Ilphaesn. Working there might provide a different perspective. Maybe *there* you can gain the necessary strength of will. At the least, it will keep the rest of us safe from your..." He shook his head, unable to even finish as his jaw clenched, as if biting back his anger.

Rsiran felt as if an icy hot hand squeezed his heart. The Ilphaesn Mountain mines were a dark place, a place where men were sent to serve out their penance when punished by the ruling Elvraeth council. And his father intended to send him to work alongside them. He opened his mouth to say something—anything—that might sway his father, but nothing came out.

"I can see from your expression that I finally have your attention," his father said. "Finish your work today, and then you are dismissed. We will talk later about getting you to Ilphaesn." His father turned, walked into the back room, and closed the door, saying nothing more.

Thenis looked at him and started to open his mouth but bit back whatever he had intended to say, turning his attention back to his project.

Rsiran stared at the fire burning in the forge. He didn't blame Thenis for turning away from him. Angering Rsiran's father only risked his journeyman status. Better to pretend not to have heard.

Long moments passed before Rsiran finally managed to get himself moving.

CHAPTER 5

RSIRAN RAN FROM THE SMITHY and spent much of the day wandering. He had walked aimlessly, letting his feet and the sounds of the city pull him. Somehow, he ended up making his way into Lower Town, toward the tavern from the night before. It was a mistake coming this far, especially as it risked him running into Brusus or Haern again. He couldn't get caught up in what they were doing.

Maybe it was best he was sent to Ilphaesn. At least he wouldn't be able to make any more of the knives that could get his father into trouble, and risk whatever Brusus might have in mind for him now that he knew Rsiran made knives of lorcith.

He had no one he could go to. Not his mother—she would side with his father, never speaking against him even when Rsiran saw in her eyes that she knew his father was being unreasonable. Not his sister either—she had made it quite clear she would be happier were he to live elsewhere. His time spent as an apprentice had separated him from any of the friends he had as a child, but even those were few. He had always struggled with opening himself to others, always fearing they might turn on him as his father had.

He thought of leaving Elaeavn, leaving the comfort—such as it was—of his home, to live and work in the mines of the Ilphaesn Mountain. There were stories of what it was like from those who had been sent to work and returned to Elaeavn. Most were surprisingly tight-lipped, probably fearing to do anything that might get them banished to the mines again.

He paused at the tavern and glanced in the window. A few people sat at the tables but none he recognized. One of the servers spotted him and motioned him in, but he shook his head and started down the street. The buildings in this part of town were smaller, more compact. Most appeared somewhat run down. Large cracks ran up the sides of many, and the once-white stone now appeared grey and dirty. A few had vines creeping along the face of the building, the leaves at this time of year brown and falling off.

Other people began filling the street. A stream of wet and dirty men smelling of fish went past, likely returned from one of the fishing vessels. Women wearing high-necked dresses more tattered and worn than those found in the upper city wandered past. Children ran by screaming as they raced toward the shore. Others, obviously finished with their labor for the day, wandered the street with a bit more direction than he had.

It wasn't until Rsiran reached the edge of the Lower Town that he stopped. The road he followed took him to the southern edge of the city where it abutted the bay. The Lhear Sea stretched out before him and huge rock cliffs towered on either side, framing the bay. Water splashed steadily along the rocky shore. Tall-masted ships moored out in the bay, and smaller boats slid through the water, ferrying people to and from the ships. To the north, the docks were busy with workers helping with the day's catch or moving crates off a few of the shallow-er-keeled boats. Past the docks, beyond the sheer cliff wall rising above the water, Rsiran saw the snow-white peak of Ilphaesn Mountain.

He climbed down onto the rocks and crept carefully toward the water. There, he sat close to the edge of the bay as salty spray splashed against him. Sunlight glittered off the water, sweeps of color stranding across the sky as the sun faded behind the horizon. He could leave Elaeavn, simply disappear like one of the Forgotten, and start anew in one of the lesser cities. With his abilities, there were other things he could do, skills he could learn. Maybe he could even continue working as a smith. No lorcith was found outside the city, so the temptation would be lessened.

Except, Rsiran was not sure he could leave Elaeavn. Only the For-gotten, those banished by the Elvraeth, ever really left the city. He might not be blessed by the Great Watcher, but he was still of Elaeavn. More than that, though. He was a smith. His father was right—the lorcith called to him, demanding that he shape it. And when he stood before the forge...everything felt peaceful. For him to learn what he needed left him with one option—doing as his father demanded, working in the mines alongside criminals, and returning to Elaeavn to prove that he could be trusted again as an apprentice. Only then would he be able to become the smith he wanted so badly to be.

He shuddered to think of what the mines would be like. His father spoke about learning to control the lorcith, but from what Rsiran had seen, he was barely aware of what he was doing when forging some-thing with lorcith. The knives and the blade simply came into being. How did he know how much was him and what was from the metal? And did he care?

Rsiran sat staring at the water until the sky had darkened complete-ly. Flickers of light sprang up behind him from candles and lanterns set into windows. A few lanterns flickered out on the ships, though most remained dark. Stars twinkled into being, bedazzling the sky like the sea spray reflecting the sunlight. A pale sliver of moon appeared in the west, high and distant.

He finally stood and made his way back toward town. Perhaps in returning home and facing his punishment he would find his father had changed his mind, though he did not have great optimism.

In the darkness, he considered Sliding home rather than walking all the way back up the sloping streets, but decided against it. The cool air cleared his mind, and he would need a clear and calm mind when he returned home. Besides, if he was going to do as his father commanded, as hard as it was, he had better start by ignoring that particular ability as well. He would show that he had control of himself.

So it was that the street again led him past the tavern where he had diced with Brusus and Haern the night before. A dark shadow separated from the street as if it had been watching him, and approached. "Do you normally make it down to Lower Town daily?"

Rsiran stared through the darkness, shadows shifting and lightening enough for him to see that Brusus stood in front of him. He wore a heavy brown cloak of fine quality, almost too warm for the weather, and his hair was wet and slicked back atop his head like the first night he met him, only then it had been raining. Moonlight bounced off the stone on his ring.

Had Brusus been watching him? Worse, had he *followed* him? "Not usually," he said carefully.

Brusus smiled and nodded toward the tavern. "You don't have to have permission to enter. Besides, there are other things we need to talk about."

Rsiran's heart fluttered. Brusus would want more knives, but now that he'd been exiled to Ilphaesn, that was one thing he *couldn't* do. "I shouldn't be out late again."

"Trouble?" Brusus watched him with pale eyes. "We can't all be blessed like those who live in the palace, Rsiran. The rest of us have to make our own way."

The comment made it even more likely that Brusus was a part of the rebellion. He needed to be careful about what he said to Brusus. "Some of us aren't blessed at all," Rsiran muttered.

Brusus looked at him strangely, and Rsiran realized his mistake. With his pale eyes, Brusus would not have much strength in whatever ability he possessed. Discussing strength in one's ability was considered taboo. He should not have said anything.

"I'm sorry," he began. "I didn't mean—"

Brusus shook his head. "No offense taken. I have lived within Elaeavn my entire life as one of the palest-eyed people here. There is more to a person than their ability, more to me than my weak Sight." He shook his head and smiled. "Besides, I like to think I have other unconventional abilities."

Rsiran nodded carefully. Though Brusus said he did not take offense, he should step lightly. Now that Brusus had admitted to his Sight, would he expect Rsiran to share his ability? With as angry and suspicious as his father was of Sliding, he dared not say anything about it to a virtual stranger.

Besides, what did he really know about Brusus? He wanted the knife Rsiran forged and knew how to sell it. Did that make him some sort of smuggler, the sort of criminal the ability to Slide would lead him to become? But the conversation he'd overhead made him wonder what else Brusus and his friends were. How would his father react if he knew Rsiran had somehow gotten caught up in something more?

"And one of my abilities is the capacity to hold my ale. Come in, Rsiran, and see if you have an unconventional ability." Brusus smiled again, draping an arm around his shoulders and steering him toward the tavern.

As much as he didn't want to get tangled in whatever Brusus planned, Brusus knew too much of him. What choice did he have but to be guided into the tavern?

* * * * *

The following morning, he awoke early, nearly shaking with nerves. In spite of knowing that he should not, he had Slid home from the tavern, smelling strongly of ale, with pockets slightly heavier after winning his share at dice. Haern had welcomed him to the table as if he were an old friend. Even Jessa seemed nonplussed that he had returned, this time wearing a blood red flower, the color practically dripping from the petals. Two others joined, Tagus and Nesin, both fresh off their ship, and both treated him warmly. Brusus might have watched him carefully, his gaze every so often drifting to Rsiran's pockets, but he'd always smiled at him, and made him feel welcome. Strangely, for the first time in as long as he could remember, he felt welcome in Elaeavn as he was about to be sent from the city. If they were criminals—or something worse—they were at least *friendly* criminals.

He arrived home after his father, and by Sliding into his room, he bypassed any possibility for encountering his sister. Too often she slept by the door, as if hoping to catch him to report to their parents and raise herself even higher in their eyes. In spite of that, he could not bring himself to hate her.

Dressing quickly, he decided to stuff the lorcith knife and his growing coin purse into a small hidden section of his trunk. He looked around the room, considering what he would bring with him to the Ilphaesn mines. Other than the trunk, his room consisted of his bed and a small shelf. A few books were stacked on shelves from his earliest school days, a time before he disgusted his father. He realized he probably would not even take his trunk with him. That meant that he would have to hide the knife and coins somewhere else while he was gone.

He left his room and went into the kitchen, feeling the growing fluttering of nerves in his stomach, fearing what his mother and father would say to him this morning. Would they even acknowledge that he had returned home late again last night? Would that even matter?

In the small kitchen, there was only his sister. She stood beside a counter, rolling bread, a strand of her dark hair hanging in her face. The aromas of flour and yeast brought back pleasant memories of when he had helped his mother as a child. The oven radiated a warm heat in the corner. A tub of water sat along one of the counters.

Alyse looked up as he entered but did not say anything. He stepped up to the counter and helped her knead the dough, pressing on it and rolling it as his mother had once taught him. His sister watched a moment before stepping away and turning toward the oven. They worked silently together as they prepared breakfast, and soon the kitchen was full of the sweet aromas of baking bread and the spice of cooked sausages.

"Father told me that he plans to send you to the mines. I am sorry, Rsiran," Alyse said. She stood in front of the oven before a pan simmering with the sausages, her back to him.

He leaned against one wall, watching her. "The fault is my own."

She nodded. "Still."

He sniffed. The response was typical of Alyse.

"Perhaps you can use the opportunity he has given you to—"

"Opportunity?" Rsiran stepped away from the wall.

Alyse turned to face him, her eyes flaring green. Rsiran strengthened his barriers to keep her from Reading him.

40

"Yes, opportunity." She stood with her back straight as she chastised him, looking so much like their mother that it nearly unnerved him. "Without him, you would not even have your apprenticeship. Then what would you do? Work in Lower Town on the docks? Learn to fish? Use your ability to become some sort of thief?" she finished, lowering her voice.

With each question, his irritation with her faded. As usual, she was right. There was nothing else for him to do, nothing that he *could* do. Soon he would travel to the mines, repress his ability to Slide, and focus on whatever his father wanted to earn back his apprenticeship. Alyse only reinforced that decision.

"I don't want to go to the mines," he said softly, pulling a chair from along the wall and sinking into it. There was no argument left in him, only sadness.

Alyse came and stood behind him, setting a hand that smelled of flour on his shoulder. She squeezed once and let go. "I know."

CHAPTER 6

THE JOURNEY TO ILPHAESN took the better part of three days. Rsiran could have Slid in a heartbeat. The only advantage of leaving the city, as far as Rsiran could tell, was that he didn't have to fear Brusus demanding more knives from him. During his last night at the tavern, Brusus had alluded to needing more knives. At least away from the city, he didn't have to fear what would happen if he didn't make them for him.

The white peak of the rocky mountain rose high overhead, contrasting with the overcast sky. A winding trail led to a darkened cavern mouth. The bitter scent of lorcith hung on the air, so thick Rsiran could taste it. Only when they reached the mouth of the mines did the man leading them speak.

"Your entire sentence will be served here," he said. His voice was thin and high, as if rarely used. "Davin will show you where you will sleep." He nodded toward a man emerging from the wide mouth of a cave on the side of the mountain. "You earn one percent of all that is mined. No more than that." He grunted. "Work harder, and your time here is shorter. Work slower…" He shrugged. "Food will be brought in twice a day and members of the mining guild will be present, but unseen."

"Didn't say anything about luck," one of the convicted men muttered.

"There is always an element of luck. The Great Watcher gives what he gives. Lately, he hasn't given all that much," the other guard said, waiting until Davin neared to turn and started back toward the village.

Davin looked at them carefully. His eyes widened when he saw Rsiran wore no bindings on his wrists. "What is this?"

Rsiran glanced at the other men. "My father sent me here to work," he answered softly.

One of the convicted men from Elaeavn snickered. He was thin, his eyes a pale watery green, and his hair shorn close, revealing a long scar along his scalp that he seemed to wear with pride.

Davin frowned. "Neran sent word," he said. "Didn't think he was serious that he was sending his apprentice to work in the mines. Didn't know you were his son too. Did he tell you how much you needed to earn?"

Rsiran shook his head, confused.

"Gryn told you one percent is earned," Davin said, nodding toward the man walking back toward the village.

Rsiran stared ahead. His father had said nothing about how long he would need to serve, saying only that he needed to learn to control the lorcith. Perhaps when he managed that he could return.

The thin man snickered again.

Davin shot him a look. He had eyes of a medium green and an intense stare that dared the other man to challenge him. "Then you'll work until we hear from him. Don't expect special treatment. Neran was clear about that. You'll work the same as the others. Share the

43

same sleeping quarters. Eat the same food. The mines are meant to be punishment."

Rsiran only nodded.

* * * * *

The sleeping quarters turned out to be a large hollowed out section within the mountain. The stone along the walls was rough and damp, and the air smelled heavily of the bitter lorcith mined deeper below. A single lantern glowed with a soft orange light somewhere in the cavern, but Rsiran could not see where it was. Shadows shifted around the edges of the cavern, strange and twisting, and—not for the first time since leaving Elaeavn—an uncomfortable feeling worked through him.

They were given a pair of thin blankets to sleep upon and a battered metal bowl and cup. Other blankets were scattered across the floor of the cavern, clustered most heavily near the single light, almost overlapping. Rsiran took his blanket and set it down away from many others, unwilling to sleep so close to men he had not met. He set his bowl and cup next to him.

He looked around, taking a quick count of the people. Nearly one hundred men moved around the cavern. Supper had recently been served, and most still ate, sitting atop their blankets. His stomach grumbled at the sight of the bread and the bowls of stew, but he tried to ignore the sensation. They had not been fed well while traveling, mostly jerky and stale rolls. The last good meal he had eaten had been the breakfast with Alyse. Strange that he should have a fond memory of her.

The floor was dry and dusty as he unrolled one of the blankets. He had not brought anything with him other than his clothes. His father had made it quite clear that was not allowed. In the darkness, surrounded by others he knew to be criminals and thieves, it was the lorcith-forged knife he missed the most.

The walls of the cavern seemed to press in on him, squeezing him, and he closed his eyes to distract from looking at his surroundings, trying to imagine open skies and water stretching as far as he could see. He could not shut out the sounds.

The other men who had come with him made their way toward the lantern. Rsiran heard them greeted as if recognized by others already there. A few men laughed.

"Finally got caught?"

"Damn Elvraeth," someone said.

Rsiran opened his eyes and turned cautiously toward the lantern. He wasn't accustomed to anyone speaking of the Elvraeth with such disgust.

The thin man hunkered near the lantern, a circle of others surrounding him, light reflecting strangely from his scar. He leaned toward the others as he spoke.

"What did you do?" someone asked.

The thin man shrugged. "Got caught outside town with an Asador merchant trying to sell silks."

"That's not a crime."

The thin man laughed. "It is if they aren't yours!"

Everyone around him laughed. One even clapped him on the shoulder.

"Any word on the—"

The thin man raised a hand, cutting the other off. He looked around, casting his gaze around the cavern, settling briefly on Rsiran before turning back to the others. "You think they don't have ears, even here?"

"Not in here," another said. "They want nothing from here."

"'Cept the ore."

"Yeah, that. I hear it's coming slowly."

One of the men grunted. "That's what we've been told to do."

"We're still moving it, only not to the city," one of the men said.

"Why are you here?"

Rsiran jerked around at the sound. The voice was soft and thin. A face that looked no older than ten peered at him from a half dozen paces away, squatted down atop a blanket. Dark hair was long and lanky, pushed back behind his ears.

"Does it matter?" Rsiran asked. He tried listening, feeling a growing unease about what the other men had been talking about. The way the men spoke sounded nothing like anyone he'd ever met in Elaeavn. In some ways, they sounded more like Brusus and his friends.

Rsiran's heart skipped. What if Brusus had connections to the men in the mines?

He needed to keep away from them, and not let anyone learn who he was. Already, he might have said too much, revealing the fact that his father had sent him to Ilphaesn.

The boy laughed softly as he crept closer, crawling on hands and feet and looking animal-like as he did. "Does it matter?" he muttered, mostly to himself. "Always matters. To them, at least," he said, motioning toward the men around the lantern. "Surprised you didn't want to be closer to the light."

Rsiran shook his head. "Too many people there," he said. Too much risk, he didn't say.

The boy smiled with a flash of pale teeth. "That's why they like it. The longer you're here, the more you'll want to be around others."

"How long have you been here?"

The boy tilted his head as if trying to remember. "Nearly a year."

46

Rsiran struggled to keep the surprise off his face. From what he understood, most sentences were for six months, rarely longer. "Why aren't you near the light then?" He avoided the question he wanted to ask.

The boy smiled again. "Some of us like the dark," he answered and scurried off toward the back wall. Soon he was a shadow in the darkness, watching Rsiran intently, his eyes the only part of him clearly visible.

Rsiran lay down on his blanket and closed his eyes. He struggled to ignore the sounds around him, the conspiratorial voices of those near the light now speaking in quieter tones, the occasional cough, and a steady tapping from deeper in the mines he did not understand. Sleep came slowly the first night.

Chapter 7

THE FOLLOWING DAY HE AWOKE with his back throbbing as a loud gonging startled him from a restless sleep filled with dreams that he vaguely remembered. The light in the cavern had not changed; the same lantern glowing a soft orange making morning look no different than night. The only difference was the fact that everyone had moved.

At some point, a large pot had been set near the lantern. A line of miners took their cups and scooped food from the pot before retaking their places and eating in silence. No one really spoke.

Rsiran stood and carefully stretched his legs. He took the battered cup and bowl he had been given and wound his way toward the line, waiting patiently for his turn at the pot. The boy he had seen the night before stood a few paces in front of him, small and thin. Fresh wounds crisscrossed his arms, blood dried and caked onto them. He looked around nervously, and Rsiran realized he had several scars on his face as well. None of the others in line had such injuries. What had happened to this boy?

At the pot, he scooped without looking, his hand slipping into a warm slop. The smell was unrecognizable, certainly not the sweet smell of bread or the tasty bite of sausage that he suspected Alyse made again this morning. He took his bowl and looked around for water but saw none. Licking already dried lips, he made his way back toward his blanket and took his seat to eat in silence.

A few of the men spoke as they ate. Rsiran recognized the soft cackle of the thin man who had traveled to Ilphaesn with him and looked over as he took his first spoonful of tasteless mush. The man sat amid five others, each dressed in the same dark grey clothes, the others content to eat silently. He laughed and gestured as he spoke, having far too good a time for the assignment. Every so often, the man's eyes wandered to their guards. Once he'd caught Rsiran looking, his hard eyes fixing Rsiran with an intensity that reminded him of the way Brusus had watched him, and he turned away quickly.

He finished his meal and looked around for some way to rinse out his bowl but did not see anything. Everyone else appeared to simply wipe the bowl clean with their sleeves. Grimacing, Rsiran copied them, hating that he was forced to live this way. A line began forming near the mouth of the sleeping cavern, and he stood and made his way to stand with the others. He focused his attention out of the cavern, staring into the darkness. Behind him came the occasional cackle from the thin man.

Once everyone had lined up, they were marched out of the cavern and into a wide tunnel that veered steadily down. An occasional orange lantern lit the tunnel. They gave off weak light, leaving everything in shadows that grew long and deep before the glow of the next lantern began to appear.

Somewhere ahead of him, someone stumbled, grunting as they did, and then uttered a moan of pain. The group did not stop, simply veering around the downed man. Rsiran looked down as they neared but could not make out anything other than the dark outline of the fallen.

The farther they walked, the stronger the bitter smell of the lorcith became. The air was heavy and stale, and a soft, fluttering, cool breeze drifted through the tunnel. Something else as well, a sensation that he felt at first was imagined. There seemed to be something pulling on him, as if dragging him forward. Probably the grade of the slope, he decided. He didn't know how long they walked before they finally reached an area where the ground leveled off.

The group stopped and divided into smaller groups. Each was directed to grab a small hammer and a pick out of a long bin, and he shuffled forward, taking the tools when it was his turn. They were well used, the point of the pick blunted. The wooden handles were worn smooth.

Rsiran recognized one of the foremen as a man he had seen in the village at the base of Ilphaesn the day before. He had ragged hair and a thin beard—something never seen in Elaeavn—and hard angry eyes flickered at everyone around him. His eyes reminded Rsiran too well of his father, especially how he became when he was drinking. Rsiran knew immediately to stay away from this man.

"Anything not returned at the end of the day is taken from your profits," the foreman said in such a way that told Rsiran he said the same thing every day.

How often did tools disappear? Normally such a thing would seem unlikely, but he suspected there were some among the workers who would take any opportunity at freedom, especially if the price they must repay was high enough. And how would they even know? There was no way out of the mines. As soon as they'd entered, a massive gate set into the stone around the mines had been locked. Only the guards could come or go. Would they really know if he Slid away?

Rsiran was sorted with the rest and directed down a smaller tunnel. Stairs were cut into the mine here, a single lantern marking the change to the ground, as the tunnel narrowed drastically. The steps were steep, and he pushed out his hands to keep his balance, careful not to bang his tools against the wall.

As he went down into the darkness, the air began to warm. The breeze that he'd felt while in the upper tunnel faded until it completely disappeared. Another lantern was set into the wall, giving enough light for him to see there were countless more stairs ahead of him. He marveled at the work that it must have taken to build these tunnels, to form each stair, before realizing it all came from forced labor. Men like him had created these tunnels over the years.

Or not like him. The ruling Elvraeth family had sent everyone else as punishment. He served because of his father.

The farther they descended, he began wondering how they would get any lorcith back up the stairs once it was mined. Would they have to climb with the ore strapped to their backs? From his time working in the smith, he knew that lump ore was heavy. He did not look forward to such a climb. Or was it collected in another way?

Unless he wouldn't be getting any lorcith out. Hadn't he overheard that the supply of the ore had slowed? Strange, considering Rsiran felt nothing but lorcith all around him. But then, he'd also overheard men saying they were moving the ore away from the city. What was that about?

Rsiran decided he didn't care. None of that was the reason he was here. Better to fade into the background, have the others ignore him, than draw attention.

No one spoke as they descended. Only the sounds of boots on the stairs mixed with heavy breathing accompanied them on their climb.

Finally, he saw another faint light in the distance. When they reached it, the ground leveled off and opened into a slightly wider tunnel that eventually simply ended. Here the foreman assigned to their group motioned, stepping back and leaning against the wall.

The others in Rsiran's group started forward, all seeming to know what to do. The thin man with the angry cackle was part of his group. He eyed Rsiran briefly before turning to the wall and starting to work. As he did, the man whispered to the others working next to him.

Rsiran backed up. He didn't need to draw the man's attention. Maybe he should have gone down a different tunnel, anything but near the man with the hard gaze, and the far too familiar stare.

He felt a tug at his sleeve and looked. It was the boy from the night before.

"Watch," he said. He took the pick and demonstrated chipping away at the rock.

The boy worked steadily and slowly revealed the dull grey reflection of a chunk of lorcith. His face twisted with the effort, and he chewed his lip as he swung the pick, the rest of his mouth tight. He worked around the ore until the small nugget was freed. Though it was much smaller than anything used in the shop, the boy still wore a look of satisfaction as he took the metal and slipped it into a pocket.

"Like that," he said, turning back to Rsiran.

"What do you do with the lorcith you mine?" Rsiran asked, careful not to look to closely at the others.

The boy frowned and wiped a drip of sweat from his brow. "Lorcith?"

"The metal," Rsiran said.

The boy patted his pocket. "Keep it." A grin spread across his face. "Until we're done. Then you give it to the Towners." He motioned toward the foreman. "They keep a record of how much you've collected. When you earn back your sentence, you're released."

Rsiran looked at the pick in his hands. The others might be released, but not him. No matter how hard he worked, no release would come.

The sound of the other miners chipping away at the wall became a steady beat, and Rsiran joined in, slowly fading into the rhythm. He moved to a section of the tunnel where he could be alone and began. After working a while, a flash of grey metal rewarded him, and he slowly managed to peel a small chunk of metal no bigger than the tip of his thumb from the stone.

He held the lorcith in his palm and closed his eyes. As he stood there squeezing it, the steady sounds of picks striking the stone echoing throughout the mine, he felt a stirring sensation deep within come from the metal itself, the lorcith resonating with something inside of him. Before he had felt it while working the heated metal, the lorcith directing his hammer, guiding each blow so he had little choice in what was forged.

Would he feel the unmined metal? He stepped toward the wall and pocketed the small rock and swept his hand out over the stone, letting his mind go blank as he strained to feel for lorcith hidden in the rock.

At first, he didn't think he'd feel anything. Then he became aware of a steady throbbing sense as he swept his hand over the rock above his head. He glanced over and saw the other miners all working at an easy angle. How strange it would look for him to chip away near the ceiling of the tunnel?

He started anyway, settling into the rhythm again, letting the pick rise and fall steadily as it struck into the stone. The first glint of dull grey metal told him he was on the right track, and he picked up the intensity. Soon it became clear that this chunk was larger than the last, possibly even larger than the usual lumps that he worked with in his father's smith. This much lorcith would be incredibly valuable.

As he worked, the lorcith seemed to call to him, as if he could almost hear it in his mind like a song. What shape it would demand of him? Part of him regretted the fact that he would never know. Someone else would get the opportunity to shape this metal, someone more like his father who would force the ore into a shape of his choosing.

Rsiran shook the thought from his head. Such thoughts were the reason he was sent here in the first place. He had to return from the mine to resume his apprenticeship; only then would he again be allowed at the forge.

He needed to ignore the lorcith, but he couldn't. The ore pressed on his awareness, demanding his attention.

Rsiran didn't know how long he worked, chipping away the rock with the dull pick, but he slowly freed a sizeable chunk from the wall. He set it on the ground at his feet and ran his hand over it, his heart trembling. He should have ignored the way lorcith called to him. Wasn't that what his father had wanted? Pieces of rock mixed with a fine powdered dust were scattered around him.

As he crouched in front of the lump of lorcith, he didn't notice the boy approach. He slid toward the other side of the metal, kneeling in front of it. "You'll learn to avoid finds like these soon enough," he whispered.

Rsiran pulled his eyes away. The strange sensation of the lorcith calling to him faded. "Why?"

"Too dangerous," the boy said.

"I thought we wanted to find this." He made a point of glancing at the other miners, but none seemed to be paying him any attention.

The boy shook his head again. "Too dangerous."

A shrill whistle sounded, and they both turned to look. The foreman stood near one end of the tunnel, whistle in hand. He wore a bored expression on his broad face. He motioned toward the tunnel and the stairs looming in the darkness and started toward them. Most men followed. A few finished picking at whatever they had found, but soon gave up and wandered toward the stairs and the others.

The boy gave Rsiran a worried look, biting his lip as he did. "Got to carry what you collect," he said and hurried down the tunnel.

Rsiran grunted as he lifted the large hunk of lorcith off the cavern floor. It felt heavy, but he should be able to get it up the stairs. Perhaps the find would impress his father. Enough like this, and he might be allowed to return home soon.

He didn't know how many stairs he had climbed when he felt something sharp bite into his back, pressing through the fabric of his shirt. He'd heard nothing warning him that anyone still remained behind.

"Set it down and keep climbing."

Rsiran felt the hot breath on the back of his neck and started to turn. The sharp tip of a pick jabbed deeper into his back, and he froze.

"Turn, and you don't live through the night."

Rsiran nodded, suddenly understanding why the boy said it was dangerous to find such large collections of the ore, and remembering how he'd overheard the others talk of controlling the flow of lorcith. The pick pressed harder, and he winced as a slow trickle of blood washed down his back. He had no choice but to do as instructed.

He set the lorcith down. The pick relaxed, just a bit, and he started forward again. As he continued up the stairs, he wondered who had stolen from him, and why. Had they stolen to take credit for the lorcith, or was there another reason, the same reason the flow of lorcith had slowed?

He didn't dare turn and look back. In the darkness, it might not have mattered anyway.

CHAPTER 8

RSIRAN SAT BY HIS BLANKET that night, holding the dented metal bowl, the soft light from the lantern leaving everything around him in shadows. Voices around the lantern were occasionally boisterous, and the men sitting near the light seemed to be having far more fun than Rsiran. Was it his imagination, or did they look his way at times? Which of them had taken the lump from him?

And why?

His body ached, arms and legs fatigued from hammering with the pick all day, freeing the large piece of lorcith.

The pain in his back seemed worse. He couldn't see the injury where the pick had stabbed into him but still felt the effects. His skin felt hot around where the tip had punctured his flesh; he wondered if infection had already set in.

When he'd reached the top of the stairs and rejoined the rest of the miners, he had simply trudged back up the tunnels, ignoring the foreman with the scale documenting the day's collection. The small lump of lorcith that he found first still tucked into his pocket.

"I warned you."

Rsiran turned, pain in his back flaring slightly as he did. The boy crouched out of reach. Shadows covered his face.

"A find that size probably paid for someone's freedom," he whispered and laughed. He skittered forward a step. "And kept you from yours!"

Rsiran shook his head. He shouldn't have listened for the lorcith. It didn't really matter that the lorcith was stolen—not for his freedom at least—but if he managed more finds like the one from today, how long before his father learned? If he couldn't ignore unshaped lorcith, how could he ever expect to ignore its call while shaping it? Unlike the others, he needed *not* to find lorcith. "Doesn't matter," he muttered.

The boy moved another step closer, enough to reveal the scratches on his arm and face. The pain in his back gave new meaning to the boy's injuries. He pushed back a strand of his lanky hair as he stood on the edge of Rsiran's blanket.

"You hear it, don't you?" the boy asked.

Rsiran looked around. Near the lantern, the occasional grating laugh of the thin man overpowered other sounds as he gestured to a few of the others while lording over the lantern. His voice sounded forced, and there was a hard edge to his words. Rsiran made a point of ignoring him, but failed. He couldn't shake the feeling that the man watched him.

There was a steady tapping sound, faint and distant, that he did not recognize. The soft whisper of a breeze blew through the cavern, playing across his cheeks with its cool touch.

"Hear what?" he finally asked the boy.

The boy's smile widened. "You hear the song of the ore."

Rsiran blinked and shook his head, pulling his gaze away from the lantern. "I don't know what you mean."

But he did. The sound of the lorcith, like soft voices in his head that had drawn him to the find. The same sound had guided his hammer while working in the forge. It was the sound his father wanted to drive out of him.

The boy narrowed his eyes. In the darkness, they reflected a soft green, almost glowing, so that he looked more like a cat crouched nearby. "There's few enough of us who can, you know. Not really an ability, not like Sight or what the Seers have, but useful enough here." The boy shifted, sliding to the side on his hands and feet. "Not sure how useful it is anywhere else but here."

He looked at Rsiran, waiting for some sort of reaction. When he didn't give one, the boy continued. "Don't let others know you can hear it. You've seen what happens. Everyone wants to earn their freedom, but there are others who want something else—" He cut himself off with a shake of his head.

"What else?" Rsiran asked.

The boy raised a finger to his lips. "Can't talk about it, even here." He glanced to the lantern. "Maybe especially here." He smiled again and looked at Rsiran. "You'll learn to ignore the song. Especially if you want to survive. Better to bring it out in small pieces than all at once. Otherwise, the others…" He trailed off, turning to look toward the lantern with eyes that went wide.

Ignore the song. The same thing his father wanted of him. The pain in his back was punishment for not following his father's instructions.

"Is that why you've been here a year?" Rsiran asked.

The boy shrugged, not turning toward him. "Better here than some of the places I've been. Here, I get food and a blanket. Same can't be said on the streets."

What must this boy have experienced to choose to remain in the mines, harvesting only enough lorcith to keep from drawing attention to himself? Compared to that, was his life so bad? "What did you do to earn this punishment?"

The boy turned. His smile had returned though his eyes looked hollow. "Punishment? I've had worse punishments. This is …work." He laughed to himself then skittered back a step, crawling on hands and feet until the shadows nearly swallowed him. "And I didn't do anything wrong. Just found in the wrong place."

"What kind of place?"

There was a flash of teeth as the boy's smile deepened. "You're not supposed to sleep in the palace unless you're one of the Elvraeth," he said. "But I couldn't help it. I was cold and that fire looked warm."

The comment finally pulled his attention fully away from the lantern and Rsiran laughed. A few by the lantern looked over. He hoped the shadows were deep enough they couldn't see him, but anyone with Sight would have no difficulty with the darkness. "You snuck into the *palace*?" he asked. "How?" Only the Elvraeth entered the palace. Barriers were in place to keep everyone else out.

The boy slid another step closer, his smile unchanged, obviously pleased to tell the story. "The windows. Most of the time, they leave them open. Something about the sea breeze. If you ask me, the air in Elaeavn smells more like fish than salt, and I'd as soon shut that out."

Rsiran bit back another laugh.

"Of course, up in the palace, they might be too far from the sea to appreciate the difference. Only when you get down near the docks do you notice the stink."

"Why did you choose the palace?" Rsiran asked. There were plenty of other places to find warmth in the city.

The boy shrugged. "It was one of those rains that didn't stop. None of the taverns would let me in. Too young, they said." He shook his head. A strand of his hair came loose and he flicked it back. "More likely they knew I didn't have any coin. By the time I reached Upper Town, I needed a place to dry off and the metal drew me to it. You know how much they have there. Saw the fire and the open window. Only learned later that it was part of the palace. Seems to me the family wouldn't take such offense to me sleeping in front of the fire, but here I am." He flicked his gaze around the cavern. "Can't say this is too bad, either. Blanket keeps me warm. Food keeps me full. Work isn't so bad, as long as you're careful."

The boy crept a little closer. "Take out the small pieces, like the one in your pocket. Ignore the music from the bigger ones. Let them be found by accident."

Rsiran looked down toward his pocket, patting the small lump of lorcith still there. When he looked up again, the boy was gone, having disappeared once more into the shadows.

Rsiran did not sleep well again that night.

CHAPTER 9

THE NEXT FEW DAYS WERE MUCH THE SAME. Each day he awoke to the whistle, having lain awake so late into the night that when sleep finally found him, he did not want to get up. Each meal consisted of the same mush and slice of crusty bread. Other than the work, he had little way of knowing day from night.

Following the boy's advice, he made a point of avoiding the larger veins of lorcith, as well as the thin man who seemed to watch him. He knew where the lorcith veins were, could *feel* them hidden and buried within the rock, almost clamoring for him to free them. But he resisted, choosing instead only the smaller nuggets that fit within his pocket. Of these, he kept a few.

Every day he wondered how long he would be left mining. How long before his father learned he ignored the lorcith and allowed him to return to his apprenticeship? How long before the thin man came to him with questions?

Rsiran had decided the man *had* to know Brusus. There was a similarity to their gaze, and the intense way he stared, and the almost knowing look he wore on his face. And if he knew Brusus, Rsiran wanted to stay as far from him as possible. When he did finally get free of the mines, he didn't want to end up drawn into Brusus's plans. He wanted to return to the smithy, and complete his apprenticeship.

He heard no more talk about why the flow of lorcith had slowed. Mostly because Rsiran simply didn't listen. If he stayed in the shadows, the others would ignore him. He needed to bide his time until his father summoned him back, and do nothing more.

But the days went by painfully slow. Rsiran had been amazed at how quickly the first day had gone, but in hindsight, that was likely because of his focus on freeing the lorcith. Once it was taken from him, he found his time spent more on clearing the loose debris from the floor of the tunnel than actual mining.

He had been working the mines, day sliding to night with nothing other than the steady hammering of the pick upon the stone, for over a week when he lost himself again.

He didn't know how it happened. One moment he worked on a smallish nugget of the ore of the size he could drop and leave behind. Never anything larger. Those he made a point of avoiding, of straining to ignore the music like the boy suggested. Rsiran started working in a remote part of the tunnel, away from the others as much as he could manage. The pick started falling almost on its own. Before he knew it, he had freed a sizeable chunk of lorcith. This was almost as large as the one he had found the first day. Both were much larger than what he normally saw in his father's shop.

Today, the boy was not in the same tunnel as he was. So often they managed to work in the same mines that Rsiran began to find his presence reassuring. He moved to block the lorcith as it sat near the tunnel wall and quickly moved to another part of the wall, chipping away at the stone as if he had not found anything.

When the whistle sounded signaling the end of the day, Rsiran quickly grabbed the lump of lorcith and shoved it under his arm, hurrying forward so he would not be trapped in the back of the line. He could leave it near the foreman or let someone else take credit for the find. Somehow, as the men nearest the stairs leading out of this section of the mine jostled forward, he still managed to end up near the rear.

Pressing forward as he held onto the metal, he had gone nearly a dozen more steps when he felt something stab into his back, almost in the same spot as the last time. He froze, recognizing it as the sharp point of a pick.

"Set it down and keep climbing."

The voice was soft but menacing. Was it the thin man? One of his friends? The voice sounded the same as before, but that didn't help him know who.

Rsiran knew he should listen, but felt a strange fluttering in his chest when he considered it. He shook his head. "No," he whispered.

The person in front of him turned and looked at him. Dust from the rock stained his face and sweat dripped down his brow. Seeing the mass under Rsiran's arm, his eyes widened, and a dark smile crept across his face. Rsiran considered handing the lorcith to him, but he flickered his gaze past Rsiran and turned away suddenly.

The pressure on Rsiran's back intensified.

He took a step forward. The pain from the pick went with him.

"Set it down or you won't make it through the night."

Rsiran suppressed a shiver at the callous tone. What did he care if someone else took the lorcith? He was *supposed* to ignore it. As he started to set it down, he felt an urgency to the soft murmuring that came from the metal itself, demanding that he not.

"No," he said again. Then he scooped the lump of lorcith into his hands and spun. The pick scratched deeply across his back, tearing his shirt and flesh with the same blunt ease. Thrusting the lorcith out like a weapon, he halted in the middle of his swing. There was no one behind him.

He tucked the lorcith back under his arm. His back throbbed, and blood ran from between his shoulder blades toward his waist. The pain almost caused him to drop the lorcith, and he struggled to steady his breathing. He had to lean against the rough wall of the stairs as he turned to climb, hurrying as much as he was able to catch up with the remaining miners.

When he finally reached the top of the stairs, he hugged the wall as he waited for his turn to meet with the foreman, staggering forward so that he almost fell. Most of the miners had already disappeared, but a few lingered. Rsiran hesitantly pulled the lorcith out from under his arm. He could have left it, but that would open him to more questions.

The foreman's pale green eyes widened as he showed him the lorcith. He smiled, flashing yellowed teeth, scratching his beard. "Quite the find," he said. "Miners haven't seen one like this in months."

The words seemed a little too loud, and Rsiran looked around, worried others might hear. The few remaining miners seemed to be ignoring him, but that didn't change the itching in his back. How deeply had he been cut?

"Months?" he asked. The one he found the first day had been even larger. Hadn't the person who stole it from him turned it in for credit?

The foreman nodded, knuckling his forehead. "Time was when this was common. At least once a week, usually more. Now?" he shrugged. "Some think the mines are dry. Others think the Elvraeth need to send more miners. Or maybe the guild just doesn't want more lorcith." He shrugged again, as if that answered the question.

Rsiran shifted on his feet, feeling weak and trying to keep from falling. He laughed nervously.

The foreman hefted the lump of lorcith. "Well, maybe the mines aren't as dry as some think. And you'll be pleased with the credit for this. Name?" the foreman asked.

Rsiran coughed. "R-Rsiran Lareth," he whispered.

The foreman eyed him a moment before taking the lump of lorcith and turning it in his hands. "Nice nugget too. Not much stone to clean off it. Smiths like it that way, you know," he added. "Curious what this will weigh." He hefted it again and set it on his scale, flicking the weights until he was satisfied. He looked up at Rsiran. "Depending on your sentence, this might be enough to get you back to Elaeavn." He turned to search through the names on the paper in front of him.

"Weight doesn't matter," Rsiran said, wanting to get away now. He felt weak and a little dizzy. Rest and water should help, but more than anything, he needed to get out of the tunnels.

The foreman looked up. "Weight *always* matters. How else you going to earn your freedom?" When he finally came across Rsiran, he chuckled. "Ahh. Lareth." He shook his head. "Too bad, I guess. Guess you're right—weight doesn't matter. Maybe a couple more like this might impress your father, though. How long did he say you would be here?"

Rsiran shook his head. "He didn't."

"Shame." He tapped the stone. "These used to be called the gift of freedom, as if the Great Watcher himself decided your sentence had been served. Not many gifts recently. Maybe the Great Watcher is displeased, keeping men here longer and longer, only releasing his gift to someone who can't use it." He looked at Rsiran and his mouth twisted into a dark smile. He shook his head. "A proper shame."

Rsiran swallowed, unable to say anything. Maybe the Great Watcher, like his father and family, had abandoned him. Letting him hear the lorcith and pull the massive deposits from the stone seemed a cruel gift. Of course, gifting him with the ability to Slide felt as cruel.

"Maybe your luck will turn. Enough finds like this, and your father might let you return."

Rsiran shrugged. He wasn't supposed to find lumps of ore like that, but how to explain to the man that he wasn't meant to find lorcith?

Pain shot through his back, and he winced as he started out of the tunnel.

CHAPTER 10

THAT NIGHT, HE SCOOPED HIS MUSH and moved his blanket even farther away from the light of the lantern, almost to the far wall of the cavern. His back throbbed and occasional spasms sent shooting pain down toward his toes. A soft tapping echoed distantly. Had the other men near the lantern watched him even more closely tonight? Did they know about his find? He thought others watched him more closely, but he wasn't sure. At least along the back wall of the caves, they wouldn't see him as well. It was better for him that way.

"You got careless again."

Rsiran squinted against the darkness. The boy crouched out of reach, leaning forward on his hands. "I didn't mean to."

The boy laughed. "You and I could have finds like that every day if we wanted. The others," he said, flicking his head toward the lantern, "barely manage that once a month if they're lucky. You've now done it twice since you came. Things like that get noticed."

"Foreman said nothing of much size for months."

The boy shrugged. "Maybe months, who knows, really? Dangerous for us."

Rsiran ignored the pain in his back. "Who has the highest price?" The question had bothered him since handing over the day's find to the foreman. He could not be certain, but it seemed that the same person had attacked him both times, but why not turn in the lorcith that first day?

The boy shrugged. "That's not really talked about here. Least, not to me. I stay away from the light as much as possible. Stay away from them as much as I can. Less they see me, the less they think of me, I figure. They already think I'm too lucky as it is." He paused, looking from the men sitting around the lantern, their voices muted this far back in the cavern, before turning back to Rsiran. "Well…they did until you came." He laughed, and the sound bounced strangely off the walls. "Now they might leave me alone."

"Thanks."

The boy smiled. "Your own fault. Warned you to be careful. Small nuggets. Avoid the song. The mines are full of finds like you had today. Let someone else be the one to make them. You'll earn enough if you're careful."

"Why haven't they been found by others?"

He shrugged, skittering along the ground on hands and feet, his eyes darting around the darkness making him look wild. "How should I know? Bad luck, probably. Great Watcher doesn't want them found?"

Was he right or was there another reason? And did it matter? He still hadn't decided if finding lorcith would please or anger his father. What lesson did he intend for him to learn? If he mined more lorcith like today, would he survive another attack? He shifted and the pain in his back shot through him again. He bit back a cry.

"Let's see it."

"See what?" Rsiran asked.

The boy moved up to him. This was as close as he had ever come when not around the other miners. "See your cut. What did they use? Knife? Shovel?"

"Pick, I think. Couldn't see."

The boy nodded as Rsiran slowly turned, letting the boy look at his back, knowing he needed to know how badly he was injured.

The boy lifted his shirt slowly. Crusted blood clung to it, sticking to his back, and Rsiran winced as the shirt lifted away. Small fingers worked along his back. There was a sudden shot of pain, and the boy jerked his hand back and dropped the shirt.

"Sorry," he said.

Rsiran turned carefully. "So?"

The boy bit his lip and shook his head. "It's deep. Probably needs stitching. And it's too dark to tell if it's infected. You'll need a healer. No physicians here or down in town, though there is local woman who dabbles in healing most end up seeing. You'll have to show one of the Towners your back before they'll get you to the healer, but they will. Can't have someone dying in the mines."

Rsiran nodded. "And no foreman until morning."

The boy shook his head. "Nope. The mine is locked until morning. At least you won't have to worry about ignoring the song from the ore tomorrow."

Rsiran grunted softly. "There is that."

"Try to rest. I'll watch for you tonight."

Rsiran looked at him. The boy was thin, his hair scraggly and long, an outcast as much as he was but in a different way. This was his protection. "Thanks."

As he curled up on his blanket, careful to keep pressure off his back, he saw the outline of the boy crouching out of reach. For the first time since he had been in the mines, he fell asleep quickly.

* * * * *

Tossing and turning, Rsiran dreamt he was back in Elaeavn. Rather than dreaming of his home or his father's shop, he dreamt of the ocean, the waves crashing along the bay, and of sitting in a tavern. Distantly he was aware of pain and darkness. It seemed a strange song sung quietly in the background, but he couldn't make out the voice.

When he awoke and saw the dimly lit cavern, the single lantern barely giving enough light to the far reaches, he felt empty. The boy rested nearby, sleeping with his arm nestled under his head and one of the blankets now balled up under one arm. Rsiran always thought he looked young, but lying helpless and snuggled into his blanket, he wondered how old the boy actually was.

Rsiran pushed himself up, wincing as pain streaked down his back. He felt hot and sweaty. His shirt and thin blanket were soaked. How late was it? Usually he struggled so hard to fall asleep that he awoke to the morning whistle. Now, other than an occasional snore, the cavern was silent. Everyone slept, resting as peacefully as possible on the hard ground.

The air was still and heavy. He felt none of the usual soft breeze that seemed to blow steadily through the tunnels and wondered what that meant, if anything. The stink of sweat hung over everything, cloying at first, but now Rsiran only noticed it occasionally. Mixed with his sweat was the rotten stink of his drying blood, and he breathed through his mouth to avoid the smell.

Fatigue that had not left him since he first left Elaeavn made it difficult to know how much sleep he had gotten. In the cavern, every moment looked the same as the last with only meals and work giving meaning to time. For all he knew, it was early morning, before the whistle and breakfast and almost time to return to the caves. Or it could be after midnight, much of the night in front of him.

He tried lying back down but stared up at the ceiling, longing to see stars. The pain in his back and the steady nocturnal tapping that came each night made it difficult to return to sleep. Finally, he decided to stand and limped around the edge of the cavern, dragging his hand along the stone. He felt deposits of lorcith even here where the mine seemed to have begun.

There were no other blankets around the periphery of the cavern. Other than he and the boy, most kept closer to the lantern, preferring the light and the comfort of others sleeping nearby. Even those who did not want to sleep next to the light still kept their blankets close together. Rsiran preferred the solitude.

A voice drifted through the cavern, seemingly coming from the entrance to the mines. Rsiran paused, resting his hand on the wall and listened.

"Not much found these days," the voice said. "I think the guild does something to prevent it."

There was something familiar about it, but he didn't know what.

"You know that they want all they can find." This was from another voice, deep and harsh.

"Yeah, well so do I."

"Your price will be paid when you—" The voice cut off suddenly.

Rsiran backed up, afraid that he might have been seen. He pushed against the wall, pain shooting through his back. What had he overheard? There shouldn't be anyone near the entrance to the mines, not at night after the guards left. What were they talking about?

He reached the end of the cavern where it led into the main tunnel of the mines. The hushed voices resumed, but Rsiran feared getting too close. He wanted nothing to do with whatever he'd overheard.

Then there was the strange tapping. It didn't get louder as he walked. He never heard it during the day. If he wandered far enough, would he eventually reach whatever made the sound?

He hesitated. Sleep was precious, and his tired body certainly needed more rest, but he couldn't stand lying awake as he stared at the shadowed roof for the rest of the night, and he didn't want to risk whoever was at the other end of the cavern. So he started down the tunnel.

He touched the wall as he walked, dragging his hand along the stone to guide his way. The slope dropped off as it carried him deeper into the caves. A fearful thought threatened to overwhelm him, that of being lost, wandering the caves in the dark, before he remembered he could simply Slide out if needed. He almost laughed to himself; perhaps his father would get his wish and he would simply abandon that ability, forgotten by his time in the mines.

He reached the flat area where the foremen weighed and logged the collection each day, his feet rather than his eyes telling him where he was. The tunnel breeze blew across his face, rising up from each tunnel. His back throbbed from the effort of walking down the slope.

How badly was he hurt? The boy had dropped his shirt awfully quickly when he saw the wound. With a mirror, Rsiran could at least see the injury himself, not that he could do anything about it, trapped as he was in the mine. Had he been in Elaeavn, he could seek out a healer, even at night.

Why couldn't he simply Slide to Elaeavn? He could find a healer and return before morning. The boy would have questions, but Rsiran could fend those off.

But if he were discovered—if his *father* discovered—Rsiran would never be able to return to his apprenticeship. He'd never be able to work in front of the forge. And then what would he do?

He wandered. The steady tapping seemed to be coming down one of the darkened tunnels.

Rsiran usually went into whatever tunnel seemed to have the fewest miners. Less people trying to talk to him that way. Now that he had been mining for over a week, few even bothered to try. He had never mined in the tunnel where the sound seemed to emanate.

Curiosity spurred him on.

He moved toward the tunnel, drifting into deeper darkness. When he found the first step, he nearly fell. His back sent out a jolt of pain as he caught himself.

Rsiran should not be here. Not at night, not in the dark, and certainly not injured, but something about the strange tapping drew him forward.

He continued down the steps. The farther he went, the darker everything seemed to become, soon leaving him immersed in pure black. Only his hand along the wall and his boots on the steps connected him to the world, anchoring him. His heart fluttered, and he considered turning around, returning to the sleeping cavern, but the draw of the tapping proved too much to overcome.

He had gone only another dozen or so steps when he felt something on the steps with him. He couldn't be certain, and in the darkness he saw nothing, but he froze and listened.

There was only the tapping.

Rsiran took another step, cautiously now.

Air blew against his face. He could not be sure that it was only the usual breeze. Something about the air felt different. Warmer perhaps. Wetter.

He panicked.

Trying to turn, his back spasmed, and he could barely move. The feeling of something near him, overpowering him in the dark, made his mind race. He did the only thing he could think of.

He Slid.

One moment, he stood frozen in fear on the stairs deep within Ilphaesn Mountain. The next, he stood along the waterfront in Elaeavn, waves crashing along the shore and the salt breeze blowing in his face.

Stars shone brightly in the sky. The moon was a thick curl in the sky overhead, almost too bright.

He staggered forward and fell.

He couldn't push himself back up. He hurt all over. His heart hammered, fear and the jolt from Sliding causing it to race. Waves of nausea coursed through him, and he heaved once, leaving whatever was left of the soft mush from the evening's meal lying on the stones near the shore.

A gull cawed overhead, circling slowly. If he rested too long, the gulls near Elaeavn would become aggressive and peck at his flesh. More questions he'd have to answer.

Somehow, he crawled along the shore. Back aflame, his brow dripping with sweat, he didn't know how far he could walk. Sliding still took focus and a fair amount of energy—energy he just expended reaching Elaeavn. He needed healing. That meant moving into the city, risking questions, but if he didn't try, he wouldn't be able to make it back to the mines.

Ambling along the street, he was startled to realize where he was. Awareness slowly sifted into him, like a film pulled away. Waves splashed along the docks farther to the north, a few ships moored for the night along the docks themselves with more anchored farther in the bay. A wide street led toward the main of Lower Town, toward the massive market that provided the only reason for most in Upper Town to make their way to the water's edge.

At night, the market was still and silent. Wind flapped the canvas covering a few of the stalls. A bright-eyed cat prowled near the shadows, watching him as he struggled along the street. Dim lanterns glowed with a warm orange light along street corners, different than those within the mines. With the bright stars and the glowing moon, such light was not truly necessary tonight. Most nights Rsiran felt as he did in the caves, wishing for Sight. Tonight he was thankful he could Slide.

He stood, staring into the market. For a moment, he forgot what he needed to do.

Wind blew up from the sea, caressing his face. If he closed his eyes, he could almost imagine he was back in the mines.

With another jolt, he started forward. Now he had no doubt—the injury was severe. Likely infected. Pain throbbed, gripping his back angrily. If he didn't get attention from a healer, he wouldn't survive.

He recognized the street meeting the market but could not recall why. Rsiran shook his head, hoping to clear the fog that had fallen over his mind for a moment.

Something grabbed his ankle, and he stumbled. The cobbles of the street tore at his face, his arms and hands. He struggled to push himself back up, but pain and weakness pinned him to the street.

A voice called nearby. He thought he heard his name but couldn't be certain. Hands scooped under his arms and lifted him. He tried to look, to turn his head and see who had picked him up, but the night was too dark and what he saw was blurred.

CHAPTER 11

RSIRAN AWOKE TO THE WARMTH of a fire crackling somewhere nearby, tendrils of pale smoke reaching his nostrils. Other smells drifted toward him, all pleasant. There was a savory spice to the air, like that of cinnamon and thyme. Distantly he smelled bread baking. An oil lantern flickered nearby. Hushed voices murmured.

The pain in his back was better.

Not gone, but the raging heat, the angry agony he had been feeling had receded. Some of his strength had returned as well, though the heavy wash of fatigue still rolled over him.

He looked around, not recognizing the room. He lay upon a low cot near the fire. Somehow, he had lost his shirt. A small chair rested alongside the cot. Shelves on one of the walls were lined with books. He could not see the source of the voices.

He started to push himself up, but a hand grabbed him and held him down.

"You need to rest. That was quite the injury. Much longer, and the infection would have taken you."

Rsiran turned to look at an older woman. One hand gripped his shoulder and the other anchored to the cot, braced to hold him down. She had dark hair pulled into a tight knot on her head and deep green eyes. Wrinkles lined her face.

"Where am I?" he asked.

The woman laughed, touching his forehead with a long bent finger. The green in her eyes deepened momentarily, so fleeting he might have missed it, and she pulled her finger away, nodding as if satisfied. "My questions first," she said. "How did you get that injury?" She pointed to his back.

Rsiran turned and looked around the room but saw no one else. Turning back to the woman, he met her eyes. Something told him that she wasn't someone he could lie to. "A pick," he answered softly.

She touched his side, murmuring to herself inaudibly for a moment. "A pick, you say? Strange choice."

Rsiran closed his eyes, remembering the way the pick bit into his flesh, tearing as he turned. "Not really. The only choice."

She shuffled backward and opened his eyes to look. "Great Watcher! You were working in Ilphaesn," she whispered, glancing at something lying near the fire.

Rsiran looked away and saw his damaged grey shirt lying next to the fire, now cleaned and drying.

"What was your crime?"

He laughed weakly. "No crime."

She narrowed her eyes. "Men do not get sent to Ilphaesn unless they have committed a serious offense."

He thought of the men he had seen in the mines, particularly the thin man who had traveled with him from Elaeavn. "I'm guilty only of angering my father." When he saw the look of confusion, he followed with, "He's a master smith. I was sentenced to serve not by the Elvraeth, but by him."

She stepped closer. "Unusual. Such a thing is rarely done and only for special circumstances. Once it was common for many to work the mines. Some even considered it an honor, but no longer. Now it is punishment, forced labor." She frowned. "You are young to have been sent to work in Ilphaesn, but if any were to send a child to the mines, it would be one of the smith guild."

She thought him a child, and he didn't have the strength to tell her that he was nearly seventeen, and already three years into his apprenticeship. Still, there was another in the mines younger than him. "Not just the smiths send children to the mines."

"The Elvraeth do not send children to serve in the mines. The punished must be apprentice age or older."

Rsiran shook his head but did not argue. The boy was nowhere near apprentice age.

"Why did he sentence you to the mines?"

"Because I am not what he expects of a son. Or an apprentice."

"How did you..." She trailed off, looking from the tattered shirt near the fire toward her door, eyes slowly going wide. "I should have known."

"Known?"

She nodded. "You can travel. Slide. Not common, not like it once was." She paused. "That is why he sent you?"

Rsiran didn't answer. He did not need to; the guilty expression on his face was answer enough. He knew of no other who could Slide. From what he had learned, few even knew such an ability existed. When his ability manifested, Rsiran had gone to his father. His father didn't understand and had gone to the smith guild, asking about strange abilities. He returned thinking Rsiran a criminal, forsaken by the Great Watcher. Rsiran's apprenticeship had changed since then.

The woman pulled her chair over toward him and sank into it. She sighed in a gust of mint-scented breath. "Shameful, it is."

He nodded, looking away. She knew of Sliding. Few did, and those who did recognized it as a twisted ability.

She grabbed his face and turned it back toward her own. Only when he finally reopened his eyes did she continue.

"Once, such ability was considered a great gift. And when we lived among the trees in the Aisl, such an ability was almost the only way to connect our people to the outside. Over time, we migrated, moving away from the trees, building along the shores of the Lhear Sea where food and fresh water were plentiful. Eventually, one of the Great Watcher's greatest gifts became viewed as dirty, unsavory. A dark ability. Even the Elvraeth tried to eliminate it." She shook her head.

Her eyes had taken on a faraway expression as she stared at the fire, flaring green. She blinked, and the deep hue faded, leaving her with little more than a pale green film. Rsiran had never seen such a change before.

Could Sliding have ever been viewed as a great ability? Sliding gave him nothing like the ability of the Seers who guided their people through the years. Even the Sighted and Readers were well respected, with gifts that while common, were nonetheless useful. From what his father learned, Sliding would only be used for dark and dangerous purposes, except Rsiran had never used it that way.

Rsiran sighed. "How did I get here?"

The woman looked over at him and narrowed her eyes. She touched his forehead again, shaking her head as she did. "Do you not remember Sliding back to Elaeavn? Such a thing is dangerous. Some are rumored to have died Sliding where they did not intend."

"I remember Sliding." The memory of the presence on the stairs in the darkness as he chased the steady tapping deep in the caverns of Ilphaesn would not be easily forgotten. "But not getting here. Where am I?"

The woman laughed then. "I suppose you would not remember, would you. You were quite sick when you came to me. Lucky it is that she found you. Most get left on the streets, especially in Lower Town. Much longer, and the Great Watcher knows you would have died."

Part of Rsiran wondered if that would have been such a bad thing. "Who found me?"

The woman tilted her head, watching his face. "Thought you knew her. She said she knew you. Of course, perhaps you don't even remember that?"

He had a vague memory of a voice calling his name but even that seemed improbable. Few enough women knew him. Mostly his sister and mother. Other than them, old school friends who he had not seen in years would likely not recognize him.

"She brought you to me for healing. A good thing too. Not many healers could have helped with that infection. Something tainted the wound, something I have not seen in years." She frowned and shook her head. The firelight flickered, casting her wrinkled face in deeper shadows, leaving Rsiran wondering how old she was. "Don't worry, though. She will be back. Said she would return soon with your friends."

Whether it was the effect of the healing or the heat from the fire, he felt his head swimming. "Friends?" He had no friends. His apprenticeship and the demands his father placed on him assured him of that. "I can't stay. I need to get back. If I don't return before morning…"

The woman nodded. "I understand. But it will be dangerous for you to Slide tonight after such an injury. The healing will take its toll as well. You will feel tired and weakened for days." She patted his arm. "Perhaps it is best you do not return."

Rsiran pushed against her hand but she held fast. "My father will find out if I don't return. I'll lose my apprenticeship. I'll have nothing…"

"Nothing? Did the Great Watcher not give you an ability?"

He shook his head. "Nothing of use."

Her face darkened, and the green in her eyes deepened. "Nothing of use? You think you know better than the Great Watcher? Did your ability not save you tonight? Without Sliding back to Elaeavn, you would likely have died within Ilphaesn."

"Without Sliding, I never would have been sent to Ilphaesn." But it was more than that. Rsiran hadn't been able to ignore the call of the lorcith, either.

Silence stretched between them for a moment with only the crackling of the fire breaking the quiet. Finally, she smiled sadly at him, releasing his arm. "True enough, young man. Perhaps the day will come when you will no longer think of your gift with such contempt."

Rsiran pushed himself up from the cot. A wave of dizziness threatened to knock him back down before it passed. "Thank you for healing me. I wish I could pay you—"

"My fees have been paid," she said, her tone more abrupt. "At least stay until your friend returns. You owe her nearly as much thanks."

He stood and grabbed his shirt from near the fire before taking a step toward the door, already thinking of where he would Slide into the mines. Probably inside the gated entrance. Since there was no light, it would be dark, and he could wander back to his blanket as if he had never left.

"You know I can't." Outside the small window, two figures approached. "Please don't tell them."

She studied him before nodding.

As he took a step, Sliding between the planes, he thought he saw a sun-weathered face, hair peppered with black, wearing a finely em-broidered cloak. He almost halted but stepped back into the darkness of the mines of Ilphaesn.

CHAPTER 12

BEING BACK WAS HARDER THAN RSIRAN EXPECTED.
The first thing he had done was rub his shirt into the loose dust on the floor of the cave, dirtying it so he didn't look as if he was fresh from the city. The healer had even taken the time to stitch his shirt with such small stitching that it was nearly invisible. Not that in the darkness of the caves anyone would notice the stitches anyway, but Rsiran felt pleased that it was less likely.

He had avoided the boy as much as he could. The boy tried to get him to go to the foreman so they would take him to town and find a healer. Rsiran argued, pulling away from him. "I'm fine, really."

"I saw your back."

"And yet I'm still here," Rsiran argued.

The boy left him alone, skulking off to a darker part of the cavern to eat, a hurt look twisting his face. Rsiran hated that he had to upset the boy, but if others learned he could Slide, his apprenticeship was lost.

He spent much of that first day back thinking about who he had seen outside the healer's house. Could it really have been Brusus? If that was true, that meant the girl had been Jessa. Lucky for him someone who recognized him had found him. Luckier still that she knew of a healer who could help at that late hour.

But it meant that he was pulled further into whatever they did. It meant that he now owed Brusus more than knives; he owed him his life.

Wrapped up in thinking about what had happened the night before, he did not find any lorcith that day. Sleep deprivation probably contributed to his distraction as well.

The next few days went much the same. The boy began to leave him alone at night, either upset that he had not gotten the help he thought Rsiran needed or for another slight that Rsiran had not recognized. Rsiran worked hard to ignore the sounds of the lorcith buried in the walls, taking only small nuggets of the ore to stave off boredom, nothing more substantial—certainly nothing that would draw the attention of any of the other miners. Each day he pocketed his small quantity. Hopefully his father would learn that he managed to ignore the call of the lorcith.

The other men watched him, especially the thin man, but they never said anything to him. Rsiran wondered who he'd heard near the mine entrance, but chose to hide in the shadows as much as possible rather than risking himself more. He'd done that enough already.

Nearly a week after his return, he awoke suddenly in the night.

Something had startled him, some sound he could not quite place. Was it the steady tapping, the rhythmic sound that never came during the day while they worked, only beginning as the miners were served the soft mush each night? The sound was never consistent, coming and going until late into the night when it became like a steady hammering.

The air held the same strange, humid stillness to it that he had felt the night he Slid back to Elaeavn. Then he had not been certain whether it was related to his injury, but there was no doubting it this night.

He didn't know how long he'd been sleeping. None of the other miners stirred. The lantern glowed softly, nearly a dozen men lying on blankets at the fringes of its light. Other blankets were staggered in a more organized line, filling the lighted space in the cavern. Some men breathed heavily or snored. A few turned occasionally.

He couldn't tell what had woken him.

His back felt tight and itched. Each day the pain receded, and now it was little more than a dull ache that seemed to stretch his skin. Since returning from Elaeavn, he'd slept better. He still missed the comfort of his bed, even his home though it had been years since he had felt really welcome there. But the blanket under him kept him off the cold stone of the cavern, and he had learned to sleep differently, ignoring the small aches from the rough ground poking into his sides as he shifted to find a comfortable position.

Sleep would not reclaim him.

Rather than stare at the dark shadowed ceiling, he stood and slowly walked out of the cavern, glancing toward the entrance. He heard nothing tonight, and breathed out carefully. He considered Sliding, leaving the mines and returning to Elaeavn, but what would he do there? Hide somewhere in the city? Find a tavern and drink like his father? Or would he abandon his punishment and stay in the city?

He shook his head. He wasn't ready to abandon his apprenticeship. He was a Lareth, born to be a smith. He knew nothing else.

The tapping rang distantly, steady, and rhythmic. Rsiran couldn't shake the curiosity he felt about the source of the sound. The last time he tried to find out what caused the tapping, he had been so scared in the darkness that he had Slid to Elaeavn. At least now he wasn't injured.

He focused on the flat area before the branching mines and Slid there.

A wave of nausea and weakness washed over him. Darkness enveloped him, swallowing him. That was almost enough to make him return to the sleeping cavern, but he pushed back the fluttering nervousness in his chest and listened. The tapping sounded closer, echoing toward him on the faintest breath of air. Still distant, but he could tell direction and moved toward the same tunnel that he'd heard the sound coming from the last time. Rather than taking the long stone stairs down into the depths of the mine, he decided to try and Slide.

It was risky. He did not know each of the mines nearly well enough to make such a Slide safely, but he had spent days working in each of the various branching tunnels and used that memory of place to guide his path.

He could appear inside the stone of the mountain, trapping him. Such a Slide would be fatal; each Slide required *some* movement on his part, and if he Slid into the stone itself, he would not be able to Slide back out.

When the sense of movement stopped, he tried to look around, but there was no light. Utter blackness surrounded him. The air moved here, soft and cold against his face, and he shivered.

The tapping was closer still but muted, as if coming through an unseen wall. He stood in the darkness, listening. The sound was familiar, and it took several moments before he realized why. It sounded like a pick striking the stone, chipping away to reveal lorcith.

Rsiran took a tentative step in the darkness, sliding his foot along the stone, his hands stretched out before him. In spite of the cool breath of air blowing through the mine, sweat coated his back, dripping down his spine and pooling along his waist. His hand reached the damp stone wall, and he used that to guide him down the tunnel, dragging his hand along the rough stone.

When he reached the end of the tunnel, he stopped and listened.

The tapping paused.

When it resumed, he *felt* the sound as much as he heard it.

Standing staring in the darkness, this close to the wall of the tunnel, the air nearly still, his palm flat against the stone, he heard the lorcith buried in the wall. The sound was like a steady murmuring voice, quick and anxious, almost eager. There was a musical quality to it, a song rising in expectation.

Moments passed before he understood. Expected freedom.

Could someone be mining the lorcith at night?

He remembered the foreman telling him that the mine used to give up large deposits regularly, at least once a week, but they had become uncommon over the last few months. The boy had told him the mines were full of the large deposits. Rsiran knew that to be true as well. Each time he worked, he struggled to avoid the sizeable nuggets, not wanting to draw the attention of any of the miners, unwilling to risk injury. Then there was what he'd overheard the night he was injured.

What if the reason no one managed to find any larger collections was that someone mined them at night? But where would they take them? Who other than the Elvraeth wanted lorcith?

The tapping stopped. Rsiran pulled his hand away. He felt a fluttering of the air, as if something—or someone—disturbed it, and he took a step back.

He waited, thinking the tapping would resume, but it did not.

As he stood in the dark, his imagination began to get the best of him. Was it the change to the air blowing through the tunnels or was there something else? Was he even alone in the tunnel? In the dark, anything could happen to him and no one would know. Likely as not, no one would even care.

There was another fluttering to the air. His heart raced, and fear got the best of him.

In a panicked flurry, he Slid out of the tunnel and out of the mine.

CHAPTER 13

H E STEPPED ONTO THE COBBLED STREET in Lower Town. Fatigue washed over him as it always did after Sliding, leaving him weakened. Distances seemed to matter; the farther he Slid, the more fatigued he felt.

Again the moon shone too bright, stars blinking brightly overhead, and moments passed as his eyes adjusted. From the angle of the moon, it didn't seem as late as the last time he Slid to Elaeavn. Pale lantern light lit the street. Waves washed against the shore. A gull circled and cawed in the sky.

Rsiran looked around and realized he had Slid to near the tavern.

Movement up the street made him hurry to hide in shadows along the building. A young couple wandered past, the woman dressed in what would be considered finery in Lower Town and clutching the man's arm as they strode down the street. The man glanced over at him, deep green eyes flashing with Sight through the shadows to look at Rsiran suspiciously before looking away.

Rsiran stepped back into the street and started away from the couple. His wandering took him to the water. There was something soothing, calm, to the huge expanse of the ocean. It was a feeling that seemed to be otherwise lacking from his life. Near the shore, he turned toward the docks and wandered past the closed booths of the fishmongers and locked doors of massive warehouses that filled much of the space in front of the water.

"Why did you leave?"

He spun quickly. At the edge of the street, near the corner of a darkened warehouse, a lone figure stood leaning against the wall.

Rsiran edged forward, curiosity making him abandon caution. "Who's there?"

A slender figure stepped away from the shadows. Close-cropped hair framed an angular face. It took a moment for him to recognize Jessa.

"Why'd you leave?" she asked again. She sounded hurt.

Rsiran looked around the street guiltily. At least she confirmed what he'd suspected—that she was the one that found him when he Slid to Elaeavn, injured and nearly dead from the poisoning of the pick. The healer was probably right that he should have stayed and thanked her for saving him, but that left him open to questions he didn't want to answer. It was bad enough the healer now knew. Had she told Jessa? Brusus?

"I—" He couldn't finish. How to explain in a way that didn't reveal too much? "Thank you," he said instead.

She stepped up to him. She wore a small pale flower tonight, white petals nearly translucent that smelled dark and bitter. "Thanks?" What she did next was unexpected. She punched him in the arm.

He winced and pulled away, looking at her and trying to decide what to say.

She balled up her fist as if to hit him again. Rsiran tried to prepare for it; she hit hard, especially for someone as slight as she was. "What happened to you?"

"I was attacked."

She pushed him. "I could see that. Where've you been?"

Should he tell her that he had been sent to the mines? Doing so would only open more questions, questions about his ability, about Sliding. Dangerous topics. "I've been working for my apprenticeship." And if he kept leaving the mines, he would likely lose it.

"Brusus brings you to the Wretched Barth, you dice with us for a few nights, then you disappear."

At least now he knew the name of the tavern. No place on the street had a sign, simply a small stone signaling that it was a tavern. "Brusus only brought me because of the—"

She punched him in the arm again and cut him off. "Is that what you think? Is *that* why you've been hiding?" She pushed him and put her hands on her hips. "You know, Brusus is too welcoming, but even Haern let you join us, and he isn't as easy to please. I had half a mind to leave you on the street."

"Why didn't you?" The anger and hurt in her voice was different than what he expected. She had been the least welcoming of the regulars at the tavern.

"And now you ask me why I didn't leave you?" she asked. "You don't know anything about people, do you?"

Rsiran could only stare, unsure how to answer. The group that Brusus had introduced him to at the tavern were not his friends, not really. How could he call someone a friend when he had only met them a few times?

Rsiran didn't really know *what* they were. Brusus bought a knife forged out of lorcith—a forbidden forging—with few questions and planned to sell it. Hearn had a scarred face and looked far too at ease in the shadows of the tavern. And Jessa... Rsiran hadn't decided what to think of her yet.

"So what happened?" Jessa asked.

Rsiran sighed. "It's a long story."

"So tell it," she demanded.

"I'm not sure you want to know."

"I think I have a right to know."

He sighed again. "I guess you did get me to the healer."

Jessa narrowed her eyes at him. "Could also be that we befriended you as well."

"Is that what we are?"

She flung up her hands, striking Rsiran again in the chest as she did. "The Great Watcher help me! Who else do you dice with?"

When she saw his face, she tilted her head, stepping closer. This close to her, he smelled a mixture of sweat and fish and a hint of something floral, as if she tried to cover up the others.

"You don't have many friends, do you?" she asked.

At that, Rsiran turned away. The comment hit too close to his heart and his own thoughts. If even his family didn't want him, how could he expect anyone else to want to be friends with him?

Had that been all there had been? He had thought the only reason Brusus had brought him to the tavern was for the knives, but what if there had been a different reason?

"Hey!" Jessa hissed as he turned. "Damn, I didn't mean to upset you. You Upper Towners get kind of touchy. Come on, you can still dice with us. No one was too mad that you disappeared. Brusus was mostly worried."

"Why would he worry?" Rsiran asked. He didn't think his family even bothered to worry about him, let alone someone who was nearly a stranger.

"Why? I don't know—maybe it was because I found you lying in the street with a massive wound torn into your back. Maybe because Della said you nearly died. Or maybe it's because you up and disappeared before any of us could see for ourselves that you were okay. Della wouldn't say anything about where you went or why you had to go suddenly, only that you had your reasons. She said that in time, you might even share them." Jessa pushed him, and he spun around to face her again. "Now that I see you're fine, I can go on living."

Something about the tone to her voice struck a chord within him and he laughed. It startled her at first, but then she joined in. Rsiran smiled, unsure if she could even see his expression in the darkness. He hadn't quite figured out what her ability was.

"I'm glad to be of help," he said.

"Damn!" she said. "Maybe we'll get you to lighten up eventually. More ale, maybe? Though I seem to remember you didn't particularly care for ale, only nursing your drink like a babe at the bottle."

The gentle teasing left him with a sense of belonging that he so rarely felt. He looked out toward the water where the reflection of the moon shone brightly. At some point, he would have to return to the mines, but each day there had begun to feel like every other. At some point, his father would have to take pity on him and relent, letting him return home and to his apprenticeship. But what if he didn't?

"So… are you going to come with me tonight, or do I have to tell Brusus that we lost you? Again."

Rsiran turned and looked at her. She held him with earnest eyes that flared a dark green. One finger absently twirled in her hair, and she chewed at the corner of her mouth.

If he went with her, was there any way he *didn't* get caught up in whatever Brusus did?

Did it matter?

Jessa tapped her foot as she waited for him to answer.

Rsiran laughed softly and smiled. "I'll come."

"Oh good. For a moment, I thought I would have to force you into the Wretched Barth. Now I'll only have to force you to have a drink."

Rsiran laughed as he followed her as she started up the street. "I'd like to see you try."

She turned and punched him again. "Don't start thinking about running away now that you've promised me you were coming."

He held out his hands in a gesture of peace.

They walked back down the street running along the waterfront. She veered up sooner than Rsiran would have expected, taking a different path than the one he knew. "You haven't said what you *thought* we were doing."

Rsiran lagged a little behind her, wondering where she was leading them. "I thought... I thought maybe Brusus was part of a rebellion." He flushed as he said it, feeling foolish.

Jessa glanced back at him. "There's no rebellion. You really think the Elvraeth would allow something like that? Damn, but their Seers would pinch that out quicker than anything."

"It was only something I'd heard," he said softly. What had he overheard with his father, then? Maybe nothing more than guild business. "Where are you going?" he asked, changing the subject.

"I have to make a quick stop," she said when she turned and saw him watching her.

"Where?" he asked.

"Errand for Brusus. Not the rebellion," she said with a smile.

They turned onto a smaller side street where no light from the streetlights reached. Shadows lengthened and darkened, but Jessa moved easily, comfortably. Either she knew the way well or she was Sighted, he decided. He'd thought her a Reader, but maybe he was wrong. Along this street, the smells changed. No longer did he smell the heavy odor of fish. Now an oily and thick stench seemed to cling to his nostrils.

"Where are we?"

She spun and slapped a finger to his lips, hushing him. "Be quiet!" she hissed. "We can talk more when we get closer to the Barth."

Jessa moved slowly now. Her head turned as if on a swivel, peering into the darkness and shadows. Then she stopped, placed a hand on his arm, and held him in place. With her other hand, she motioned for him to stay.

Without saying another word, she crept toward a shadowed door. Rsiran could not see what she did—not from where he stood and not without additional light or Sight—but a soft metallic sound pierced the night, as if she scraped at something. Or poked. Then a *click*.

The door opened, and Jessa slipped inside, leaving him standing in the darkness.

Long moments passed with him standing alone. After a while, he began wondering if this was some idea of a joke, Jessa leaving him standing in some hidden alley, lost in a city he thought he knew well, like he had left her and the others wondering about him after he Slid away from the healers.

A cat hissed down the alley, followed by another low growl. Something stirred nearby, a soft swish and the slight shifting of shadows. Another cat likely. Rsiran wondered at their significance. Cats were felt to be both lucky and unlucky depending on their numbers. The two he had heard growling at each other were felt to represent balance. Neutral. If there was a third, that meant luck.

Too much time had passed. Jessa clearly played a joke on him. He turned and thought he saw two other pairs of eyes down the alley. They seemed to be watching him.

Rsiran swallowed. Tradition held that five cats were unlucky. Once he knew why, but right now he couldn't remember anything.

He shuffled quietly back down the alley the way he came. He considered Sliding but wanted to save his energy for the return trip to the mines. Too many attempts in the night might leave him without the strength to return. He didn't want to consider what would happen if he suddenly was gone from the mines.

As he moved closer to the two pair of eyes, they stared unmoving. Should he simply Slide back now? Jessa would be angry, but he didn't owe her anything, not really.

Just his health.

And if they had healed him out of friendship, rather than a desire for anything more, didn't he owe it to her to wait? If she was going to play games on him, well… he probably deserved it for leaving the healers the way that he had.

As he stood debating, something touched his arm, and he jumped.

"Damn, Rsiran!" Jessa hissed. "Easy!"

She held a long box tucked under one arm. Pulling him along with her, they moved quickly toward the street. Under lamplight along the street, he noted the clasp of the box was bent and broken. A sheen of sweat coated her brow.

Rsiran struggled to keep up. "What is that?"

She shook her head, and her short brown hair swished slightly. "For Brusus, I said."

Rsiran glanced back the way they'd come. "Why are we hurrying?"

She slowed at the next intersection and led him up the slope toward Upper Town. "I'm late."

"I thought you were getting back at me," he said.

She turned toward him and smiled slightly. "Aw, damn! Wish I would have thought of that. Don't worry. I'll make sure to do that another time."

She continued up the street, and Rsiran hurried to keep up. At each intersection, Jessa paused, hanging back and away from the streetlamps, before hurrying across. It almost seemed as if she intentionally took the narrowest streets as they wound their way through a section of Lower Town that Rsiran did not know.

A few scraggly trees attempted to grow in the rocky soil. Fewer than were found higher up, though those were groomed and watered in an attempt to mimic the twisting delicate branches found within the Elvraeth palace. Small pale flowers bloomed on some of the trees, the petals damp and glistening in the moonlight. They had a soft sweet aroma that mingled with the usual scents of Lower Town. In spite of their hurry, Jessa paused and plucked one of the flowers. She slipped the one on her shirt out and replaced it with the one from the tree.

After wandering for a while, she finally led them back onto a main street and one that Rsiran recognized. A large statue—worn and weathered by years of salty wind—stood overlooking a small square. Telvrath Square, named for one of the first of their kind who left the trees of the Aisl and dared to brave the waters of the bay. The sculpture made him appear thin, his narrow face pointed like his hand pointing at the water, and Rsiran wondered how any with the fortitude to venture out onto the vast water could looks so frail. Probably the effect of time wearing away at him, leaving him less than he really was.

Rsiran felt a little nervous about seeing the others. How long had it been since he last diced with them? How long had he been working the mines, toiling away like the other criminals for the crime of being given the ability to Slide? Would they ask him to explain? Or would they—like Jessa—simply be glad he was unharmed and welcome him back?

"You coming?" Jessa asked.

"I'm coming." He glanced up at the sky, noting the position of the moon. Another hour, possibly two, before he would have to Slide back

97

and try to get whatever sleep he could before the morning whistle blew and he had to return to the mines.

Outside the tavern, a hint of nerves rolled his stomach as Jessa pulled open the door and slipped inside. Rsiran paused, again debating whether he should return to the mines, but decided that he did not want to leave Jessa feeling abandoned again. He understood all too well the hurt look on her face when she asked him why he left. It was the way Alyse made him feel about returning home.

CHAPTER 14

Taking a deep breath, Rsiran stepped nervously into the tavern. Flickering light from the fire in the hearth at the back of the room gave a warm glow. The tavern was busier than the last time he visited. A steady chatter of voices hung over the room, punctuated occasionally by a loud laugh or, once, a fist slamming onto the top of a table. A flutist played softly in one corner, giving the room a lively feel. The smell of roasting meat wafted out of the kitchens mixed with the spice of the ale. Both smelled inviting.

When Rsiran entered, Brusus looked over from talking quietly at a table. Tonight he wore a shirt of deep green embroidered with strips of blue that matched the stone of his ring. Jessa slipped the long box over to him, and he stuffed it under the table, trapping it between his legs. When Brusus saw him, he stood and hurried over, leaving the box unguarded by the table, an unexpected expression drawing tight lines around his wrinkled eyes—concern.

Had he really misread him? Rsiran wasn't accustomed to anyone worrying about him, not even his family. Were he simply to disappear, leave the city like one of the Forgotten, he suspected they wouldn't spend even a moment thinking about him. So for this man, essentially a stranger, to worry about him…

He swallowed back a strange lump in his throat.

"What happened to you? Della said you were pretty badly hurt. Some sort of poison? Who would try to poison you? Are you mixed up in some kind of trouble?" His words all ran together. "I tried to see you, but by the time I got to Della's place, you had already left!"

"I'm sorry, Brusus." Seeing the mixture of relief and anger that crossed Brusus's face as he spoke made Rsiran feel even worse. He didn't really have any answers for him, either. It was not like he really understood what happened to him, only that someone had wanted the lorcith he mined for himself. "I…"

Brusus sighed and clapped him on the shoulder, his pale eyes flashing a dull green, barely deepening any at all. Again Rsiran wondered about Brusus's ability but such things were not polite questions. Almost as bad to comment on someone's relative strength—a mistake Rsiran had already made with Brusus.

His mind crawled with the sense of someone trying to Read him but it passed quickly. Rsiran glanced at Jessa, but she seemed more interested in the cup of dice.

"Say no more, Rsiran. I'm pleased Della could heal you. Maybe later we'll get you relaxed enough to tell us what happened. The way Jessa explained it, you damn near died from some sort of knife wound to your back. You have to anger a man pretty badly for him to want to stab you in the back! Even Haern hasn't managed that."

Haern looked up, a serious look on his scarred face. He idly spun a fork on the table. "What haven't I managed?" His deep brow furrowed as he looked from Brusus to Rsiran. He spoke slowly and deliberately, his half empty glass of ale sitting in front of hands steepled together on the table.

"To get stabbed in the back," Brusus said, sliding back onto his seat near Haern. His feet cupped the box under the table again.

Another man sat at the table next to Haern and smiled at the comment. Rsiran didn't recognize him.

"As far as you know," Haern said. "Of course, I know better than to come to you for help with something like that. Poor Rsiran has much to learn."

Rsiran smiled and sat in the free chair Brusus offered. Jessa watched him, a satisfied look on her face.

Brusus motioned to the other man. "This is Firell."

Firell nodded. He had long black hair, pulled back behind his head. Unlike most others in the city, he had a small patch of hair on his chin. His eyes were a moderate green and stared at Rsiran intently.

"Hear you let Jessa save your life," Firell said. His voice was soft and lilted with a deep musical quality.

Jessa flashed him a smile. "Worst mistake of his life."

"Probably doesn't even know what a mistake that is," Haern said.

"She's already promised to get me back," Rsiran said.

Firell's eyes widened. "Careful with this one," he said, nodding toward Jessa. "Even Brusus don't want to tangle with her. That's why I prefer to keep out on my ship, away from dangerous girls like her. At least there you see them coming."

Brusus nodded seriously. "Nearly slit my throat the first time I met her."

"On accident!"

"Doesn't mean it didn't happen. The Great Watcher knows that another finger more, and I wouldn't be sitting here."

"But you are. Unfortunately for us," she said.

A small smile pulled on Rsiran's lips, listening to the quiet banter. The teasing felt different from the criticism he usually experienced, all good-natured instead of hurtful. He looked around the table: at Jessa who had saved his life though he had only met her a few times, at Brusus who was making a joke with Firell and had been so concerned about him, and at Haern who watched him closely, a faraway look on his face, his eyes flaring deeper green. Rsiran realized he felt comfortable.

Yet, should he be comfortable? They accepted his injury without too many questions. Brusus dressed like one of the Elvraeth but hung out in Lower Town. He wanted lorcith knives, so maybe feigning concern was his way to convince Rsiran to help. And from what he could tell, Jessa had stolen that box for Brusus. As far as he knew, they were criminals, the kind his father warned he would become with his ability.

Why, then, did he feel at ease?

"Now that we have the boy back, should you tell him your news?" Haern asked, the distant look to his face now gone.

Brusus shrugged, a laugh trailing off as he motioned to one of the servers to come to their table. "Not so much news, but a possibility. And only if our Rsiran here were so inclined."

"What possibility?" he asked.

Brusus pointed toward his glass of ale when the server approached the table, motioning to everyone at the table. The server was thin and with a round face, her black hair curling around her shoulders looking much like Alyse. She smiled fondly at Brusus before turning toward the kitchen.

"Ah," Brusus started. "Well… it has to do with that knife of yours."

Rsiran shook his head. "Not mine. You bought it."

Brusus smiled, twisting the ring on his finger. "And then sold it. Got a fair price, I might add."

Haern snorted.

Jessa punched him in the shoulder.

He looked at her, feigning a hurt expression. "What? He got triple what he paid!"

Brusus's smile deepened. "Two talen! Could probably get more once the quality is known. As of now, Rsiran's mark isn't well known. But with enough time and a few more blades like that, I'm sure that will change."

"Wait," Rsiran said, understanding where this was leading. "I've already told you that I can't make any more like that."

Brusus nodded, taking a long drink of ale. "Don't worry. I'll make sure you keep your cut of the profits." Firell snorted, and Brusus turned to glare at him. "Not like I can cheat him now that he knows what I got, right?"

Firell shrugged. "Not like you wouldn't try."

Rsiran shook his head. "You don't understand—"

If his father learned of that, he would lose his apprenticeship for sure. And he would never be a smith.

"Hold on before you answer. Think on it. You make a dozen of those knives, and we can sell them for ten each. Let's say you keep half. I figure for a longer blade we might be able to get that to five talen. Possibly even a guilden. That kind of money adds up. How long it take you to make one of those knives? Couple of days?"

Rsiran shook his head, realizing now which of the two men he'd overheard that night Brusus was. He owed someone money. "No more than a few hours." Even that was probably a long estimate. With enough focus and the right lorcith, he could probably make one of the knives in less than an hour. And pocket a talen each. That was more money than his father made for some of his most intricate work, but what Brusus asked was forbidden by the smith guild. Too many knives and he would surely be discovered.

"A few hours!" Brusus said too loudly. He glanced around and lowered his voice. "Damn, Rsiran, if you can make them that quickly we could turn out a couple dozen a week!"

"I can't, Brusus."

"I think if we can make a few longer blades, we can drive up the value even more," he continued, as if he hadn't heard Rsiran.

"I can't," Rsiran repeated.

Haern watched with deeply green eyes, still spinning the fork. Jessa chewed her lip, head tilted forward as she softly inhaled the smell of the flower. Rsiran wondered if he was the only one to notice.

Brusus kept talking for another moment before what Rsiran said seemed to register. "What do you mean you can't? That knife was simple. Elegant." He shook his head. "Nothing like that is made anymore!"

Rsiran swallowed. His father would argue that knives were no longer made of lorcith for good reason, though Rsiran never really understood the reasoning. Iron or steel were fine but only for eating or decoration. Never for weapons. If the guild discovered, he wouldn't have only his father to fear—he would be forbidden from working in a smithy by the guild.

"I'm not exactly in good standing in my apprenticeship."

Brusus's eyes widened. "Still can't believe you're just an apprentice. Damn, Rsiran, that knife was..." He trailed off. "How did you manage to make the others?"

"At the end of the day. My role is to keep the shop clean, manage the forge, run supplies." He shrugged. "I don't really get much actual time working at the forge. That's more for the journeymen."

"Life of an apprentice," Firell said and smiled.

Haern nodded as well.

"So we go a little slower," Brusus said, his enthusiasm not waning. "You make one blade a night. Even that production is more than has been seen in several centuries."

"Brusus... I can't." Rsiran didn't even have access to a forge, at least not until his father allowed him to return from the mines. Even were he to risk his apprenticeship then by making knives, there was the small issue of whether the lorcith would even choose to become a weapon. As much as his father wanted him to learn to command the lorcith, to ignore the way it called to him, demanding he draw out the desired form, Rsiran had barely been able to ignore the soft murmuring music while working in the mines. And when he listened, it nearly killed him.

Brusus blinked, excitement finally fading. The others around the table sat still, as if waiting to see how he would react. Finally, he clapped Rsiran on the shoulder. "Well, think on it, at least. You have a gift that we can use. Not many opportunities to make this kind of profit." He waited until Rsiran met his eyes that flashed a soft green. "Please, think on it."

There was a desperation to Brusus's voice that Rsiran hadn't noted before. How much did he owe? And to who?

Rsiran suddenly wished he could help Brusus. The man had helped make ensure he was healed. *Shouldn't* he help him if he could?

"Can we dice now?" Jessa asked.

Haern laughed, and Brusus shot him a look. Haern ignored him and pulled a stack of dronr and set it on the table. "If Rsiran won't help Brusus, looks like he'll have to earn his coin another way. Too bad he never has much luck!"

Jessa stifled a laugh.

Brusus set a similar stack of coins atop the table before pulling out his leather pouch and dumping the carved dice out in a clatter. He scooped them up and waited for Firell until he set coins on the table.

Jessa shook her head. "No money tonight. Though I think you owe me, Brusus."

"Do I? Ow!" he yelled as Jessa kicked him under the table. Brusus's eyes looked down, considering the box he held between his legs, before he turned and smiled. "Maybe I can cover you for a hand. I'll be earning my own money back anyway."

She kicked him again, and Brusus slid back to avoid her feet.

"You in?" Jessa asked Rsiran.

He shook his head. "No money, either."

Brusus turned and gave him a sly smile. "I think I heard of a way you could make some pretty good money. I'll even let you keep the full price for the next one."

"Let it drop, Brusus," Firell said. "I think Rsiran fears losing his apprenticeship if he accepts your offer."

Brusus eyed Rsiran for a moment before raising his hands. "All right! Besides, I couldn't let him keep the two talens anyway. He owes Della two dronr for his healing."

"As if Della charged you two dronr!" Jessa said. Rsiran suspected that she tried to kick Brusus again but he was out of range.

"One?"

She shook her head. "I've never been charged by her once!"

"Well, damn. Guess I will have to let him keep the two talens."

"Here." Haern slid a handful of coins toward Rsiran. "You can play with my coin. I keep whatever you win."

"I wouldn't want to lose your coin."

"Who said anything about you losing?"

"That's not right!" Jessa argued, looking from Brusus to Haern. "None of the rest of us are Seers!"

Brusus frowned and shook his head. Firell simply watched Haern.

Haern only shrugged. "Not Seeing anything. Watched him dice before. Kid's lucky."

A smile spread across Brusus's face. "You'd better hope so, otherwise you'll lose twice as much tonight!"

As they began dicing, sitting around a table comfortably with others who actually wanted him there, Rsiran smiled. Maybe Haern was right. Tonight he did feel lucky. How else to explain that Jessa found him twice—first to save him and the second time to bring him back to the tavern with her. Lucky.

He smiled. It was the first time in his life he'd felt that way. But he couldn't help but worry: how long would it last?

Chapter 15

THE NEXT DAY WAS DIFFICULT. Fatigue made focusing on mining more challenging than he had expected, and Rsiran hammered away at the stone with his dull pick without paying attention to what he was doing. Only when he'd cleared a good-sized chunk of lorcith did he realize what was happening. The work, much like it did when he was working the forge, heating the lorcith and hammering it into shape, took hold of him, demanding what it would.

He looked around. None seemed to see the size of his find, and he pushed it toward a pile of loose debris, covering it as well as he could. Thankfully, the boy had been leaving him alone, choosing to mine down a different tunnel, else he might have been seen. For some reason, Rsiran didn't want him knowing that he was still removing the lorcith from the walls.

The other miners worked in a staccato rhythm. A few worked smaller pieces out from the walls while most simply worked at removing stone, widening the tunnel as they went. The thin man worked in his crew today, but Rsiran didn't think he'd seen him pull the piece of ore from the rock. The foreman assigned to them stood chewing a length of tobanash, its tangy scent hanging in the otherwise bitter air. Flames weren't allowed—something about how the dust could ignite, the same reason the special lanterns were used rather than real flames—otherwise most preferred to smoke it rather than chew the rolled leaves.

Sweat coated Rsiran, and his back ached where he had been cut, though not as bad as it should after such an injury. His skin felt tight, pulled and stretched as he worked, and now itched as he looked around. He dared not stand too long or else he would attract more attention. Better to work slowly than not at all.

Turning back to the stone, he was careful to keep his lump of lorcith near his feet as he chipped away at the cave. Before returning, he had Slid home and grabbed the other knife, taking the coins with him as well. He kept the knife tucked into his pants, making certain not to move too quickly so that it didn't dig into his flesh. The few coins he had in his pocket weighed as heavy. Were anyone to know that he had either, they would be ripped away from him, leaving questions Rsiran was not prepared to answer.

After a while, the whistle sounded. He was careful to let the others move ahead of him. The foreman always made sure to leave the cavern first, never checking for stragglers as he carried the lantern out. Few, other than the most powerfully Sighted, would dare remain in the blackness without the meager light.

Once everyone had moved ahead of him, he dusted the loose debris from the larger lump of lorcith and carried it toward the stairs. After a few steps, he thought he felt motion behind him. This time he was certain he had been the last to leave the cavern. Rather than linger and risk another pick wound to his back, he Slid, taking the lorcith with him.

Stepping from the Slide, trees within the Aisl forest surrounded him, a place his mother used to bring him when he was younger. The air was damp and earthy, and broad green leaves coated the branches. Small bushes attempted to creep from the underbrush, but most were stunted, starved of light with the trees pushing together. A small clearing was nearby, one he had often explored before his father agreed he was old enough to apprentice. He had rarely returned since then, only occasionally when he needed solace. He was not sure why he chose this location for his Slide.

Daring not to linger—there was another roll call in the evening to ensure everyone made it out of the mines—he looked for a place to stash the lorcith. He found a large tree with twisted roots coming from the ground outside the clearing. Burrowing into the ground with his pick, he freed enough space to store the lorcith and quickly covered it with loose leaves and dirt, careful to keep it as hidden as possible. He made a mental note of the tree before taking a step away and Sliding back to the staircase leading out of the tunnel. All told, he had been gone minutes, but he feared it might have been too long.

Only after he returned did he realize that he was now what his father feared he would become—a thief, stealing lorcith from mines owned by the Elvraeth and hording it outside the city.

Now unburdened of his load, Rsiran hurried up the stairs. There was no light, nothing for him to see by, and he worried the foremen would begin to wonder what happened to him. He doubted anyone would worry.

He paused at the top of the stairs, seeing light and a couple dozen miners lingering near the foreman weighing the finds from the day. As he readied to step out and join them, he felt pressure at the base of his neck, cold and sharp. Wetness trickled down his neck.

"Don't move any farther."

Rsiran recognized the voice. It belonged to the same person who had attacked him twice already. How had this person managed to stay behind him on the stairs and how did they know that he had collected a large quantity of lorcith again?

"Where is it?" the voice hissed.

"Where is what?" Rsiran already prepared to Slide. There was no mistaking the threat in this person's voice, no way to mistake the intended use of the pick stuck into the base of his neck. Any more pressure, and he would be dead.

"The ore," the voice hissed. "Where is the ore?"

Rsiran shifted forward and felt the pressure on the back of his neck push harder. Somehow, he stood at the edge of the stairs, right before the ground opened up, but no one saw him standing there. As he moved, something shifted on his back, and he remembered the slender knife tucked into his pants.

"I don't have it."

"Where did you leave it?" The blade pressed harder.

Rsiran nearly screamed but suspected that if he called out, his attacker would only finish him off more quickly.

"Not here. Down in the mine," he said, hoping to buy some time.

"There is nothing but dirt and stone down in the mine. Where is the ore you harvested?"

His mind raced. Somehow this person knew he had a large find today and also knew that he no longer had it with him. Had they seen him Slide? At least he didn't feel completely helpless. He could move, Slide himself to safety, even if only forward a step…

Rsiran had never tried such a short Slide. Even a small step would be useful, likely tiring, but would at least get him up into the open where the other miners would see him.

Would his attacker dare follow him?

"I don't have it," Rsiran said angrily.

Then he Slid forward two steps.

Such movement was like a flicker. One moment he was on the steps, the pick jabbed into his neck, the next moment he was two steps out into the openness of the cavern, a pair of miners standing nearby. One looked up and frowned, surprised to see him, but shrugged and turned back to the line in front of the foreman.

Rsiran sagged, after Sliding to the Aisl forest and back, he felt weakened by even that short Slide. With his fatigue, he might not even have been able to manage a more significant Slide. He shuffled toward the table where the foreman sat, pulled out a few pieces of smaller lorcith, and set them on the table.

The foreman glanced at them and then looked up at Rsiran, his eyes widening. "You're bleeding," he said.

The words took a moment to register, and then Rsiran reached behind his head and felt his neck. There was a long slice deep into the flesh of his neck, nearly as deep as had been in his back. Blood stained his hand as he pulled it away.

"Stones fell," he muttered, knowing the foreman wouldn't ask too many questions unless Rsiran said anything. Falling stones frequently injured men, and though Rsiran had never seen anything more than minor injuries, supposedly a few had even died.

The foreman nodded. "If you need bandaging..."

Rsiran nodded. Nothing until morning. "I'm fine." He wobbled slightly on his feet.

The foreman looked back down to his log and nodded, making a few notes. He waved Rsiran on and didn't look back up.

Rsiran took a weak step and nearly stumbled, catching himself by leaning on the wall of the cavern. Even without looking, he knew this was worse than the injury to his back.

He staggered down the tunnel toward the sleeping cavern, dragging his hand along the wall as he walked. After taking a few steps, he dared not walk any further. His face felt hot and flushed, his legs weak and unsteady. His mind swam remembering what the healer had said about the other injury.

Poisoned.

Not bothering to look, he Slid. What other choice did he have it he wanted to survive? Everything blurred around him, and he staggered forward rather than stepping, and feared he had gone too far.

CHAPTER 16

WHEN HE OPENED HIS EYES, he was in the healer's home, lying on the floor near the fireplace. His pick and small hammer fell to the floor with a clatter. There were no other sounds, only the soft crackling of flames. He tried to cry out but nothing more than a moan made it through his lips.

He lay motionless for long moments, fearing that the healer wasn't home. Finally someone moved behind him.

"Great Watcher!" the healer said. As she reached him, she ran her hands along his neck and back, probing the wound. "Again?"

Rsiran could only nod weakly.

"The poison set quickly this time," she murmured. "I'll need to try…"

Rsiran didn't hear what else she said; everything suddenly sounded muffled. Pain seared across his back as her hands ran over him. His head throbbed, and the lights swirled with bright colors. Muted and muffled voices spoke around him, and more than once, he thought there was someone else in the room with the healer. Slowly his head began to clear, and he could make out what she said.

"Some of it remains inside. Can only wash the wound now."

Something wet and icy hot touched his neck. Rsiran didn't know if it was blood or some healing concoction. It poured over him for what seemed an eternity and then subsided. Della muttered something else, but he didn't understand what it was. Then he felt a steady stabbing along his neck.

"Hold still!" she commanded. "Got to stitch this one. No other way to hold the flesh together, not as damaged as it was. Won't heal on its own any other way. Might not heal as it is, but at least this gives it a chance. There will be some scarring…can't help that anymore. Skin around it might be different too. Not sure if there will be other complications. Have to wait and see on that."

She prattled on as she worked. Rsiran felt each jab of the needle as it went through his skin and the steady pulling of the thread as she pulled it taut. After a while the sense faded and he could tell she had stopped.

"Not at all pleased with this one. Not at all. Messy work and looks like it was done by those without any talent, but it will have to do. At least you'll survive."

She patted him on the head. Her hand was cool and moist. Rsiran managed to blink open his eyes. He was lying on a cot near the fire. Somehow she had managed to lift him to the cot and had worked on his neck.

"Done?" The word croaked out of him. He licked his lips and found his tongue and mouth had gone completely dry and tasted of blood, as if he had bit himself somewhere along the line.

Della tipped a cup to his lips, and cool liquid ran into his mouth. He tasted a bitter flavor mixed with honey and rinsed his mouth as he swallowed.

"That's the first thing you think to ask?"

He pulled himself up. His head felt heavy and wobbly. Pain still pierced his neck, but better than before. "I didn't want to move too soon," he said, trying to explain.

She looked at him with her deep green eyes. Her dark hair was twisted atop her head, and a long stick stuck through it seemed to hold it in place. Wrinkles on her face seemed to have deepened since he last saw her. A sheen of sweat coated her face. "Think you'll Slide away again?"

Rsiran blinked once and then nodded. "I can't be gone too long." All he could think of was returning to the mines. If he didn't, his absence would be discovered, his father would learn, and his apprenticeship—the ability to work the forge—would be taken from him.

"Who attacked you? Same weapon, I think," she said, motioning toward his back, "but a little different poison. More refined. Next time might kill you before you get a chance to jump here."

Next time. Rsiran didn't think he could handle a next time. "I don't know who attacked me. I thought I was clear, but they found me anyway."

"Did you fight back?"

Rsiran tried to shrug but the movement was too painful, causing a flaring pain to shoot up his neck. "Tried. Not much I can do with a weapon pressed against my skull."

"You can Slide."

"I can Slide. Not fast enough."

She frowned, the wrinkles on her forehead deepening. "Only because you refuse to practice. You think they hesitate to use their abilities on you? This gift of yours—and make no mistake that it *is* a gift, young man—does not make you into something you are not. You *choose* how you use it, choose whether to be like the men assigned to the mines…"

He arched an eyebrow at the comment but said nothing.

"Or whether you will find a way to honor the Great Watcher for his gift."

The words washed over him. He didn't know what to say.

"And in spite of how you've been made to feel about your ability, still you use it. Especially when needed. Only you do not practice to gain strength. Each Slide weakens you?"

"How do you know?" he whispered.

"You think all abilities are so different? The Great Watcher grants us our gifts and expects us to use them. Mastering them takes strength. Until then, we are weak."

Rsiran swallowed. His mouth and lips were still dry. "The weakness will get better?"

"Until you barely notice it," she said softly. She leaned back and watched him. "Why don't you give them what they want? Why let them attack you at all?"

Rsiran considered the question and was unsure of the answer. Why had he hesitated to give his attacker the lorcith? He had not the first time, choosing his safety over the ore. When he refused the second time, he had been injured. This time had been the worst, nearly killing him. But even if he had the lorcith, would he have given it to his attacker?

"I don't know."

"And yet you will return."

"It's what my father requires. If I don't, I'll never be a smith."

She smiled sadly. "Your father demands that you suppress another part of your bloodline, young smith."

He looked up. Could she know?

Della nodded, as if Reading him. With as weak as he felt, maybe she had. "The oldest smith families can all sense the lorcith, can all *hear* it. Over time, most have chosen to ignore the call, and in doing so, they ignore who they are, who they should be. That talent, another from the Great Watcher but no less important, has been destroyed over time almost as much as your other gift."

He grunted. "And I am cursed with both."

"Cursed?" she said sharply. "Gifted. Blessed. You should not turn away from anything the Great Watcher gives. Can you turn away from your hands? Ignore the color of your hair or eyes?" She shook her head. "Your abilities are much the same. There is nothing shameful about you, only how you behave."

Rsiran was taken aback. He pushed forward on the cot and started to stand but found that his legs did not want to support him yet. "How do you know so much about all of these abilities?"

Della smiled. "I have lived many years. As a healer, I am privy to much that others are not. I also see how destructive people are to themselves, especially when they try to deny an aspect of who they are. As you attempt to do. Eventually, they harm themselves as much as others. There are injuries even a healer cannot mend."

"What else other than a smith can I be?"

"Why must it be one or the other? Why can it not be both?"

"My father..."

"Ignores a part of himself as much as you have, only he is far enough along, recovery is unlikely. There is still a chance for you."

Rsiran thought about his father, thought about the way he spoke of controlling the lorcith, ignoring the call of the ore, and wondered if that was the reason for his anger, the reason he turned so heavily to the ale.

"He won't accept me if I continue Sliding."

"Then he is the wrong mentor for you."

Rsiran blinked. "There are no smiths in Elaeavn who would accept someone interested in listening to lorcith. At least not that I've met. Every time I let the lorcith guide me, I make a weapon. Knives or sword blades. Such things have been forbidden by the guild."

Della nodded as he spoke. "Then there are no master smiths in Elaeavn who could mentor you."

It dawned on him slowly what she implied. "You mean I should seek apprenticeship *outside* Elaeavn?" He wouldn't even know where to start.

"Why learn from one who would suppress who you are? Suppresses all the abilities that you possess rather than attempt to draw them out? That would be like me ignoring my gift at healing and simply letting you die. To do so is to deny the Great Watcher himself."

"I…" He'd never before considered leaving Elaeavn. Few ever *chose* to leave the city.

She shook her head. "You can choose where you learn, young smith. Especially you. Your ability to Slide can take you as far as you can *think*. Why restrict your education to those who have forsaken so much of what made them great?"

She smiled, and the wrinkles in her forehead deepened, making her look ancient. Rsiran suddenly wondered how old Della was and how she had learned so much about things that few spoke freely of.

"You have not decided," she saw, reading his face. "For now, that is probably fine. You still have time. Soon you might find that you must make a choice—suppress who you are and be who you think you should be or become the person the Great Watcher intended you to become. The choice is not easy, not in Elaeavn as it exists today, but vital to you." She watched him another moment. "Returning to Ilphaesn puts you at great risk. Whoever has attacked you knows much about a particular poison. I don't know why there would be anyone in Ilphaesn with that knowledge, but I also don't think you will survive another attack. Consider, at least, remaining in Elaeavn while you decide. There is safety here."

"They will know if I do not return. My father will know."

Della sighed. "They will know. And so will whoever attacked you. Have you considered why you have been targeted? Could there be another reason?"

"Most men must collect enough lorcith to purchase their freedom. I've been lucky and found large lumps of ore."

That wasn't the only reason, he knew, but the only one that made sense to him.

"Not lucky. You have listened for the lorcith. Quite a difference. The others depend on luck to find even a small nugget. You can listen for the lorcith and target your efforts. You could have a large find each day if you so wanted." She sighed again. "You may not believe this, but you have people who care about you—even if you do not care for yourself."

"I have no one," he muttered.

"No one?" Della repeated. "No one should have let you die on the street then. No one should not have brought you to my home to seek healing. No one should not have returned to check on you, only to find that you had already departed." She shook her head. "You are right. You have no one."

Rsiran did not know what to say and so sat silent, watching the fire. Della let the silence between them linger. He felt her eyes upon him, watching him, waiting. He suspected she would not speak first.

"What should I do?" He looked away from the flames and met her eyes.

She frowned, narrowing her deep green eyes. "Do you think you are the first person who felt they didn't fit within the confines of Elaeavn? Sometimes you have to make your own place, even if it is not the place you thought it would be."

Rsiran stood for another moment, but Della said nothing more. She stood and started organizing the small bottles on a nearby shelf, her back turned to him. He considered Sliding but didn't think he had the strength to return. At least that was what he told himself.

He set the coins in his pocket on the cot before he left.

The door to Della's home closed with a soft jingle as he stepped into the street.

CHAPTER 17

RSIRAN SLOWLY WOUND THROUGH DARKENED STREETS. Could Della be right? Should he return to the mines or should he stay in Elaeavn? Staying meant losing his apprenticeship, but would his father ever really welcome him back?

How long would he be stranded in the mountain? How long before his father cared enough to check on him? Maybe he would never check, deciding instead to let Rsiran linger and fade while working in the mines.

If not for Sliding, he would have died there. Maybe that was what his father wanted.

No one cared for him, so what did it matter if he returned?

Only, that wasn't true. Brusus seemed to care, and his friends. And Rsiran had told Brusus he couldn't help him, couldn't help the one person who had bothered to reach out to him in the last five years. Turned his back on something he asked…something *small* that Rsiran could do.

He spent so much time denying his abilities, that maybe it was time he embraced them. If not for Sliding, he would be dead in the mines, poison and a massive wound in his back leaving him to die in the darkness, no one to find him until the following morning. If not for Sliding, he wouldn't have been brought to Della's home. If not for Sliding, he would have died… not once, but at least twice.

Why should he deny himself an ability like that? Why would he deny his ability to listen to the lorcith?

Why would his sister, his mother, his *father* want him to be anything other than what the Great Watcher made him to be?

He turned and started toward Upper Town. The wind gusted against him, swirling through the buildings and seemingly pushing him as he walked. He passed by a small florist, a sign above the door that of brightly colored petals and a deep green stem, and wondered if this was where Jessa would find her flowers, before deciding she would not. Jessa would find her own, always had flowers that fit her. None of the beautiful and delicate flowers in the window seemed like her. The flowers she wore were different, unusual, and yet still beautiful.

He passed one of the other smithies. The lights were out, the scent char and hot metal radiating to the street from a cooling forge within. A sense of longing stirred in his chest, a sense of something missing. He walked on.

As he walked further up the street, the roadway widened gradually to wind its way up the cliff side toward the palace. In the distance, the peaks of the small outermost spires rose above the city, the twisting towers mimicking the natural stone of the rock. But from his angle it stood out, making it appear to be floating. The farther he walked, the more the palace shifted, each of the many spires taking on the illusion.

Rsiran stopped when the entire palace seemed to float.

This was the point in the city where the Floating Palace took its name. In the daylight, the sun struck the rock so that the walls simply vanished, the spires and towers seeming to float unattached to the rest of the cliff. In the moonlight, it looked impossible.

Time passed as little more than the shifting of clouds and the fading moon. The Floating Palace did not change—had never changed—but lights in the windows came and went. The wind blowing up off the sea, skittering across the dusty streets of Lower Town, blew up toward him, losing the fishy stink of the harbor as it stretched toward Upper Town, always holding the salty hint of the sea.

The healer was right. Now was a time for deciding, a time to choose whether he would Slide back to the mines, return to his life, to the chance of his apprenticeship resuming, or whether he would not. There seemed to him no other choice to make.

Returning would be easy. The pattern to the mines was now familiar: awake, eat, mine, eat, try to sleep, and hide from the others in the mine. Only Rsiran never managed to hold to the pattern, always finding some way to disturb things. Whether it was struggling to sleep or finding some massive lump of ore, he never really held to the pattern. Even there, among criminals and thieves—maybe worse—he did not fit in.

Not returning created new challenges. Did he dare stand up to his father, tell him that he could not stand another day working the mines, trying—and failing—to ignore the call of the lorcith? Did he dare admit that mining had almost killed him?

Would his father even care?

As much as he did not want to admit the truth to himself, that last bothered the most.

Finally, Rsiran stood. The stillness and the cold had stiffened him, and he stretched. Pain pulled on the tight flesh of his back. The freshly stitched injury on his neck burned but not with the pain he knew it should, and he was thankful for whatever the healer had done to lessen his injury. Rsiran Slid.

Familiar walls of his home pressed upon him. Down the hall, toward the kitchen, he smelled the remnants of last night's dinner. The other end of the hall opened into the small sitting quarter. Once a place of happiness for him, a place where he and Alyse would play, a place where his parents would sit and talk, a place where they read to him and his sister. But those were times *before*.

Standing in the room, looking down at the small metal sculptures made by his father over the years that lined the hearth, at the solid wooden chairs and the simple rug thrown across the floor, he felt as if he didn't even recognize the place.

He turned. There, standing in the hallway, was Alyse.

"Why did you come back?" she hissed. "He sent you away. Sent you to the mines."

Away. That had been what she said first. "And that pleased you?"

Alyse's face softened. "Whether it pleased me or not makes no difference. It was for the best."

Something in what she said struck a nerve. Only then did Rsiran move, stepping back. "He was never going to call me back."

Alyse hesitated, and in that moment, Rsiran knew the painful truth. "I don't know."

For a moment, he considered returning to his room and grabbing the remaining items he felt were his. A long coat. A few puzzles. A couple of shirts. But he decided against it. Other than the knife and the coin he had taken the other night, there was nothing else of value.

Turning his back on his sister, he prepared to Slide. "Goodbye, Alyse. You will not see me again."

Then he Slid from the house.

* * * * *

Dawn dusted the horizon, grey light filtering through clouds. Overhead, the gulls still circled and cawed. He was not sure whether they chased or supported him. This close to the water the heavy crashing of the waves thundered against the shore. The sound of fishers and dockworkers filled the harbor.

The tavern was silent. Rsiran realized that he had never visited it this late in the night—or early in the morning—but it was the only place he thought to go. He was tired, his body aching and feeling like he had not slept in weeks rather than missing a night of sleep. Hunger rumbled his stomach.

If he did not return to Ilphaesn, he had no place to go.

Part of him struggled with his decision, a distant part of his mind pleading with him to return to the mines, to do what his father asked of him so he could return home, could continue his apprenticeship, could return to work the forge.

Rsiran shoved that voice aside.

"You look lost."

Rsiran jumped at the voice and turned. Brusus stood near the corner of an alley that led up and around the tavern. He was dressed in a dark brown overcoat and had a small wooden box like the one Jessa claimed for him clutched under his arm. His pale green eyes seemed to flicker as he looked Rsiran over, glancing only briefly at his dress. Rsiran wondered again at what Brusus's weak ability might be; probably something useful even weakened, something like Sight.

"Brusus..." His heart hammered for a moment, and he felt guilty about how he had left things the last time he saw the man. Brusus had helped him without any expectation of repayment, and now, if he stayed, he would never be able to repay him. But Brusus had

126

welcomed him, worried about him. It was more than could be said about his family.

"I... I don't have anywhere to go," he finally admitted.

Brusus didn't hesitate. He simply moved forward, shifting the wooden box under his arm, and placed the other arm around Rsiran's shoulders, pulling him down the street. "You can't sleep in the street," he said as they walked.

This close, Brusus smelled of aged cedar and dust. A grey film covered his collar and smeared across his coat that reminded him of the mines.

"Your 'ship?" Brusus asked, steering him toward a side street that looked vaguely familiar. Small twisted trees grew between the buildings, barely rising over the rooftops. Weeds peeked between the stones. There was garbage and the hint of sewage in the air. No one else walked the street at this time of night.

Rsiran sighed and nodded. "My... father," he started. "He is displeased with my work. I am no longer welcome at his forge."

Brusus led him to the back of a small squat house and twisted a small key in the lock. He paused before opening the door. "You know the thing I hated most about the 'ships?"

Rsiran shook his head.

"It's the way the masters make you feel. The way they think they *have* to make you feel. Like you're worthless... until suddenly you aren't. Then they call you a journeyman and let you do actual work. You know the difference between some of the apprentices and the journeymen I've met?"

"The journeymen have mastered—"

Brusus shook his head. "You're falling into their trap again. Sometimes, the only difference is a day. Just *one day* separates a higher apprentice from a lower journeyman. The guilds can't be satisfied with teaching their craft, they have to make a game of it, torment those working through their 'ships, have tests which never serve to test your skill—only your loyalty to the guild."

Rsiran wondered what guild Brusus had served. What skill set did he have that he no longer used?

Brusus pushed the door open. "Sorry, but as you can see, I don't have much space. You're welcome to stay. Can't have you sleeping on the street. Too cold at night. Too many dangerous people out."

Rsiran felt a small smile come to his mouth. "You were out."

Brusus flashed a smile in return as he pushed him through the doorway. "You don't think I'm dangerous?" There was a hint of something dark in his tone, and Rsiran remembered the way that he'd felt about Brusus when he first met him.

Rsiran shook his head. "Not like some."

Brusus lit a small candle, lighting the room. He was right… he didn't have much space. A small room, barely more than five paces each way, held a hearth and a single chair. A plush woolen rug stained in a red and green checked pattern was the only real decoration. Two metal cook pots lay unused next to the hearth. Another darkened room led off to the side.

Brusus grabbed a rolled blanket and handed it to Rsiran. "You should get some rest. We can talk in the morning."

Rsiran smiled. "I think it is morning."

Brusus shrugged. "Later then. We'll figure this out, Rsiran. I know it can be scary not knowing what to do next, but some of us have been there before."

He started past, walking toward the unlit room. As he passed, Rsiran shifted the blanket around him and lay upon the carpet. It was as soft as it looked and much better than sleeping on the rock inside the mines. "Brusus?"

"Hmm?" Brusus paused in the doorway, the box he carried tilted. Strange writing was scrawled on the side in faded black lettering.

"If you can find me a forge, I'll make more of the lorcith blades."

Brusus shook his head. "Don't. No obligation for letting you stay. Just friends, Rsiran."

Rsiran nodded. "No obligation." It was more than the desire to help Brusus. That was part of it, but what Brusus had said resonated in him like a hammer striking ore with the right speed, the way he usually felt when in the thralls of the lorcith. It wasn't that he wanted to help Brusus. He wanted to stand before a forge again, wanted to feel the sweltering heat as he took the lump of metal and shaped it into something else, something *more*.

Whatever else he was, there would always be a part of him that was a smith, and he would no longer deny that any more than he would deny his ability to Slide or listen to the call of the lorcith.

"It is the only thing I know," he said softly.

Brusus watched him for a moment, his face unreadable. "We can talk after you rest."

"But, Brusus, I…" He hesitated before pushing forward. Brusus deserved some measure of truth from him. "I heard you that night we met. I know you're in debt. If I can help—if the knives I can make can help…" Rsiran shook his head and met Brusus's eyes. "I want to do what I can."

Brusus watched him, considering. "I know what this means. Unsanctioned smiths are punished by the guild. Doing something like that risks more than your future."

"I've already risked my future. I just want to stand before a forge again." He couldn't hide the longing in his voice.

Brusus nodded. "We'll talk in the morning." Then he disappeared into the room.

As Rsiran lay on the rug, blanket covering him, he knew that Brusus was right. The guild was possessive of the smiths. Anyone not operating within the guild was subject to fines. Sometimes worse.

He sighed. If not the forge, then what? He truly didn't know anything else.

CHAPTER 18

BRUSUS WAS GONE WHEN RSIRAN AWOKE. Instead, Jessa sat in the small wooden chair next to the hearth, watching him sleep, a pale purple flower tucked into the loose brown shirt she wore. Her hair was brushed away from her face, leaving her thin lips in a line that almost resembled a smile. Dark green eyes that stared at him intently twitched slightly, as if she wasn't certain how he would react.

"You're awake," she said. With one hand, she gripped her hair, twirling it in a way that was at once more feminine and youthful than Rsiran had ever seen of her. Of course, he suddenly realized, he had never seen her during the daytime.

He pushed himself up, shifting the blanket that had covered him. His neck hurt, aching and itching where the healer had placed the stitching. His back felt tight where he had first been injured, making his skin feel like it was too small for him, like leather soaked in water that had shrunk. Stretching helped. Would he always feel this way or would it eventually get better? If he ever saw the healer again, he would have to ask her.

"I am."

The reality of what he had committed himself to struck him. By now, the mine would be up and active, names read, and they would know he was missing. How much longer until word reached his father that he had disappeared?

"How do you feel?"

The question seemed laced with accusation. Rsiran wondered how much of his injuries Jessa knew about, how much the healer had passed on to Brusus and his friends, or was much of what they had talked about kept confidential?

Rsiran shrugged. "I feel..." He trailed off, struggling to decide *how* he felt. Pain worked through him, but he had become familiar enough with the sensation over the last few weeks that he was no longer aware of it unless it flared or changed. His stomach rumbled, demanding that he be fed. Healing and weeks without much food took their toll. His mouth was dry, and his tongue felt thick, as if he had spent the night drinking ale in the tavern. Were he left alone, he thought he might be able to lie back and sleep for another day or more.

But in spite of that, he felt a sense of release, of freedom. "I think... I feel fine."

Jessa watched the emotions play across his face, her lips twisting into more of a smile. She snuck a sniff of the flower, and again Rsiran wondered how many had noticed her do that.

"Then get up. You're coming with me." She stood and watched him, crossing her arms over her chest as she waited.

He stretched again, each time making his body feel a little better. "Where?"

She shook her head. "I'd say breakfast, but it's almost noon, so lunch? I could use a cup of tea."

She pulled open the door and stepped into the street, waiting for him to follow. Dropping the blanket, he realized he was still dressed in the dark greys of the mine and waited for Jessa to react, but she did not. Would any others in the city recognize the dress? Surely there were some who had been sentenced and managed to mine enough lorcith to earn their freedom. Most would live in Lower Town as well.

Jessa flashed him an annoyed expression, and he decided it didn't matter. He would simply Slide and grab some clothes later; change into something else.

At the doorway, he saw that the sky was blue and bright, thin clouds drifting overhead. No gulls circled as they had last night, chasing him until he found Brusus. The sky was empty, nothing but the warm sun nearly at its peak. How had he slept until midday?

"Where are you taking me?"

"Food," Jessa said. "Didn't you hear me?"

His stomach rumbled again at the mere mention of food. "I don't… I don't have any money."

She turned and glared at him. "Who said anything about money? You Upper Town folks sure think about money an awful lot."

Biting back the first thing that came to mind, Rsiran caught up to her and glanced over. "When did I say I was from Upper Town?"

Her smile widened. "Didn't have to."

She led him down the street as it twisted before meeting up with the main street running from the harbor all the way up to the Floating Palace. Rsiran couldn't remember the last time he had been this far down in Lower Town during the day. Most of the errands his father had him run under the guise of his apprenticeship were to shops between Upper and Lower Town. Occasionally, he would be sent to fetch more supplies of ore, but even that was rare since most ore merchants delivered directly to the shop. Most often, Rsiran was responsible for delivering completed projects. That was a task he always despised, especially the way the Upper Town customers left him standing on the doorstep, never inviting him in, careful to barely even touch him as they took the project his father had been commissioned to work on off his hands. Early on, Rsiran had wondered why his father never made the deliveries himself, but now he thought he understood. In that, he agreed with his father.

The street was crowded. People moved from storefront to storefront, some dressed in simple dark pants and light shirts, others more formally in long, collared overcoats. A few looked to be shoppers from the Upper Town, but most looked to come from the middle section of the city and Lower Town. Carters with wheeled pushcarts loaded with purchases moved up the street, heading toward Upper Town. A few empty carters moved down the street to begin shopping. At least with the variety of dress he didn't feel completely out of place. His mining clothing did not truly fit in, but didn't stand out as he feared they might. Only another from the mines—or one of the Elaeavn constables—would recognize his attire.

The shops even looked different in the daylight. At night, what seemed faded and rundown still had a certain washed out appearance, paint long since faded or chipped, disappearing in the harsh sunlight that beat upon the stone, but the cracked stone and unsettling feeling he had wandering the streets was gone. The activity around the stores helped, and the merchants hawking at the doors gave a sense of urgency. There was a vibrancy to the Lower Town, a sense of life that he never really felt on the higher streets.

Standing on the intersection of the smaller street as it ran into the wide main street that wound all through the city, he looked up toward the palace. From where he stood, only one of the towers seemed to float, as if detached from the rest of the palace, an arm separated from the rest of the body. Even that had a certain grace unlike any other place in the city.

Jessa saw him looking and nudged him, pulling him into the throng of people. "Keep your eyes out of the clouds."

Rsiran glanced over. "What do you mean?"

She nodded toward the palace. "None of us is ever gonna float like the Elvraeth do. Doesn't do any good to set your eyes up there in the Floating Palace. Doing that only makes you feel bad about what you don't have."

Rsiran stared at the palace and wondered how difficult it would be to Slide inside. How long would it be before he was caught like the boy in the mine? Would he have time to explore, to see how the Elvraeth lived? Surely, the life they lived was nothing like his. Theirs would be one of freedom, of excess. Rsiran wanted simply to *see* it, to know how different they were from him.

"I don't have anything," he said softly.

Jessa shrugged and turned to her flower, sniffing the purple petals briefly. "Exactly. Why would you want to stare up there and feel bad about your place in this world? The Great Watcher might have a purpose for you, but it isn't up there. Unlike those who have been simply handed their place, you have to find your own way, make your place. If you ask me, it's better that way."

Rsiran looked over to Jessa wondering if she was joking and saw nothing but an earnest expression on her face. He wondered if she had lived her whole life in Lower Town, if she had ever had a chance at an apprenticeship, if she knew what it was like to lose your future. Lose everything that you knew. The way she looked at him, the pain that hid behind her deep green eyes, told him that she had felt *something* like that in her past, even if it was not the same. Even though they had started at different places, they shared a similar future.

"Better than that?" He pointed toward the palace. Sunlight caught the stone in such a way that it nearly glowed.

Jessa looked up toward the palace, a mixture of emotions on her face. Eyes appeared distant, almost haunted, the corners twitching as she blinked against the sunlight. Her mouth was tight, and she sighed, almost a sound of longing.

"Better to be wanted." Jessa blinked again, and her mouth tightened. "If Brusus has taught me anything, it is to stay out of the clouds. We might not have the same view, but we don't have as far to fall. Besides, we can see the ground better here."

She started down the street, winding through the crowd, not waiting to see if Rsiran would follow. He hurried after her, losing her at times as she slipped between people. Finally, he grabbed at her sleeve and held her arm so as not to lose her. Jessa looked back and offered a strange smile but didn't pull away.

The crowd thinned as they neared the harbor. The storefronts looked more dingy, and the sound of the waves crashing on the shore mixed with the cawing of gulls more than the voices of the crowd. Jessa pulled him toward a side street that ran parallel to the harbor. The scent of food drifted to him long before he saw the market. His mouth immediately started salivating, and his stomach lurched in a rumble.

They stopped at a stand selling smoked meats where Jessa paid a copper benar for an arm length of sausage. At another stand, she bought two apples. She eyed a stand down the street selling flowers but turned away without buying anything.

As they wandered the market, Rsiran froze when he spotted a constable in the distance. There was no mistaking the deep green cloak hanging over his shoulders or the slender sword sheathed at his side.

In all of Elaeavn, only the constables were allowed to carry weapons openly. The man moved toward him, and Rsiran suddenly wondered if he'd recognized Rsiran's clothing. Would he know that it was from the Ilphaesn mines? Or was he simply patrolling? The constable was too far away to know with certainty whether he moved toward them intentionally, but he approached quickly.

Rsiran grabbed Jessa's arm and turned away from the market, steering her along a side street barely wide enough for them to move side by side and headed in the only direction he knew. They reached the harbor, and he hurried along the shore, glancing back over his shoulder as he went, not relaxing until he was sure the constable did not follow.

Finally, they sat on one of the massive rocks lining the water. Jessa said nothing, only pulling a slender steel blade out of her pocket. Rsiran noted that it was chipped and the tip had broken off somewhere, but it was otherwise sharp. She sliced the meat and pushed a handful over to him. She did the same with the apples, slicing them and tossing the cores toward the water.

"What was that?" she finally asked.

Rsiran took a slow bite, deciding how to answer. He tasted the smoky flavor as he ate, and even though the meat was tough, he enjoyed it. The crashing waves seemed to wash over him as he thought about what to tell Jessa. For all that she had done for him she deserved an answer.

"I—"

"Did you see someone?" She leaned forward, meeting his eyes.

Rsiran swallowed and nodded slowly.

"Was it the same person that hurt you?"

When he hesitated, she pressed.

"Was it, Rsiran? You nearly died!"

He looked down at the grey pants he wore, pants that were the uniform of the Ilphaesn mine, and decided he couldn't answer the question. Not and keep the other part of him secret, the part that his father had hated most, the reason he had been sent away in the first place.

But did he lie to Jessa? The concern on her face was real, almost twisting her mouth in pain as she waited for his answer. And yet... if he told her the truth, he didn't know if she would still stand by him. And if not telling her kept her around, then he knew what he would do.

He hated himself as he nodded.

* * * * *

After they ate, Jessa led him back up into the city. The crowd at midday had not thinned, though he noticed there were fewer carters. Jessa barreled forward, her tiny body somehow crashing through the crowd.

"Where are we going?" he asked her.

She glanced over the shoulder of the arm he had again grabbed onto so that he didn't lose her. "Got a place to show you."

He nodded but she had already turned away. "What place? Why?"

She pulled him alongside her so that she could see him without looking back. "Can't have you spending all day wandering the streets. We've got to find you some work."

Rsiran felt his steps slow and forced himself to keep up with Jessa. She was right. He needed to find work of some sort—a way to be able to repay Brusus for his kindness, to repay Jessa for the food she had bought for him—but the only work available to him would be the kind he didn't want. He had no formal training and had abandoned his apprenticeship. The only for job someone with his ability was something he refused to become.

Jessa watched his face and slipped her arm out of his grip, pressing her hand into his and squeezing. She said nothing else but did not let go of his hand, dragging him along.

Near the upper boundary of Lower Town, she pulled him onto a side street. The buildings spilled on top of one another, simply crowded together. The stone of some had crumbled, leaving piles of debris in the street. None were painted. Piles of garbage stacked in front of some of the buildings and a lingering scent of sewage hung in the air, as if it no longer drained toward the harbor as it should. A few people slunk along the street, drifting into shadows as they neared. The farther they walked, even the sound of the crowd along the street behind them became muffled and faded.

They passed a small child sitting on the ground outside. He looked sickly, his face thin and pale, and he looked up as they passed. Rsiran noticed eyes that were nearly as pale as his face. It was no part of the city that he had ever visited. For the first time in his life, he wished he had one of the blades he had forged.

"Why here?"

Jessa shook her head, and they slipped down another side street, this one so narrow that their shoulders brushed the walls of the buildings they passed. Along here, it seemed as if there was one long stone building. Cracks worked along the wall and piles of stone and dust lined the street, mixing with pools of water that still stood from the last rain. Rsiran had been out of the city too long to know when it had last rained, but the air smelled moldy and dirty and the street looked as if it never saw the sun. Narrow doorways interrupted the run of buildings, some gouged and others damaged, as if they had been broken into and set back in place.

139

Why was Jessa leading him here?

Finally, along the row of doorways, she stopped. The wood of this doorway looked newer than the rest, but still faded and worn. It was set solidly into its frame and a shiny handle with a massive lock blocked entry. Jessa glanced at the lock and smiled before pounding on the door with her small fist.

Rsiran waited next to her anxiously. If this was where she was taking him for work, he wasn't certain he wanted anything to do with it. He might be better off returning to the mines, or simply heading down to the harbor and begging one of the ships to take him onboard. He had never been aboard one of the tall-masted ships moored in the harbor, but in spite of the low pay, the captains were said to be loyal, and with luck, you could work your way up the ranks. As he stood in the dark street, buildings pressing down on him, the stench of fetid water and other things even more disgusting holding in the air, he wondered if that might not be better.

Then the door opened.

A large man greeted them. He was round and flabby and wore a thick beard around a wide jaw with eyes blazed a pale blue, looking nothing like any man he'd ever seen in Elaeavn. Long brown hair hung curly and loose, shooting up in random sprouts. Black dust or grime seemed worked into his skin, and he wiped his hands across a long canvas apron on his massive belly. He eyed Rsiran suspiciously before he saw Jessa. When he saw her, his face brightened.

"What you doin' here, girl?"

"Shael." She shook her head, and her eyes tightened. "I should have known you were back, especially with the way Firell has been acting. Didn't Brusus tell you I was coming?"

He shrugged. "Might have said sometin' about a visit. I don't always pay attention to those sorts of things."

Jessa pushed on him in his stomach with her free hand. "Don't play dumb, Shael. Suits you too well."

"Aye there, girl!" he said, backing up. "Don' be pushing me like that. You know I bruise."

Jessa shook her head. "Yeah, yeah. You say you're like an apple."

Shael narrowed his considerable brow and shook his shaggy head. "Nah, girl. Like a peach. The saying is bruise like a peach."

"I don't know what that is, Shael."

"Sometimes I forget you're so sheltered, girl. Need to get you out of this place from time to time. See a little of the world. More to it than the water and these rocks."

"Are you sure? Seems to me there is plenty right here." She jabbed him again.

He grimaced at her. "Careful there, girl. Don' be messin' around with my feelings. Jus' teasing me, you are."

Jessa laughed. She tilted her head slightly and took a deep breath of the flower stuck through her shirt. "So what is this, Shael? Why did Brusus want me to bring him here? And why you?"

"So many questions you do be asking, but you ask the wrong person. I just be doin' what I am told."

She snorted. "Somehow I doubt that's *all* you're doing."

He spread his thick hands. "Maybe a bit more than that, girl, but I've got my reputation to uphold."

"So?" Jessa tried to push past Shael as she asked.

He smiled and his mouth split his wide face. "So." He held his ground and looked over at Rsiran. "This is the boy Brusus was blathering about?"

Jessa glanced over at Rsiran and snorted. "Blathering? That sounds nothing like the Brusus I know. Now if you said rambling or...."

Shael raised his heavy eyebrows. "Nah… he jus' go on about how I needed to find a forge, something about a smith needing a fire and all that. Can't believe he was talkin' bout this boy. Barely able to hold a plow, this one is. Can't see him working a hammer over an anvil."

Jessa shook her head again. "Still don't know what that is, Shael."

He stepped aside and motioned them to enter. "You all the same here. No one knows there is other places beyond yer walls. Think this is all that your Great Watcher made."

Jessa let go of Rsiran's hand, and he felt its absence as a loss.

As she passed, Jessa patted Shael on the stomach again. "Why go anywhere else when the world comes to us?"

"Don' you go playin' with me, girl!" Shael laughed, the sound hearty and stretched out to fill the room opening in front of them.

Rsiran stepped past the door and into a wide storeroom of sorts. Much wider than he would have expected from standing on the street, it was as if walls of the neighboring buildings had been torn away, leaving a much larger space. Loose rock and dust littered the floor. Stone columns interrupted the openness. Three small iron oil lanterns hung on posts gave enough light to brighten the room. The crumbled roof in one corner let in sunlight that spilled across the floor, revealing pale red stone and piles of dust.

The far wall of one room caught Rsiran's attention. An immense old forge rested along the wall, metal chimney dull and faded, cobwebs spilling out on the ground around it, and a few loose stones cracked along the wall. A huge anvil was set onto the floor. The smell of fresh oil lingered on the air, and he suddenly understood what Shael had been doing when they arrived.

Rsiran started toward it before he even knew what he was doing.

"So you like it, do you?" Shael asked.

Rsiran caught himself and froze. Wasn't this what Brusus had wanted—his own access to someone to make lorcith weapons that he could sell? And Rsiran had offered.

He turned and looked back. Shael watched him with a curious expression, strange blue eyes narrowed and his generous brow furrowed. Rather than annoyed, he seemed amused, as if he would start laughing at any moment.

"Seems Brusus read you right. Aye, but he got a gift for that, don' he? Took me all morning, but I think I got mos' of the rust worked out. Jus' need someone who knows how to work these things and you might have yourself a smith, not that I would tell the guild 'bout that." He eyed Rsiran again, and his expression changed. "You sure you be the one who knows how to work this? Shael here spent a good bit of coin to get this 'ol shop. Not sure Brusus can afford to lose any more coin to me. Not with what he owes…" Shael caught himself and laughed again.

Instead of answering, Rsiran walked over to the forge. Blocks stretched from floor to ceiling, framing the outer edges of the forge. An open pit for coals was stained black from ancient soot. The wide metal chimney jutted out overtop, looming like a protective hood. In front of the forge was an anvil even larger than the one in his father's smith that stuck up like a stump into the room. The surface gleamed, and he slipped his hand across, feeling the slick sheen of oil. A huge cracked slack tub was next to the anvil, full of cobwebs and dead carcasses of insects. The only thing missing was the bellows.

Rsiran could practically hear the activity within the smith as it once had been, could nearly envision smiths moving carefully about, tongs holding red hot metal as they turned simple lumps of metal into useful items.

"Is this yours?" he asked, turning the Shael.

The large man wiped his hands across his stained apron. Even given the scale of the room, he seemed to fill it, looming in a way that reminded Rsiran of his father. "This not be mine, boy. Brusus simply ask that I find a suitable place for yah. Mos' of these buildings been deserted for years, squatters only livin' here, and this one be no exception. Another week or so, and I might make it legitimate, but for now you do be running off the books. Takes money to bribe the right constable, and from there I do be having to convince the Elvraeth that I have the right bloodline to own property in your fair city." He shrugged. "If it don' work out for me, might be that you have to fight to keep it to yourself."

Jessa walked past Shael, patting him on the wide shoulder as she passed. He glared at her, but the expression looked more affectionate than angry. "So you know what all this is?" She leaned forward and looked at the stone forge with uncertainty. "Seems to be nothing more than a pile of rocks."

Rsiran nodded. "It is a pile of rocks. But the right kind. If I can get some coals, a working bellows, and some water, I could get this to work." He said nothing of the tools or the ore that he would need. This was a start. With a simple hammer and enough iron, he thought he could make most everything he needed.

Shael watched him. "So, boy, you do be thinking you can make more of those lovely blades here?"

Rsiran glanced from Shael to Jessa. Was this what he was to become? An unsanctioned smith, violating the most sacred of their conventions? Shael spoke of bribing constables, *lying* to the Elvraeth. Had he already become the criminal his father feared?

And if he had, did Rsiran care? Brusus and Jessa were kind to him, unlike his family. What did it matter that they wanted him to forge lorcith knives?

As he watched their faces, concern flashed across Jessa's eyes, as if she feared he would make the wrong choice. Such concern would never have been seen in his father. Even Shael looked as if he only wanted Rsiran to do what was best for him. There was no threat, no intimidation, in spite of the fact that the large man could clearly harm him.

Rsiran decided he could work the forge, could finally listen to the lorcith speak to him, directing his hands, and not fear that he was upsetting his father as he worked. Regardless of his other abilities, he had always accepted that he was born a smith.

Finally, he nodded. "If you can get me enough lorcith, I can make more of the blades."

Shael's face turned into a frown. "What do you be meanin' get you the lorcith, boy? Brusus said nothing about that. I secure the building, the forge, and that be all. You do be working the rest out with Brusus."

Steel and iron were easy to acquire—there was enough waste and loose material that he could simply take what was needed to get started—but how would he obtain lorcith? The supply was tightly controlled from the mines all the way to the smiths, delivered to each smith directly. Only the guild could license a new smithy to enable them to acquire the precious ore. Without a supply of lorcith—more than the simple lump he had buried—the forge would be no more useful to him than it was to Shael.

And if he couldn't, how would he repay Brusus?

CHAPTER 19

"C AN'T YOU SIMPLY MELT DOWN THINGS LIKE THIS?" Brusus asked, shaking a small lorcith forged bowl as they sat at a table in the tavern. A steaming mug of ale rested in front of him, untouched since Rsiran told him of the challenge, dashing the smile that had split his face only moments before.

Rsiran recognized the quality to the bowl, the way the silvery metal dipped and rolled over at the edge, etched with a pattern that had taken a steady hand. He may not have known the smith who'd produced it, but knew that whoever had made it knew what they were doing.

He shook his head. "Lorcith isn't like other ores. Once shaped, the metal holds the shape, almost as if it remembers."

"You talk about it as if it is alive," Haern said. He spun a dronr on the table before him, lifting it and flicking it between his fingers.

"Well… it almost is. With most any other metal, you get it hot enough, you can melt it down, change its shape. Take a spoon," he said, holding one up for demonstration, "and turn it into a chain." He mimicked bending the metal for them. "But with lorcith, it's something different. Once set—once whatever you make is pulled from the metal—it's almost like it fights to keep from changing."

Firell frowned. "Metal is metal. One's more pricey than the next." He shook the dice in his hand absently, almost as if annoyed that they weren't playing, but Brusus would have nothing of dicing until learning if his plan with Shael would work. The disappointment playing across his face was almost more than Rsiran could bear.

"Not the same." Rsiran felt suddenly like he was giving the same talk his father had once given him as they stood around the forge, heating copper and iron to demonstrate how quickly one reached the right temperature compared to the other. Rsiran had been five then and happy, thinking that his family was everything to him. "Does anyone have a guilden?" He waited with his hand outstretched.

Brusus watched him with a curious expression before pulling a thick gold coin from his coinpurse. The top was stamped with an image of a massive Eareth tree, the kind that grew only around the Floating Palace, while the other side had an etching of the city of Elaeavn as seen from the sea.

Rsiran took the coin and held it in his palm. "Now the bowl."

Brusus pushed the lorcith bowl over to him. "Careful with that, Rsiran. Lianna will have my hide if something happens to one of her precious bowls. Took a near miracle to have them made, she says." His eyes drifted to the short thin woman wiping the counter near the taps. She had flowing black hair and fixed Brusus with eyes that blazed green.

"You'd like it," Jessa said.

Rsiran glanced over. "Nothing will happen to it. Nothing *can* happen to it."

He took his spoon and pressed it against the coin as hard as he could. The surface dimpled slightly, deforming the stamp of the city. The spoon was unharmed. He did the same with the bowl, pressing the spoon as hard as he could into the bottom of the bowl. This time it was the spoon that deformed, the end flattening out slightly.

"So... the bowl is the hardest?" Jessa asked. She perched on the chair next to him, lips pursed together as she twirled a finger through her hair. A large, pale yellow flower was stuck into her shirt, looking almost like it blossomed from her chest.

Rsiran smiled at her and immediately felt a flush wash through his face. He glanced at the others nervously, but they didn't seem to see anything. "Yes. And no. Not only harder or softer. Each metal is unique. Different heat makes it act differently. Some—like the gold in the guilden—are soft even when cool. If I had enough time, I could reshape the coin into something else entirely."

Brusus snatched the coin from the table and stuffed it back into his purse.

Rsiran ignored him. "Others, like the steel in this spoon or the lorcith the bowl is made of, are harder. But even though lorcith is the hardest, it conducts heat better than steel, taking a different amount of time on the forge before you can do anything with it." He shrugged. "They have other qualities that would take more time to explain, but those are the easiest. Some metals can be mixed with other metals to make them stronger—like the steel in that spoon—while others won't mix at all."

Haern set his arms onto the table and looked Rsiran in the eyes with a heavy gaze. Rsiran couldn't look away. "You seem to know more than most smiths I've met. The alchemist guild wouldn't like it if you shared their secrets."

Rsiran glanced at the faces around him. Most thought of smiths as simple bangers, using hammers to shape the metal. And most were.

His father thought differently, learned how to smelt down the ore, even if he would never have to do the work himself, feeling that it was important enough for what they did.

"No secrets. Just experience."

"So tell me why we can't take this bowl and heat it to turn it into one of your blades?" Brusus asked, running a hand through his grizzled hair.

Rsiran shrugged. "I'm not sure. Maybe if you ask the alchemist guild," he said, looking over to Haern.

Haern laughed and shook his head.

"The bowl will take heat fine. But you will never be able to change its shape now that it's been set. Now it's a bowl, nothing more."

"Then how did you make the knives?"

"Lump ore. You have to take it fresh. Then it seems willing to be whatever you want it to be." Rsiran didn't say anything about how the ore seemed to guide him to what it wanted. How to explain something as strange as that? Even trying to explain things that had taken him years of learning with his father seemed difficult.

"Then we need to get freshly mined ore," Brusus decided.

Haern leaned back. "How do you think you can accomplish that, Brusus? The mining guild controls the lorcith from the mine all the way to the smiths. Only the master smiths can take delivery of lorcith, and only the guild can register a master smith. Otherwise, the mining guild closely monitors the flow of lorcith out of Ilphaesn."

Brusus sat back and tugged on his loose brown shirt. His brow furrowed as he considered the problem, and he tapped a finger on his cheek as he thought. "We could borrow some from the smiths."

Haern shook his head. "If you're caught, you would get sentenced to the mines. How often do you remind me of the need to avoid attention?"

Brusus shot him a look. "Only if we're caught."

"I know she's a skilled sneak, Brusus, but it only takes one time for it to get noticed before all the smiths put out a watch. And from there?" Haern asked.

Rsiran tried to fade back toward the wall and the shadows, anything to hide the dark shirt and pants he wore. Shifting in his seat, he could almost taste the bitterness of lorcith dust on his tongue; could almost hear the hammering of the picks on the stone within the mines. He remembered the paralyzing fear of having the pick gouging into his neck, tearing through his flesh. He wrapped his arms around his chest, covering the mining shirt with his arms. How much longer before someone recognized what he wore and began asking questions?

And if they did, what would he say? Would he admit to his ability to Slide? Brusus proved he had no qualms about stealing from the guild, what would he ask of Rsiran once he learned of that ability? After what Brusus had done for him, how could Rsiran refuse if he did?

And then he would truly be the thief his father expected.

Rsiran looked at the faces around the table and had another idea. He could get lorcith straight from the mine if he was careful enough. He could Slide into the village outside of Ilphaesn before the ore even left for Elaeavn. But doing so would feel too much like stealing. Of course, he had already taken a large lump of ore from the mines and hidden it in the Aisl Forest, so would what he was considering be any more stealing than that?

And he knew that it was. What he had hidden in the forest was ore he had mined himself, ore that had called to him, demanding he pull it from the rock. Anything else was taking from the efforts of others. He might not be able to ignore the pull of lorcith, but he *could* avoid becoming a true criminal.

These people had helped him, for no reason other than friendship. They were more family to him than his real family; had showed him more kindness than Alyse or his parents ever did. There was another option. One he didn't want to really consider.

He could return to the mine, work under the darkness of night, and pull what he needed.

While he'd been thinking about what he would do, the others had continued to speak around him. He caught pieces of their conversation, enough to know that Brusus considered breaking into another smith and stealing ore. Rsiran knew what would happen: the master smith would blame the journeyman, or worse, the apprentice.

"No," he said. "Too risky."

"If we don't have lorcith, then all we can use are the common ores. Iron, copper, and the like. I'm sorry, Rsiran, but that won't really make much profit."

He nodded, hoping the anxiety gnawing at his stomach didn't show on his face. "You're right, Brusus. We need lorcith for this to even make sense. I think I know a way to obtain it."

Haern leaned forward, and Brusus frowned. Jessa reached over and rested a hand on Rsiran's leg. He didn't try to move it.

"How?" Brusus asked.

Rsiran struggled with what to tell them to hide his ability before coming up with an answer. "My father—" he started.

"Rsiran," Firell said gently, cutting him off, "you understand what happens if you're caught? The Elvraeth do not take kindly to theft of their property, and they can be quite particular when it comes to this ore. Are you sure you want to be the one to do this?"

He didn't want to explain to them that what he suggested was nothing like they suspected. How to explain that he would mine the lorcith himself, pull it from the stone of Ilphaesn, rather than simply steal it?

Whatever he was, whatever he would become, it was not a thief.

"I understand." He shifted on the stool, feeling suddenly uncomfortable, all too aware of the warmth of Jessa's hand on his thigh, the smell of her sweat mixed with the fragrance of the flower she wore. She watched him with an unreadable expression.

"I can do this. Really," he said.

Brusus watched him for a moment, then sighed. "Okay."

* * * * *

Rsiran stood in the broken down smithy hidden deep in Lower Town. The few lanterns glowing in the room gave off enough light to see by, especially since his eyesight seemed to have improved from all the time he'd spent in near darkness, and reflected dully off the metal of the anvil. The air mixed with the odors of oil and the foul stench of sewage drifting through the solid door, now safely locked. Other than his heavy breathing, there was silence.

The others left him alone. Rsiran had told Brusus he needed time to work on the forge, but really he had something else in mind.

He Slid back to the door, checking to make sure it was locked. He didn't want any surprises when he returned. He considered turning down the lanterns, but he would want light when he returned.

He turned to the forge, inspecting it fully for the first time. Stone crumbled on each side, the mortar failing, but the overall structure was intact. He brushed the loose stone off and kicked it away from the anvil so it could not trip him. One misstep, especially with lorcith, and a project was destroyed. Once he managed to get a broom, he could do a better job cleaning, but for now, this would do.

Blackened coals lined the pit, leaving a layer of soot and crust he couldn't scrape off. He hoped that with enough heat, the layers would soften and loosen. According to his father, care with the forge meant care with the forging. Someone clearly hadn't been careful with their forge.

Once he was satisfied, he leaned over the pit and looked up the chimney. Darkness greeted him. He would have to inspect that sometime in the daylight to make sure the smithy didn't fill with smoke.

A crate of coal had been set next to the forge. Had he anything to work on, he would have lit the coals. Instead, he set a layer into the pit, stacking them carefully so it would light easily when he was ready.

Rsiran stood, realizing that he was putting off what needed to be done.

The forge *did* need to be prepared, but he could do so during the daylight. Now that it was dark, he needed to fulfill his promise to Brusus. There was lorcith to gather.

He sighed. It did nothing to slow the steady pattering of his heart. Then he Slid.

He appeared in the small clearing in the forest. Moonlight seeped through the branches overhead, and a distant call from a wolf made him jump. The steady rushing of the Lneahr River as it flowed out to sea made its presence known. He remembered days spent wandering the shores of the Lneahr, feet dragging through the sandy shores as Alyse chased him down the river or into the forest, back when she still cared about him.

Shadows shifted around him, and he didn't want to linger. Not in the Aisl at night. Though their people had once lived within the trees, they no longer had mastery over the forest, and many dangerous things wandered at night. Best to keep this visit brief.

He hurried toward the massive tree where he had hidden the lorcith and kneeled in front of the twisted roots. He looked for the disturbed earth. Finding the spot where he had buried the ore, he quickly dug it out and dusted loose earth from the metal as he had once chipped rock from it. The lorcith gleamed and shimmered in the wan light. Already it called to him.

Another sound interrupted the night, like an angry scream. Whatever made it was nearby. The shrill cry tore at his ears.

Rsiran stood. There was nothing else for him here in the forest, nothing but nightmares.

He Slid back to the smithy.

The lanterns were a welcome sight. Even the foul air from the street outside didn't bother him. He shivered from the memory of whatever had made the scream, and then tucked the lorcith into a corner, hiding it behind some of the loose rock crumbling from the ceiling.

He again considered simply Sliding into another smithy—it didn't have to be his father's—and taking what he needed, but doing so would only draw attention from the guild, which would gain the attention of the Elvraeth and the constables, especially with how the price of lorcith had gone up so drastically over the last year.

Once, his father had been able to acquire huge nuggets of lorcith, large enough to make platters or bowls, all of which the Elvraeth eagerly bought. Over the last year, however, the cost to acquire such deposits from the mining guild had nearly become prohibitive. Now his father only bought when he had commissions lined up, and those were rare. But after working in the mines, the only reason he had as to why lorcith production had diminished, especially with as much of the ore as he felt hidden in the walls, was that someone *wanted* it that way. But now that he'd abandoned his apprenticeship, that wasn't his concern.

Rather than risk harming one of the master smiths and gaining the attention of the guild, it was better to Slide to the mines.

Taking a deep breath, he sighed, dreading what he needed to do. There was really no other way to do it, though. No way that would keep the others from harm.

He Slid.

This was the first time he appeared in the healer's home without an injury, but his neck itched where the stitching pulled his skin together, healing slowly. He would have to return soon to have the stitches removed, but this was not the time for that.

The same small fire crackled in the hearth. The scented air smelled of honey and flowers, reminding him of Jessa. He felt a pang of guilt that he had deceived her by not sharing how he would acquire lorcith. The small cot was folded and pushed against the wall. A plush rug that Rsiran hadn't noticed before was woven in a circular pattern that drew the eye outward and lay in front of the fire. Small shelves lined either wall.

He scanned for his pick and hammer, wondering if the healer had thrown them out. He hated coming in this way, knowing it would have been better to simply knock rather than sneak in, but justified his decision since he was only reclaiming what was his.

"I'm not sure I can heal you again."

Rsiran spun. The healer sat on a small wooden chair. The faded stain that made it look worn and comfortable reminded him of the chair his father always preferred. Her dark hair was still twisted in a knot on her head, and the smile on her face deepened the wrinkles around her eyes.

"I'm not injured this time."

She stood slowly, pushing herself up and stepping carefully around the chair, showing her age. Della looked at him with her deep green eyes, her mouth thinned to a line, and sighed. "No. I believe you are not. But still you place yourself at risk."

Rsiran wondered how much she knew. Had Brusus shared his plans with her, or was she simply a Reader? If she was, he hadn't felt her trying to crawl through his mind, nothing like he did when he was around Jessa.

"I can help them."

She tilted her head and looked at him. "So you have made a choice, then?"

"I tried with my family…"

"So you have chosen another."

Rsiran shrugged. "They're friends. I can help them," he repeated.

"That does not change the fact that you put yourself at risk."

"I think they would do the same for me." Rsiran had not been around them long, but Shael made it clear when Rsiran first saw the smithy that Brusus was reaching beyond what was probably safe for him.

"That they would. They're good people. But still you don't fully trust them."

"I don't know what you mean." He turned away guiltily. Jessa, at least, deserved to hear the truth. He tried to make it look as if he was simply looking around Della's room, staring at the small window that ran along the side street. The curtains were pulled slightly, letting a small salty breeze blow in.

She stepped up to him and set strong hands on his neck, turning him so she could see his injury. She grunted as she ran her fingers along the wound. "I think you know exactly what I mean. Maybe in time you will learn to trust."

He felt her pulling on his skin, as if plucking at the wound, and winced. "I trust—"

Rsiran wasn't sure exactly what he would say. That he trusted the healer enough to keep coming back? That he feared losing his new friends by revealing his dark ability, the ability that he somehow couldn't keep from using? That he wasn't sure who he was anymore?

"There," she said. "Stitching is out. I am surprised you have healed so well, especially as badly as the poisoning had set."

"Thank you."

She pushed on his shoulders and turned him around. "Promise that you will be careful. I know what you think you need to do, that you think you must help your friends. And for all that he has done for me, I would never tell you not to help Brusus. But use your ability if you find trouble. Or it finds you."

She shuffled over to one of her shelves, pulled his pick and hammer off the shelf and handed them to him. "Remember someone there who wanted to harm you."

He shook his head. "It had nothing to do with me. They wanted the ore."

Her brow furrowed, wrinkles deepening. "If you are so certain, then why risk injury again by returning?"

"The other option is worse."

She sniffed. "Are you certain you have considered all other options, including doing nothing? I do not want to see you hurt again. More than that, I do not want to see Brusus suffer."

Rsiran blinked. "That is why I must do this."

The healer turned to another shelf and picked something up before handing it to him. It was a long, slender cylinder made of solid metal. A slider bar ran along one side of it.

"What is it?"

"Light for you in the darkness. Were your Sight greater, you would have no need. As it is, use this to keep the shadows at bay. Perhaps it will keep you safe."

Rsiran tucked it into his pocket. "Thank you."

"I will pray that the Great Watcher turns his gaze upon you," she said solemnly.

Rsiran nodded and turned away from Della, not certain he wanted the Great Watcher to notice him. Then he Slid to Ilphaesn.

CHAPTER 20

THE STALE AIR HIT RSIRAN IMMEDIATELY, the bitterness of lorcith dust seeming to hang in it, biting at his lungs as he took a deep breath. He staggered forward, a wave of weakness washing over him. Would the weakness following a Slide ever disappear? Perhaps if he practiced it like Della suggested he would eventually grow accustomed to its effects.

He targeted this Slide to enter the upper level of the mine. Since he still didn't have perfect control, sometimes with a Slide he had the potential to overshoot, especially when traveling long distances, like from Elaeavn to Ilphaesn. Shorter distances were easier to pinpoint, but he didn't dare Slide straight to the deepest part of the mine or else he might end up buried in rock, unable to Slide out.

He wasn't sure how late it was, but the sleeping cavern was quiet. An orange glow from the lantern spilled over toward where he stood near the entrance. The miners murmured softly, broken every so often by a burst of laughter before quickly dying down. Behind him, the entrance was barred, and a heavy lock kept the miners trapped inside. No one moved along the mining tunnels at this time of night; the only sound was the distant, steady tapping.

He swallowed a mouthful of dry air and steadied himself, readying for another Slide.

As he began, there came a movement of shadows, and he hurried forward, Sliding out of the upper part of the mine and into the deeper, darker heart of Ilphaesn.

Rsiran stood motionless as he waited for his eyes to adjust. Gradually, the darkness faded but not enough for him to see exactly where he stood.

Had the Slide taken him as planned, he should be near the end of the farthest mine. He stretched out his hand and felt along the wall. The rough stone was cool and damp under his hand. Rsiran took a tentative step, sliding his feet along the floor, following the curve.

Satisfied he was where he had intended to emerge, he stood and listened.

As usual for night, the steady tapping echoed through the mines, but sounded distant. He didn't want to be near whatever it was making the sound, uncertain as to its source.

The lorcith called to him, like a song sung under water. Leaving his hand on the wall, he moved it until he felt a reverberation, almost a thrumming, like that of a hammer against steel, on his palm. The sensation went up his arm into his head.

Rsiran positioned the pick over the wall and began to chip at the stone, using his awareness of the lorcith to guide each blow. He decided to keep time with the tapping, hoping that his picking would be lost in the sound of the other. He worked carefully, always watching for signs of light to know if any of the foremen came to investigate. As far as he knew, they went back to the village at the end of the day, locking the miners within Ilphaesn until morning.

Every so often, he hesitated, listening for the tapping. The steady sound continued, like a distant hammering, only never coming any closer. Rsiran did not dare investigate.

Unlike when he had mined during the day, the foreman distracted and barely paying attention, only the orange light of the strange lanterns lighting the tunnels, he worked entirely by feel. This made him more attuned to the lorcith as he focused on where he chipped away at the stone. All around him he felt other large deposits of lorcith, some buried deeply, while others like the one he freed with the blunted pick, sat near the surface.

With as many as he felt, it seemed strange that large finds were rare. Even working blindly, the others should have been found, freed by luck and time by the workers sentenced to serve in Ilphaesn.

He had nearly freed the large collection when he realized the tapping had stopped.

It was during one of his pauses, and it took his mind several moments to register what was missing. He waited, expecting the sound to resume, but it did not.

What did its absence mean? Rather than resuming work, he dusted around the stone with his hand, feeling the size of the lorcith he had freed. The lump was massive, far larger than any other he had taken, and sat loosely in the wall. Another few strikes with the pick, and it would be free.

The sudden silence disconcerted him. He worked to steady his breathing, but memories of the last time he was in the mine kept pushing to the front of his mind. That attack had nearly killed him, the poison on the pick acting quickly enough that he had been lucky to Slide from the mine when he did.

Instead of using the pick, he took the hammer and scratched at the rock, scraping it as quietly as he could over the lump of lorcith, pulling on it to try and free it from the stone.

As it began moving, the tapping began again.

This time it was close and almost loud enough it could be in the same tunnel as he was. Rsiran froze, hands wrapped around the lump of lorcith, the pick and hammer trapped between his knees.

The tapping continued, steadily, breaking occasionally. Rsiran suddenly understood what he was hearing. It paused like he did, as if to wipe dust away.

His mouth went dry. Reaching to grab the device Della had given him, he found it had fallen out of his pocket somewhere in the darkness.

There was around him but more blackness. And now he was certain he wasn't the only one mining the lorcith at night.

Barely breathing, he felt the lorcith stone begin to shift. It screamed as it came free of the wall.

The tapping stopped.

Rsiran didn't wait to hear if it would resume. He Slid.

* * * * *

The air in the smithy felt cold compared to the mine. The light from the lanterns nearly blinded him. Rsiran's arms shook as he clung to the lorcith, and his heart pounded, blood rushing through his ears. Nausea rolled through his stomach.

He staggered toward the forge, dropped the lorcith next to the other nugget, and leaned against the crumbling stone to steady himself, his mind racing with what he encountered.

Someone else mined at night.

That meant Sighted or someone who could sense the lorcith within the walls.

How many nights had he stayed awake, lying and listening to the steady tapping? Even when he went down into the mines on his own, walking through the darkness at night, he hadn't been certain what it was that he had been hearing.

There was no doubt now.

Rsiran looked at the two nuggets he had. Enough to get started. More than enough to forge a knife or longer blade. But he would need more if he was going to make Brusus's goal worthwhile, much more if he was going to actually help Brusus pay off his debt.

How could he return to the mines now? Whoever was there had to have noticed him; had stopped hammering when he pulled the lorcith from the stone. What if it was the same person who had attacked him?

To settle his mind, he set to working. The coals had already been aligned, and he used the flint and steel that Brusus had provided to build the flames. His hands shook as he started, the trembling making his work difficult, but he somehow managed to strike a fire, only injuring his hands a few times in the process.

Stoking the flames helped calm him. This was familiar. Even though the smithy was different, the forge and bellows not the same as he knew, the work was the same. Once the coals were glowing comfortably, he briefly Slid outside to ensure it vented. Only after he was convinced that smoke rose freely from the chimney did he set to work.

He had a hammer; though it was not ideal, the small mining hammer could be used to shape the lorcith. Setting the smaller lorcith nugget atop the coals—the one reclaimed from the forest—he let the heat consume it. He stared at the glowing coals, letting his mind wander as the lorcith heated. When it began glowing red, he reached for tongs... but realized he didn't have any.

In his need for familiarity, the need for something to calm him, he had forgotten he didn't have any other tools. Now that the lorcith was already glowing, he had no choice but to shape it, otherwise it would cool and become useless, no more changeable than the bowl Brusus had in the tavern.

He looked around the open smithy for anything that could be used for tongs.

The forge and bellows consumed one wall. Piles of debris—cracked and crumbling stone from the walls and the forge—scattered along the others. He considered somehow using the lanterns, perhaps pulling off the handles to twist into makeshift tongs, but they would not be thick enough to support the weight. In one darkened corner he saw a wooden bucket and thought he could use the metal support hoop—one of the few things his father sanctioned him to fashion—but as he picked it up, the iron crumbled, corroded by time and salty air. Along the wall opposite the forge, there was a small shelf, but other than dust and cobwebs it was empty, only imprints of what had once been stored remained.

There was nothing in the empty building he could use.

Cursing himself for his stupidity, he hurried back to the forge. The lorcith was glowing nicely, heated nearly to the point where it would be workable. Much longer, and it would be useless.

What was he thinking to start the coals and begin heating the lorcith without the proper tools? Had he so quickly forgotten the lessons his father had taught him?

Maybe he had been away from the smithy too long. Perhaps he couldn't make what he had promised Brusus.

The idea of letting Brusus down hurt. He had more lorcith, but how much more would he be able to obtain? If tonight was any indication, Sliding into the mines was going to be dangerous, and he would have to be extremely careful and prepare for the possibility that he would have to Slide away at any moment, abandoning his work.

It was either risk his safety or risk drawing attention to all of them. Rsiran knew already what he would choose. There was no other alternative.

He Slid to his father's smith.

Coming out of the Slide, he staggered forward. In one night, he had used his ability more often than he should, expending too much effort. For the first time, he worried about the return Slide. And he still had a night of forging ahead.

Rsiran looked around the darkened smith. Faint streetlight filtered through dirty windows. Little had changed since he had last been here. The forge cooled along the back wall, heat still radiating from the heated coals earlier in the day. Bins full of iron and steel were stationed to one side. A smaller bin loaded with lumps of lorcith was on the other. He considered taking a single nugget but decided against it. His father might notice.

Along the back wall, near his beaten and faded wooden workbench, was a line of hooks. Various tools of the trade were placed carefully on the hooks, each returned to its place at the end of the day. His father would know if one was missing, but Rsiran intended to return what he borrowed before anything was noticed. Tomorrow he could have Brusus find him proper tools; for tonight he would borrow them.

Hurrying over, he grabbed a long-handled tong, and after a moment's consideration, a heavy hammer. The small mining hammer would work fine for some of the detail work, but he needed something with more heft for striking and shaping.

He paused and looked around the shop again, thinking briefly of all the time he had spent working alongside the journeymen, the time he had spent cleaning and organizing, all the time he had spent daydreaming that one day he would work alongside his father before eventually taking over the shop. Now those were only lost dreams. He would have to find a new dream.

He worried the lorcith heating on the forge would become unusable if he waited much longer. Moving toward the middle of the shop, he Slid back to Lower Town and his rundown smithy.

The scent of the heated lorcith greeted him as he emerged from the Slide. Fatigue nearly overwhelmed him, and he caught himself on the anvil before he tripped into hot coals. He swallowed against a dry mouth, wishing for water, but that would come later.

He should rest. Pressing on when exhausted risked him simply passing out. But Rsiran shook his head, blinking to try and clear his tired mind. He had to focus on his task, use the lorcith now glowing brightly.

Taking the tongs, he lifted the nugget off the coals and set in on the anvil. He had no idea what he would forge. Brusus wanted knives, but this was too large of a nugget to be a single knife. Could he manage to split it? Maybe he could make two or three knives…

Inhaling deeply, he set the tongs next to him and lifted the heavy hammer, pausing long enough to listen for the call of the lorcith, to see if it would direct his forging as he remembered. He heard nothing.

Anxiety gnawed at his stomach. Had he been too long away from the forge? Rsiran didn't want to think of the disappointment Brusus would feel or the look he would get from Jessa if he couldn't manage what he had promised. He had not known them long, and there were no ties to him other than the casual friendship he had made. If his own family could discard him, what would stop near strangers?

Rsiran pushed the thoughts out of his mind and focused on the lorcith.

There was nothing to do but begin.

He raised the hammer and started striking. The sound of it hitting the lorcith rang out loudly, a familiar and reassuring sound. Tightness in his back quickly loosened, and his neck itched with sweat that dripped along his still healing skin. With each blow, his anxiety about disappointing Brusus and Haern faded more. Another dozen heavy strikes, and the worry about hurting Jessa faded. Soon he fell into a steady rhythm.

He was not certain when he lost awareness of the hammering. One moment, he struggled making anything appear, struggling simply to change the shape of the lorcith, hoping that the metal would trigger something within him and guide his blows, and the next moment, he was lost in a flurry of steady strikes. First he worked with the heavy hammer, flattening and stretching, using the few tools he had, and then he switched to the small mining hammer, carefully shaping and directing each strike.

At some point, he began feeling the pull of the metal, feeling as if each movement was guided, his hand directed by whatever shape was within the lorcith and wanted out. Over and over the hammer fell, his mind blank as the movement became everything, a steady jarring sensation as it worked up his arm. Heat came off the blade, seemed to know when it was time to bring it back to the coals to bring the reddish glow back to the metal. Rsiran ignored the sweat streaming from his body.

And then he was done.

Rsiran felt a sense of release from the lorcith, as if whatever had taken hold of him had given up its grip, freeing him now that the work was finished. The soft call of the metal faded, disappearing in what seemed a sense of satisfaction. Tunneled vision cleared, and slowly he became aware of his surroundings. He looked down to see what he had made.

A long blade lay on the anvil. The entire length still glowed a faint orange. The tip was wide and tapered gradually toward the blunt tang. The metal seemed to shift and shimmer, almost as if liquid beneath the surface. It shifted with a pattern formed from metal folded over in a way he could not even remember, let alone describe. He ran his hand above the blade, knew that it would be smooth, and wondered how well it would take sharpening.

If it was anything like the others he had made, it would quickly take an edge, almost demanding that it be sharpened. All this blade needed was a hilt, and it would be complete.

His heart fluttered as he realized what he had done. A sword. A tool of death, forbidden by the guild. It was enough to bring him before the Elvraeth council, possibly enough to get him banished. But why did it look so beautiful?

Rsiran had never forged anything like it before. There had been the blade he started in his father's shop, destroyed when his father realized what he made, but this was different. The only other swords he had ever seen were made of steel, carefully crafted by master bladesmiths. Never out of lorcith.

He knew how he had done it, understood that it was the guidance of the lorcith calling to him that pulled the shape out of the raw nugget. But what if it was more than that? What if the lorcith reacted to something within *him* to make this? What if this was part of the darkness his father believed within him?

A small mark was near the base of the sword, above the tang where it would be visible with the attached hilt. At some point, he had engraved a small marking, the same as he had made on the knife blades that he should not have created. He didn't know how he managed to make such fine detail along the blade, a twisted piece of the handle off one of the lanterns rested alongside the anvil.

As he leaned against the anvil, tired and sweaty, he wished nothing more than to lay on the ground and sleep. Maybe he would awaken and this would be nothing more than a dream, the sword simply part of his imagination, but he knew better.

Already much of the night must be gone, spent mining and forging, and still he must return the tools to his father's shop before he noticed they were missing. Pushing back up, he staggered toward the door and pulled it open, curious how late in the night it was, hoping he would have time to sleep before Brusus came bursting in, looking to see what else he might need.

Rsiran wasn't sure he had the energy needed to Slide back to his father's shop, but needed to try before morning came and he noticed the missing tools.

As he opened the door, his heart sank.

Reddish orange light from the sun rising over the harbor made him stagger back. Little darkness remained, only memories of shadows lingering in the spaces between the falling buildings. He swallowed against the nausea rising in his stomach as he pushed the door closed and locked. Leaning back against the rough wooden door, he steadied his breathing.

He had spent the entire night mining and forging. His eyes fell on the tools borrowed from his father's shop. How long before his father noticed? How long before he suspected Rsiran? And how long before he turned him in and the guild came searching for him? How long did he have before he was brought before the Elvraeth and banished?

Because of him, Brusus would not have the knives he needed to pay off his debt.

CHAPTER 21

R SIRAN AWOKE TO A LOUD POUNDING IN HIS HEAD.
His eyes were hazy, covered by a film from sleep, and his first thought was that he was somehow back in the mine and that the steady tapping came from deep within. In a fit of confusion, he panicked.

He sat up with a start and nearly smacked his head into the anvil.

Sleeping. Only sleeping, and fitfully at that. He remembered snippets of dreams where darkness followed him, the sense that someone loomed out of sight, and always the fear of another attack.

His back burned, and his neck ached. After running a hand across the still fresh wound, he pulled it away tentatively, fearing he might find blood. He let out a long breath when he did not.

Looking around, he was still in the old smithy, the coals cooling behind him, the long blade he had forged during the night resting on the ground near him. Bright light shone through the cracked ceiling, lighting a spot on the floor. Debris and dust scattered across the floor seemed more noticeable in the light. One of the lanterns still flickered, the oil within burning with a thin smoke. Another lantern laid near him, disassembled, the handle twisted and bent.

Above everything was the pounding.

Not in his head, though. It took him a few moments to realize what he was hearing. Someone was pounding on the door to the building.

Rsiran pushed himself up and took the long blade, holding it away from himself. Even holding it made him feel somewhat sick, knowing such a thing should not exist. In the daylight, the pattern along the surface shimmered even more, appearing to shift and slide, as if his eyes couldn't focus on it properly.

He hid it to one side of the forge, tucking it behind the bellows so the wooden frame would prevent anyone from seeing it.

As much as the blade bothered him, part of him wanted to keep the blade to himself, sharpen the edge, and attach a hilt. But he had no use for such a weapon. Likely as not, he would trip over the blade or worse, cut himself carrying it. The small knives he had made suited him better, and even those should not have been made.

The pounding came faster, more urgent. Whoever was at the door was persistent. Hopefully it was only Jessa or Brusus, but what if it was not? Could he take the chance that it was someone else? What if someone had heard his hammering last night?

If the guild learned of an unsanctioned smith, the constabulary would be notified. If Shael did not have the proper proof of ownership of the building—and Rsiran was not certain that he did, or that he'd bribed the right constables to leave him alone—the building could be raided. And then the lorcith would be found. The blade would be discovered.

Maybe his father was right after all. Had his ability turned him into something worse than a thief? But why did the sword still seem so beautiful?

Wiping the dust from the floor off his pants, he hurried to the door and unlocked it, pulling it open enough to see who battered the other side. It pushed open in a heavy blast, and Brusus barreled inside.

Brusus seemed hurried today, dressed differently than usual. He wore a heavy brown cloak overtop a red shirt and leather pants. Traces of dirt and dust marred the cloak and looked as if he had tried to carefully brush it away. Even his grey hair was combed differently. A small twisted silver tree hung on a chain about his neck. He carried a stack of clothing in his hands and tossed them at Rsiran.

"Damn, Rsiran! Why didn't you answer the door?"

Rsiran shook out the clothes. Simple brown pants but nicely sewn. The deep blue shirt had a line of embroidery, fancier than what he was accustomed to wearing. "I was sleeping." He said nothing about the blade. Not until he decided what he was going to do with it.

Brusus laughed. "Sleeping? Already?"

"What do you mean already? I'm waking up for the day."

Brusus pushed past him, and Rsiran shut the door, careful to lock it.

"Jessa said she hadn't seen you yet today. What happened?"

Rsiran moved to stand in front of Brusus so that he wouldn't be drawn toward the hidden blade. "I've been figuring out how to acquire lorcith."

Brusus's face changed, brow furrowing. "Are you sure you can do this? There are others who could help. You don't need to do this by yourself."

"I know, Brusus." But if he let others help, they would risk punishment from the guild. If everything went well, he might reveal to Brusus that he could Slide. Until then he would keep it to himself. "Give me a little more time."

Brusus turned and looked around the smithy. "Do you have everything you need here?"

Rsiran shrugged. "Most everything. Some tools still to get. Water source for quenching. Mostly, I'd like to clean the dust and stone off the floor."

"Dirt a problem?"

"Only if I trip."

Brusus looked at him and smiled. "I think I know how to work a broom."

"That would be great."

Brusus stepped past him and seemed to notice something for the first time. "Testing the coals?"

Rsiran swallowed. He didn't want to hide what he had been doing from Brusus but wasn't certain he was ready for him to know, either. Knowing meant questions. How had he gotten the lorcith? Where had the tools come from? Questions might come regardless, but he hoped to delay needing to answer a little longer.

"Trying to clean up the coal pit. Need to clean the venting." He shrugged, careful to keep himself between Brusus and where the sword hid next to the bellows. "Didn't want to get too far along and have something as simple as poor ventilation keep this from working."

Brusus turned and looked around the smithy. "Shael didn't leave you much to work with here, did he?"

"This place is perfect," he said, and meant it.

The building had more space than his father's smithy, and other than the damaged stone, the anvil was solid and useable and the coal pit massive. Whoever had once used this as their shop likely had an impressive setup. If only some of the tooling remained, Rsiran would be even more pleased.

"Need to get that hole fixed." Brusus motioned toward the ceiling. "Can't have rain coming in and damaging your projects."

172

Rsiran nodded. Rainwater wouldn't harm anything he planned on creating. Unlike iron, lorcith never corroded. It was barely even magnetic. Beyond that, he didn't think the smith guild knew much more about lorcith. Only the alchemist guild knew the deepest secrets of the ore.

"Well, now that I've found you, I suppose I better take you to find Jessa. She was all twisted when I asked if she'd seen you yet today. Maybe you'll have time to dice with us tonight?"

"I don't know," he started. "To gather lorcith, I have to work at night."

Brusus frowned at him. "Is that what you were doing last night? This isn't an Upper Town neighborhood, Rsiran. You need to be careful if you're going to be wandering at night. Especially by yourself. Dangerous things are out."

Rsiran started to smile but saw the earnest expression on Brusus's face. "I'm careful," he said. "There's little chance anyone sees what I need to do."

"Care to share what you're planning?"

Rsiran almost told him, but caught himself. "When I'm sure how to make it work," he said instead.

"You don't have to take all the risk," Brusus suggested. "If you think you're going to sneak into your father's shop and take his supply of lorcith…"

"Not as simple as that. My father would know and report to the guild. Constables would be notified—"

"We can handle constables…"

Rsiran wondered what he meant by that. He hadn't figured out Brusus's connections yet. "And the other smiths would be on edge. Worse, the mining guild might catch wind of what we're doing and limit the supply altogether." He shook his head. "What I have planned is simpler."

Brusus pinched his chin as he looked around the smithy. "I'm not sure I'm comfortable being kept in the dark with this, but if you say you've got it under control then I'll trust you. Just… be safe, Rsiran. I can't think of how you intend to acquire lorcith outside of the smiths and the mining guild, and to be honest, it worries me, but you need to be careful. There are people other than the constables to fear in Elaeavn."

The note of concern in his voice surprised him, and Rsiran almost told him everything. "Really, Brusus," he started, "it isn't that dangerous. An ability I have…" Rsiran caught himself, glancing up at Brusus's pale eyes, feeling embarrassed that he had mentioned abilities when Brusus's must be as weak as they were, and shrugged. "I will get a supply of lorcith soon and start working on the knives."

Brusus studied him for a moment and then nodded. "Get dressed and come then. Since you are taking this risk, then I'll take one with you. There is something I need to show you."

Something about the comment sounded faintly ominous. "What?" He quickly switched his clothes, ditching the shirt and pants worn by Ilphaesn miners and dumped them near the hearth. Maybe he would burn them later.

Brusus clapped a hand on Rsiran's shoulders and turned him, pulling him toward the door and out into the street. Brusus waited as Rsiran fished the brass key out of his pocket and pulled the door closed behind him, locking it carefully.

"Shael knows how to pick his buildings," Brusus said, shaking his head. "Can't believe this is even here. Probably don't even need to lock the door."

"Once we get a stock of lorcith," Rsiran reminded.

Brusus nodded, glancing back at the building. "Surprised the smith guild hasn't claimed this building for themselves before now.

And surprised Shael found it so quickly. I thought we might have to build one when he came across this."

The thought struck Rsiran. Why *hadn't* the smith guild taken over this building? Surely, they would have known that it had once been a smithy—it was too massive to be anything else. Or did the building predate the guild? Rsiran couldn't remember how old the guild was—somewhere around two or three hundred years old—but that would mean the forge here was even older than he thought.

"These parts of Lower Town were some of the first buildings constructed," Brusus went on, leading them through the narrow street. Sunlight shone between the buildings but still some shadows remained, lingering along the edges of the walls and in the small spaces between buildings. Fetid water stood in those places, leaving foul smelling pools that even overpowered the stink of sewage and garbage that otherwise filled the street. "You know that at first, most simply built along the outer edge of the forest? No one really wanted to leave the trees and try something different. Only later, the rest of the city came to be, the sprawling streets stretching up the faces of the cliffs, the engineers designing the buildings to look like natural stone, the Floating Palace."

Rsiran looked up, expecting to see the palace looming over them, but from where they were, there was no sign of it, a sheer rock wall stretching toward the sky. "How old is this part of town?"

Brusus looked around, eyes pausing on the cracking buildings, the dust and stone crumbling and spilling out onto the street, and shrugged. A few people, most of them young and thin, clothing tattered and ripped, simply sat along the streets. In most parts of town, the constables would move such people along, keep them off the streets and send them toward the harbor where they would be put to work or placed in a shelter.

"Maybe eight or nine hundred years? Older than old Elaeavn, and the city is a thousand years old. Some parts—like here along the shore—are much older. This is the only part you can really see from the water."

"I wouldn't know about that."

Brusus looked over at him. "You should really see Elaeavn from the water, Rsiran. Only from out on the sea can you fully appreciate what the city engineers managed to accomplish. Even the palace fits." Brusus's voice took on a faraway quality as he spoke, but he still said the word "palace" with a hint of disdain. His gaze drifted toward the sound of waves crashing along the shore somewhere behind the row of buildings. From where they were on the street, the sound was more muted than other places in the city, as if the buildings crouched together to shield those living here from the ocean.

"I've seen the city from above," Rsiran offered, looking toward the towering cliff face that framed the southern edge of the city. "Everything seems small and insignificant. Only the Floating Palace really stands out from above."

Krali had been one of his favorite places to Slide before his father had berated him for the ability. Standing above the city, looking down on everything, made him feel a part of something larger. Perhaps there really was a Great Watcher sitting in the stars, watching over all of creation. There, he almost felt as if *he* were a Watcher.

"You've climbed Krali Rock?" Brusus asked.

Rsiran felt his heart catch. He should have been more careful. Krali Rock, named after the people who once lived along the shores, was nearly impossible to climb, rising sheer and smooth above the city like a pillar of stone. The only way Rsiran had managed to stand atop the rock was by Sliding to the peak. From the markings he had seen there, others had been before him, but whether they had climbed or Slid like himself, he did not know.

"Not from Krali," he said quickly. "To the north. When I was younger, my father took me out of the city to the north." The answer was mostly true. The view from near Ilphaesn wasn't nearly as impressive as from atop Krali, but was easier to explain.

Brusus watched him with a quizzical expression. "Well, that's not really from above then. From the north, the city is splayed out across the bay, buildings looking like they are stacked atop one another. Can't even remember ever really seeing the palace."

Rsiran shrugged, wanting badly to change the topic. "It was some time ago," he said, not needing to say more as they reached the end of the long narrow street.

Along here, the air felt warmer, as if the sun failing to shine through those last remnants of shadow kept the temperature lower. A steady breeze blew in from the sea, carrying the sound of the gulls and the noise from the harbor. The street bustled with activity here on the edge of Upper Town with people wandering in both directions. Those coming from Lower Town always seemed burdened with heavy loads or baskets, most coming from the market or the harbor. Those moving down the street often pulled empty carts or baskets.

Stepping into the crowd, Brusus led them toward the harbor. After all his time spent in the mines and wandering at night over the last few weeks, so many people made Rsiran uncomfortable. They pressed in all around him, eager to squeeze past, always pushing from behind. His back itched, a reminder of the injuries he had sustained during the mine. A reminder for caution.

Brusus moved quickly, his cloak billowing out around his shiny boots. "Keep up with me," he urged.

"Where are we going?"

This was not the main thoroughfare leading through the city, the wide path that wound up from the harbor toward Upper Town and the palace, but was nearly as busy. As they made their way, the crowd thickened, and the sense of purpose changed. No longer were people simply ferrying items from the harbor to Upper Town. Now there were dockworkers and tanners and merchants squeezing around, all dressed for their trade. Rsiran did not recognize where they were, but if he followed this down to the harbor he could eventually figure out how to get back to Upper Town.

But if he Slid, he would never really have a need.

Upper Town was named for more than its location in the city. Set up above the harbor, above the water, it also housed many of the trades, families like Rsiran's. Smiths, weavers, potters all lived there, and many had their own stores and shops. Those living in Upper Town had a different idea of wealth compared to those in Lower Town, something Rsiran struggled adjusting to.

"We are going to see a little project of mine down near the harbor. I thought you might be interested in seeing a different part of the city."

Rsiran laughed. "I've been to Lower Town."

"Not the Lower Town I know. Living here, you'll get to know it. Different from where your father's smithy is, but still Elaeavn. Even those living in the palace couldn't manage without the harbor. Need the dockworkers to keep it running smoothly. Merchants rely on the ships to manage their trade. Food comes in and out of the harbor." He shrugged, eyes casting out toward the sea as they neared the end of the street where it intersected with the long curving road. "Once we lived differently. Once we lived among the trees, taking what the forest provided." He turned to Rsiran and smiled. "Not sure I would have been able to live that way, at least not well."

178

Rsiran laughed. Brusus walked with a purpose, eventually veering off onto a small alley between two massive low buildings that stretched back away from the harbor.

"What do these store?"

Brusus waved a hand at the warehouse on the left. "Most are temporary stores. Hold cargo and merchant goods until ships come in. Shippers like Firell and merchants rent space and the building owners pay for guards to keep watch." He motioned at a thin man watching them carefully.

He was dressed in strange black pants and a long-sleeved tunic. A heavy tan marked face and a thin moustache that wrapped around his mouth. A deep red cloak hung from his neck, loose and immobile as he moved. Rsiran was surprised to see a longsword sheathed at his waist.

"I thought only the constables were allowed swords in Elaeavn."

Brusus waved, and the man frowned at him. "These men are not from Elaeavn."

Like with Shael, Rsiran noticed the guard's eyes first. Steel grey eyes flickered around, seeming to watch everything at once. They paused on Rsiran for the briefest of moments, as if passing judgment. Even Readers trying to crawl through his mind did not make him feel as unsettled as those eyes did. Cold and callous.

The guard moved with a casually light step, but every muscle in his body seemed tensed, as if he were a coiled spring ready to unload at any moment. One hand hovered near his hip, ready to grab his sword in the blink of an eye. The other drifted toward his back as they approached, sliding underneath his cloak.

Brusus looked over to the man and held his eyes, almost as if daring the swordsman. A half smile twisted his mouth. "Neelish sellswords. Quick and deadly with the sword, but it's the weapon you *don't* see that is the real threat."

Rsiran watched the man as they moved past, his eyes never truly leaving them as he patrolled the street between the warehouses. Brusus paid him no more mind than he had anyone else, choosing instead to simply walk past, the same half smile never leaving his face.

After passing one long warehouse, they stepped into a narrow alley before reaching the next. Brusus moved more quickly now, motioning Rsiran to follow. The street felt much like the narrow alley outside the old smithy, the buildings piling atop one another as if trying to squeeze the light away. Little made it past the overhangs. Pools of water were common, and they had to step around areas where mud and other filth sat. A few rats scurried along, ignoring the sun. A single cat yowled around the corner somewhere.

Rsiran shivered. Bad luck.

Other than the shape of the buildings, everything seemed much like what he saw in front of the old smithy. The only difference was that there was no garbage here and there were no people sitting forlornly staring at nothing.

"Where are we going?"

Brusus raised a finger to his lips to shush him. "Quiet here. Can't have them see us. Not yet."

Rsiran did as Brusus asked, but felt a shiver of nerves at the comment, wondering what Brusus intended to do.

He didn't need to wait long.

Reaching a short and narrow door that looked as if it had once been a window, Brusus kneeled in front of it and took a leather roll out from the pocket of his cloak. Setting it carefully onto the dirty stone, he unrolled it and took out a slender metal rod. Then, slipping it into the lock, he twisted and wiggled it until something clicked.

"Brusus?"

Brusus shook his head as he rolled the rod back into the pack, and then tucked it carefully into his pocket. He pulled open the door and ducked inside, motioning Rsiran to follow.

Rsiran glanced up the alley, remembering the lithe movements of the sellsword, before he followed Brusus into the building.

CHAPTER 22

"CAREFUL WITH THE STEPS," BRUSUS CAUTIONED.
Rsiran was thankful for the distraction; thoughts of what he was becoming—the criminal his father swore his ability would lead him toward—led down a path he still wasn't prepared to travel. Perhaps, as the healer said, some day he could confront what he had become, look back at how he got there, and know that there wasn't anything wrong with him.

Now was not that time.

Plunging into darkness, he felt Brusus's strong hand on his arm, pulling him into the warehouse. Rsiran slid his foot forward and felt the lip of the step, easing his way down. Block walls pressed against him along the stairs, heavy with the scent of damp earth and dirt. After a half dozen steps, he reached a dirt landing, and the massive warehouse opened up in front of him.

The warehouse was mostly dark, but light squeezed through cracks in the roof. A few dirty windows set into the rafters let more light through, barely enough to keep Rsiran from crashing into Brusus as he stood at the bottom of the stairs, waiting. His eyes sparkled and a thin smile split his mouth.

"What are we doing here, Brusus?"

Brusus motioned around him. "What do you see here?"

Rsiran stepped past Brusus and looked around. Wooden crates filled the warehouse. Hundreds were stacked, some two or three high, lined up evenly and carefully, almost as if in some sort of pattern. Some had writing on them in faded lettering, the type that Rsiran had seen somewhere before. Others were blank. A thick layer of dust covered everything.

"Boxes," he answered.

Was this the secret Brusus wanted to share with him or did it have to do with how Brusus had broken into the building?

Brusus grunted. "Too simple, Rsiran. These are boxes. Shipping crates, to be exact. Carried on our ships from all over the world to be left here, in this warehouse, stacked to the ceiling and covered in dust and age. Crates stored for years, some for hundreds of years. All owned by the Elvraeth."

Rsiran's heart skipped a beat. "Brusus... I worried about borrowing lorcith from my father's smith and forging knives because I would attract the attention of the smith guild. We agreed that would be dangerous." He had risked his safety in returning to the mine. "This..." he started but didn't know how to continue. What was Brusus hiding from him? Why did he dare risk the mines if Brusus was going to taunt the Elvraeth?

Brusus laughed, and the sound flooded out along the dirt floor of the warehouse. "The Elvraeth don't even know what they have here! Their palace could not hold all of this. Some of these crates are hundreds of years old, never touched during all that time. Do you think the Elvraeth care?"

Rsiran couldn't begin to imagine what the Elvraeth cared about. They lived high above Elaeavn, sitting in the Floating Palace, ruling by the power of the abilities granted them by the Great Watcher.

"Then what is all this?"

He felt uncomfortable even being in the warehouse. Did he want to risk drawing any more attention from the Elvraeth? Rsiran imagined the council learning of him forging lorcith weapons, sentencing him to Ilphaesn, forced to find enough lorcith to earn his freedom. He couldn't go back to the mines... not to stay. But worse than Ilphaesn was banishment.

Brusus saw the anxiety on his face and set a comforting hand on his arm. "There is nothing to fear standing here," he said softly. "Most among the Elvraeth don't even know about the existence of the warehouse. How many of the Elvraeth have you ever seen leave the palace?"

As far as he knew, none of the Elvraeth ever left the palace, sending servants instead. Those servants Rsiran had met over the years carried themselves with such an air of superiority that he almost believed *they* were Elvraeth, if not for the forest green cloak they wore to mark their station.

"How could they not know about the warehouse?"

Brusus looked at him with sadness. "Even living in Upper Town didn't give you a clear understanding of the Elvraeth, did it? How many Elvraeth do you think live in the palace? How many separate families that we simply think of as one?"

"There's only one family. The Great Watcher—"

Brusus cut him off. "Not one family. There are *five* separate families—all Elvraeth and all claiming gifts given to them by the Great Watcher. But how are their gifts any more special than what he has given you or me? What has given *them* the right to rule?"

"Why are we here, Brusus?" Rsiran felt altogether too uncomfortable with where the conversation took them. What did Brusus think to do with a warehouse full of crates owned by the Elvraeth?

"Secrets." He looked out over the crates, reaching his hand to run it along one of the old and dusty boxes with faded black lettering that Rsiran could not read. "Think of what must be here, the stories that must be hidden within these crates, some here for nearly as long as this building has stood."

"Why do the Elvraeth store this here?" He was curious in spite of himself.

Brusus stepped out into the warehouse. His stepped lightly, barely stirring up any dust, a confidence in his step in spite of how dark it was. With as weak as his abilities were, how did he manage? "Because what is here is not important to them."

Brusus walked down to one of the crates and tapped the side. The lettering on this box was faded but not nearly as badly as others around the warehouse. Rsiran recognized the style of writing but not the words.

"This is from Asador," Brusus said.

Rsiran looked at the box. Asador was nearly as well known for its silks as for the university. And, to him, an exotic and foreign place. "What's inside?"

Brusus shrugged. "Don't know. The Elvraeth don't even know. And they don't care." He tapped another box farther down the line. "This is from Cort. And Thyr. And Gahlan." He said each place, tapping another crate. "Think of what could be stored within these crates. Silks. Precious stones. Swords." He tapped the Gahlan crate. "Could some have sent food? Herbs for healing?" he asked, knocking on crates from Cort. "Or had they sent fabrics, cloth so fine that even here in Elaeavn we would find them beautiful?" Brusus shook his head. "Most of what is here will never be known."

Rsiran thought of the child starving outside his new smithy. "But why? If it's all so valuable—"

Brusus nodded. "I had the same reaction, Rsiran. But as the Elvraeth have wealth, they do not value things the same as the rest of us. From what I've learned, everything stored here was simply gifted to the Elvraeth."

Rsiran looked around, seeing how massive the warehouse was and how many boxes were stored here. There were probably thousands. He could not imagine so much wealth that you simply did not care about it. "And you want to do what with this, exactly?"

Brusus snorted and wandered farther down the line of boxes. Rsiran had to hurry to catch him, feet stirring up clouds of dry dust that sifted into his mouth with each step. He quickly raised his arm across his mouth.

Rsiran almost reached Brusus as he ducked in between two towering stacks of crates that stretched nearly to the ceiling. They were carefully aligned so that they could not fall. The lowermost had barely visible lettering with lines that angled backward, sloping in harsh unreadable lines. The exterior of these was different than some of the others, and he ran his hand along the lower boxes, touching smooth wood that felt almost slippery to the touch, as if coated with fresh oil. As much as he hated the urge, he wanted to pry an end off, peer inside, and learn what secrets the Elvraeth hid here. Though they may not value the wealth stored within, Rsiran still did.

He finally found Brusus standing in a small clearing of boxes. A window above had been cleared of much of the dust and dirt, leaving it smeared but letting more light stream into the warehouse, almost as if focused on this spot. The clearing was framed with six of the massive crates, all arranged in an even shape. All looked much like the last, strange angular lettering barely visible, the same smooth and glistening wood. He touched the nearest one and ran his hand across it, rubbing the oil between his fingers.

"Why did you bring me here, Brusus?"

Brusus turned and look at the crates, shaking his head, speaking softly. "Not long ago, I was hired for a job. Brought here to see an example of something before I did the job. I cannot imagine all that is stored here. Hundreds of years of history. Items of value and power." He turned to look at Rsiran.

He led Rsiran to a crate along the edge of the small clearing. Two other boxes were stacked atop it, both made of the strange old and oiled wood, their surfaces marked with the faded lettering that he could not read.

The end of the crate had been forced open. Rather than splintering, the wood seemed to peel away in layers, looking more like stacked paper than any type of wood Rsiran had ever seen. Inside the crate, were other smaller boxes. It was then he recognized the lettering. "Jessa had one of these."

Brusus nodded and an angry tilt came to his eyes. "She reclaimed one, yes."

"What's in them?"

Brusus slipped one of the boxes out. It was long and narrow and made of the same wood that the rest of the crate was made from, the surface slightly less slick. Two faded brass hinges mounted along one side, and a solid clasp held the lid closed. The lettering appeared burned into the wood, charred into the surface with the slashing writing.

"Is there a key?" Rsiran asked.

Brusus shrugged. "Probably was once. Not sure that even the Elvraeth would know anymore. It took me quite a while to figure out how to get into the crate. The wood wouldn't gouge at all. Wasn't until I tried chiseling it off that I realized I could simply peel apart the layers. Then it opened easy enough."

Rsiran grabbed one of the stacks of peeled wood. It bent easily enough but was still stiff, like bark peeled from a tree, nothing like the stiff sheaf of parchment it appeared to be. Taken together, the stack peeled from the crate seemed more like layers of something other than wood, with whatever oily substance he felt on the surface used to hold it together.

Brusus pulled the worn leather pack out of his pocket and unrolled it again. Rsiran noted that he set it away from the crate and the stacked pieces from the end, careful to let the leather touch nothing but the packed dirt ground. Thumbing through the slender rods placed within the pack, he settled on one and took it out. As he worked it in the lock, he muttered to himself inaudibly. Finally, there was a soft *click*, and the clasp popped open.

Rsiran realized he was holding his breath. As Brusus opened the lid, he let it out slowly. Inside, tucked into a soft velvet pad to keep it from moving, was a long metal cylinder with strange markings along the side, almost runes of a sort Rsiran had never seen, running from one end to the other.

Brusus carefully lifted it and held it up, twisting it. The color of the metal seemed to shift and shimmer, drifting from gold to bluish grey to silver as he spun the cylinder. The runes along the sides took on more or less light, depending on how he twisted it, almost seeming to move.

Rsiran blinked, and the effect stopped.

Brusus handed it over to Rsiran, and he took it carefully. The cylinder was heavier than he expected, the metal denser than steel or even lorcith. Up close, the colors shifting along the shaft glimmered faintly, sliding from one to the next depending on how he held it. The markings, characters etched with painstaking detail and looking like animals or trees or even figures holding weapons, still moved, the effect unsettling this close. Each end of the cylinder was open, one seemingly tapered slightly more than the other.

"Do you recognize it?" Brusus asked.

Rsiran shook his head. "Not any alloy I have ever seen."

"What if it's not an alloy?"

Rsiran looked over to Brusus. "Then this is even more impressive. What sort of metal shimmers like this?"

Brusus placed his narrow lock pick back into the leather pack and carefully rolled it back up, sliding it into his pocket before standing. "After hearing you talk about the different metals, I had hoped you might recognize it."

"What's this for?" Rsiran held the cylinder in front of him. The craftsmanship that had gone into making it was impressive. More impressive was the level detail in the runes. He could almost imagine the tiny characters were alive.

Brusus took it from him and set it back into the box. After closing the lid, he locked the clasp again. "I don't know. I've opened nearly a dozen, and each is a similar shape but has different markings. Most seem to be made of the same metal, but a few were different. One was solid gold. Another silver. Haern thinks they are all part of something greater, meant to be assembled once the crates arrived in Elaeavn. Of course, he also tells me I should leave this place alone. Not sure how I could when they simply collect dust here in the warehouse."

"They are skillfully made."

Brusus nodded. "And likely worth nothing other than as a curiosity," he said ruefully. "Oh, the gold one has value. As does the silver. But these," he pointed to the small box, "made of some unknown metal are only valuable to collectors. The only collectors are the Elvraeth or those close to them." He shrugged and pointed toward the opened crate.

"What about outside of Elaeavn? There must be collectors in other cities."

Brusus nodded. "I'm certain there would be. The universities in Asador or Thyr would likely have interest, but there are problems with trying that. First is simple transportation. These boxes are quite heavy. Weight equals cost." He smiled and shrugged. "The other is as problematic. I'm not ready to draw the full attention of the Elvraeth upon me. So… worthless. I've sent what I can with Firell—items that could come from anywhere—but there is much more here, much that I don't fully understand."

Rsiran kneeled next to the box and ran his hand over the surface. He didn't know what the cylinders were made from or their purpose, but was sure they weren't worthless.

"This crate is probably five hundred years old," Brusus said. "And someone thought it important to ship to the Elvraeth." He thumped the crate with an angry smack. "Now we're left with questions, curiosity only, trying to understand what it is that was forgotten here all those years ago."

Each crate in the warehouse was nearly ten paces long and half as wide, standing nearly to his neck. Stacked as they were atop each other, the topmost one touched the ceiling. Inside each one there was so much wonder. Rsiran could not help but feel curious about what was in the others.

"Is this the only one you've opened?"

Brusus smiled and shook his head. "The only one that has proved interesting. Each has been challenging to open. I suspect the design is particular to the Elvraeth, something they requested, which is likely why these are so damned hard to break into. Probably why they store them here so openly. Who else would waste so much time trying to break into these crates?" he asked disgustedly. "The first took me nearly two nights to crack open. Two nights! And all it held was stacks of paper. The quality was fine enough, but had I known…" Brusus sighed. "Another held fabrics woven in a rough design and nearly worthless. There was one full of fine porcelain. Nice quality and painted with interesting detail, but *that* box took me a day and a half to crack."

In spite of Brusus's apparent annoyance, Rsiran smiled. "How long did this crate take to open?"

Brusus saw the tilt of a smile on his face and glared at him. "Nearly a week. Took me most of that time to figure out how to peel away the layers. Once I learned that, then it opened easily."

Could he Slide into one of the crates to see what they contained? Likely he would end up trapped… or worse. Injured or impaled on something inside. To Slide successfully, he needed to know there was an open place to emerge. He could not always tell that when he started. Maybe with enough practice he could get better, but for now, it would be safer to not risk it.

"What were you asked to do?"

"I wasn't asked to do anything with the crates stored here," Brusus admitted. "They were shown to me as an example. Probably a warning too. If they can leave all this wealth here, why do I matter?" Brusus ran his fingers along the nearest crate. "I doubt he even knows I've returned. Or maybe he does. The man who brought me here is like that crate. He works in layers. The outermost layer is not often the real reason. With him, I have learned to look deeper, peel away until I find something beneath. I still don't know if I have peeled away enough, but I think there was another reason I was brought here." Brusus looked with a longing expression at the crates.

Rsiran could almost see him calculating how much wealth was stored within, could sense the disappointment he would have felt when this crate was finally opened only to learn that whatever was stored inside was not something he could easily sell.

"Who showed them to you?"

Rsiran knew this must be where Brusus had gone the day after he'd first met him.

Brusus looked up and met Rsiran's eyes. For a moment, Rsiran thought there was a surge of green there but decided it must be some trick of the light coming through the dirty windows overhead.

"Someone who is more at home here than I am."

"A merchant?"

Brusus shook his head. "No merchant is allowed within this warehouse. As I said, I don't think any but a select few of the Elvraeth even know what is stored here."

"If none other than the Elvraeth know about the warehouse, then how did your..." Rsiran trailed off as he suddenly understood. "One of the Elvraeth *showed* this to you?"

Which meant Brusus owed money to one of the Elvraeth. Brusus's desire for Rsiran's knives took on new urgency. Brusus didn't simply need a little money. With the Elvraeth involved, Rsiran couldn't begin to fathom the sums Brusus might owe. And maybe the overheard comment about a rebellion had something more to it.

Brusus held his gaze. "Not from one of the high families, but he knew and showed me to this place." Seeing the puzzled look, Brusus explained. "As I told you, the Elvraeth are not simply one family—they are many, all joined by common bloodlines. But only the high families rule, the families that trace their ancestors back generations ago to when they claim the Great Watcher himself gave them a gift."

The Elvraeth were gifted with varying degrees of all the known abilities. Some manifested more powerfully than others, but every member of the family had each ability in some form. It was this that granted the Elvraeth the right to rule, and they had ruled over Elaeavn since before it moved to the sea.

"So the Elvraeth you owe money to brought you here?"

Brusus shot him a look. "He brought me here to discuss a job."

Rsiran felt an itching in his head, like someone trying to Read him, and looked around. Other than Brusus, he thought they were alone.

"Is that why you didn't fear the sellsword seeing you enter the warehouse?"

Brusus shook his head. "I'm not certain my friend was permitted to share what he knew of the warehouse."

"Not permitted? Why would one of the Elvraeth share it with you if he wasn't permitted?"

"That is another of the layers I have yet to peel away."

"How much do you owe him?" It was only one of the questions he wanted to ask.

The itching in his head continued, and Rsiran turned, pretending to look at the boxes.

"Doesn't matter. Not if I do this."

"Brusus—this is one of the *Elvraeth*!"

Brusus's eyes narrowed and his face hardened. "I think I understand that better than most. Besides, he's hired me several times before. Always the jobs have been simple and paid well. The last… let's just say it didn't go as he planned. He's offered me a way out of that debt." He looked around the warehouse and shook his head. "Probably didn't intend for me to return and open the crates, but what choice did he give me?" He shook his head again. "He knows I have to do what he asks or

193

he'll report me to the constables. And my coin won't get me out of that when one of the Elvraeth does the reporting."

"Brusus… are you sure you should be doing this? I mean, you are working for one of the Elvraeth but also against the Elvraeth. Don't you think that's dangerous?"

Brusus clapped a hand on Rsiran's shoulder. "You have been spending far too much time around Jessa."

Rsiran felt his face flush.

"That is the same question she asked. I will tell you the same as I told her—I don't know. There are Elvraeth politics at play here. I suspect even if I hadn't taken this job I would somehow end up mixed into them. I would rather be in control, if possible."

Rsiran looked around the warehouse before turning to look at the open crate, the long box still lying on the floor. Something about the dirty floor or possibly the thin light reminded him of the mines and the men sentenced by the Elvraeth council to serve, and he wondered—with the Elvraeth, could one ever really be in control?

CHAPTER 23

As Brusus tucked the box containing the strange metal cylinder back into the crate, Rsiran looked again and counted
the boxes that remained. From what he could tell, there were nearly
two dozen, all lined and stacked neatly. He couldn't help wondering
what they were meant for, what purpose had the people that made and
shipped them to the Elvraeth intended for the strange items?

Given the space remaining, it would seem other boxes had not
been returned to the crate. "What did you do with the others?"

"Others?" Brusus turned and looked at him.

"You said there was one of gold and of silver?"

Brusus shrugged. "Those I've kept."

"Will you try to sell them?" Rsiran imagined one of the Elvraeth
learning of something missing. How much more trouble could Brusus
get himself into then?

He shrugged. "Not in their current form. Too many questions."
As he led the way away from the small clearing, Brusus waved his

hands around and tried to explain. "They're solid gold, solid silver. I would have to melt them down before I could try to move them." He shrugged again. "Besides, I'm not sure I want to sell them quite yet. They're a part of whatever it is that is stored there, and until I know what that thing is, I don't want to give up any of its parts. And… I will have another source of income soon."

Rsiran felt some of the pressure coming off of him. If Brusus didn't need him to create weapons of lorcith, he wouldn't need to risk Sliding back to the mines.

Brusus turned. "If you ever manage to get that forge working, we can sell those blades of yours. If this job goes wrong…" He forced a smile. "Might need something else to offer."

Rsiran nodded slowly. How could he *not* help Brusus? "The forge isn't the issue."

"I saw that."

"After seeing this place, I do wonder if there might be anything here that we could use. Even tools that I wouldn't have to forge would help."

"There might be, Rsiran, but seeing how long it takes to open a single crate, searching through them all would take far too much time. Better to simply move forward with your plan." Brusus took a few more steps, moving away from the lighted part of the warehouse, now where long shadows stretched that reminded Rsiran too much of the mines. "You do have a plan, don't you?"

"I do," he answered quickly. Except, after what happened last night, he wasn't sure that he could go through with it anymore.

When they reached the door, Brusus motioned for him to be silent and pulled it open a crack. Sunlight and fresh air spilled through. Brusus shoved his face up to the door and looked. Once content, he slipped through and ducked along the wall, keeping his head low.

Rsiran followed, pulling the door closed behind him. Dust from the stairs stuck to his tongue.

The sun had shifted during the time they were in the warehouse. Now it glinted over the top of the roof, reflecting with a bright light that bounced into his eyes. Muted sounds of water splashing along the shore reminded him again how different Lower Town was from what he was accustomed; the waves were rarely heard well along the rock wall in Upper Town, only the circling gulls and the distant water a reminder of the bay. A single cat yowled nearby and then hissed. Rsiran paused and look for what disturbed it.

Seeing nothing, he started after Brusus, staying close to the warehouse, keeping his head ducked low under the overhanging roof. As they started down the street, a shadow separated from the buildings. A glimmer reflected sunlight.

"Brusus!" he shouted.

Brusus had seen it as well and jumped back. A sellsword—not the same man they'd seen before entering the building—seemed to melt onto the street. One moment there had been no one, the next, his deep red cloak hung limp in the slight breeze blowing between the buildings, his sword half unsheathed as he faced them.

Rsiran's heart fluttered. Old injuries on his back and neck itched. This man had the same heavily tanned face and steel grey eyes that stared icily at them. He wore dark leather pants with maroon that seemed stamped along the edges. His hand lightly gripped the hilt of his long sword.

Brusus waved his hands. "Just leaving, friend." His words had a strange inflection, almost a sense of pressure.

The man's face changed immediately, and he pulled his sword completely from his sheath. "Friend?" The word carried a thick accent, as if spoken from the back of his throat. "Not friend. You come from stores."

It took Rsiran an extra moment to process what he said. Brusus seemed to recognize immediately.

Surprisingly, Brusus nodded, tilting his head toward the warehouse they had exited. "Needed to inventory. Recent shipment received and had to make sure the captain didn't try to filch half." His tone changed, going from soothing to more conversational. Still there was a sense of pressure to the words that Rsiran could not explain.

The sellsword shook his head. "No shipment. Not to that store."

Brusus turned his head slightly. "I think you are mistaken. Check the logs if you need to."

The sellsword slid forward a step. Though wide and solid, he moved with a languid grace, only his face showing any evidence of tension. His eyes seemed to shift, darting from Rsiran to Brusus, then back. Eventually, he settled on Brusus, as if dismissing Rsiran. His sword swiveled as he held it, moving like an extension of his hand. "No log," the sellsword said. "Unauthorized. You come with me."

Brusus spread his hands, his palms facing out toward the sellsword. "Listen, friend," Brusus tried, "even though you are mistaken, we were leaving." This time, there was no mistaking the strange pressure of the words, almost as if he tried to force them upon the sellsword.

The sellsword frowned. "It is you mistaken." His voice filled with his thick way of speaking. "You Pushing will not make it so."

Brusus lowered his hands and his smile changed, twisting from the friendly grin he had been showing the sellsword to one of acceptance.

The sellsword waited, tilted on his toes as if expecting something different from Brusus.

Then Brusus slipped forward.

The movement was so sudden and unexpected that Rsiran wasn't sure what he was seeing at first. One moment Brusus had been standing, hands at his sides, and the next he practically flew forward, a slender blade appearing from somewhere beneath his cloak and flickering toward the guard.

The sellsword simply stepped to the side, moving with such speed that Brusus nearly barreled past him. His sword twisted, and there was a clang of metal, sword against sword, and Brusus jumped back.

The sellsword's eyes had changed. The icy grey seemed to dance, almost excited.

Brusus had changed too. His face no longer drawn and sallow, his greying and thinning hair pulled back behind his head. Now the flesh of his face flattened, drawing tight, making him seem years younger.

Eyes blazed a dark green.

Rsiran froze, unable to look away. How had Brusus's eyes changed so suddenly?

Brusus darted in and then back, sword tipping and swinging, but the sellsword did not back away. Rsiran knew little of swordsmanship, but it was clear that the sellsword did not fear Brusus.

Then there was a quick movement, and Brusus grunted, jumping back. Blood trickled down his side, staining his cloak and pants. The green of his eyes faded.

The sellsword moved forward, sword flashing toward Brusus again.

Rsiran saw it almost as if time had slowed. Blood drained from Brusus's chest, and his arm hung limp at his side, unable to even lift his sword. There was no way he would be able to stop the attack.

Rsiran did the only thing he could think of: he Slid.

The Slide took him to Brusus, and he grabbed the man's hands. One was wet and sticky, and Rsiran squeezed, careful not to let go. The scent of blood reminded him of the time he had been attacked in the dark. That it was not him injured this time did not make it better. The air whistled as the long sword swung.

Rsiran Slid again.

He had never Slid with another person before, never with anything heavier than the lump of lorcith. Had he not rested as long as he had during the day, he didn't think he would have the energy. As it was, he did not risk a long Slide, deciding in an instant where to emerge.

There was a warmth from the sword nearly striking him, like a hot breath of air against his arm, as they Slid from the alley between the warehouses. As he did, he thought he saw someone else come out of the warehouse.

CHAPTER 24

RSIRAN EMERGED FROM THE SLIDE into a familiar room. The fire crackled in the hearth along the wall. The scent of incense and smoke hung in the air, mixing with the metallic tang of Brusus's blood. The small cot was folded against the wall.

He staggered, more drained than he ever had felt after emerging from a single Slide. The effect of carrying another with him had almost been more than he could manage. He did not want to think what would happen if a Slide failed. Had he a mentor, someone who shared his gift, he might better understand the limitations. Instead, he had to fumble along, learning what he could alone.

Brusus groaned at his feet.

His face had gone pale and his eyes were closed. Blood slowed from the wound on his chest but still flowed. One hand somehow had managed to keep hold of his sword. Quality steel and finely made. Where would Brusus have acquired such a blade?

Brusus groaned again and jerked. Then he went still.

Rsiran prayed to the Great Watcher that the healer was home.

"I will not heal you of your foolishness again."

Rsiran spun. Della stood in a small doorway, her greying hair wild about her head, a thin blue scarf wrapped around her neck as if she prepared to leave.

"Della—"

She frowned, as if realizing something was off. "Not you?"

He shook his head. "Brusus took me to…"

He trailed off. How much would Brusus want to trust the healer?

Rsiran shook away the question. Already he trusted her with more than he trusted anyone else. Of all the people in Elaeavn, she alone knew nearly everything about him, from his ability to Slide, to the attacks, to his return to the mines to harvest lorcith for Brusus.

He needed her to help Brusus now, do whatever it was that she did for him, to save Brusus.

Della watched his face, and her eyes widened as she saw Brusus lying on the floor. "Brusus?"

The healer hurried over and knelt beside Brusus, running her hands along his sides. With a strong grip, she ripped his shirt away, revealing a deep wound near the center of his chest. The edges had blackened, and dark lines ran out from the wound, twisting like vines.

She touched the flesh and winced. Her jaw tightened, and Rsiran saw her eyes flare a bright green. Then the bleeding slowed.

"What happened?" She did not look up at him.

"A sellsword."

"Neelish blade?"

"I don't know. Probably."

She turned and looked up at him. "You were by the warehouse?"

202

Rsiran was relieved that she already seemed to know. He nodded. "Right outside. The sellsword seemed to appear from the shadows, almost as if he Slid."

She turned back to Brusus, pushing her finger into the wound. "They are not of Elaeavn, Rsiran. They cannot Slide. That is a gift from the Great Watcher to our people alone."

Rsiran watched, uncertain what to say to the healer. She continued to insist that his ability was a gift. Without his ability, would he have been sentenced by his father to Ilphaesn? Would his family have turned away from him?

Would Brusus have a chance of survival?

Della's mouth tightened, and her eyes flared again. Some of the darkness around the wound seemed to fade, slowly turning a shade of pink.

"Can you help him?"

"Neelish blades are tipped in poison. Rare to survive an attack. Most are dead before they see a healer, even if they survive the wound." She poked her finger into the hole in Brusus's chest. Drying blood stained her finger. "And this wound is particularly nasty. I am not yet certain what poison was used, but unlike some I have seen recently, I can slow it." She flicked an accusing gaze at him, as if to remind him of his own wound. "Had you left him by the warehouse, he would be dead already."

Rsiran swallowed.

Della looked over. Her eyes were moist, and she blinked away the welling tears. "Without your ability, he would have been gone from this world, returned to join the Great Watcher."

She focused on Brusus, running one hand along the skin of his chest while the other remained plunged in the hole. As Rsiran watched, the skin slowly faded, and the hole gradually seemed to shrink, the edges pulling together. She murmured softly as she worked, one hand moving over his body, the other staying in the wound, as if plugging the flow of blood.

She was a skilled healer, but he had thought she used mostly potions and powders. What she was doing with Brusus was different and much like any other ability. Only he had never seen a healer with abilities given to them by the Great Watcher. After how she had fixed his back, he should have known better, but hadn't thought to question.

"He has lost much blood already. There remains a chance that he does not awaken." Her voice became hushed. "And if he does, he will be weakened for quite some time. I do not know what he had planned with that warehouse, only that he was foolish enough to take the job." She looked down at Brusus with an affectionate expression. "This time he took on too much. Always thinking he can compensate with his abilities."

Rsiran frowned. Abilities? What did the healer mean? "Della," he began. "The sellsword seemed upset with Brusus over something. Said he was Pushing him."

She glanced up at Rsiran and her eyes flared. She seemed to consider how to answer. "We all have our secrets, Rsiran. Each of us is more than we present ourselves to be, and even the most honest still hides something."

Rsiran recognized the truth in that statement. "What did he mean? What did Brusus do that upset him so much?"

"Brusus did as he always does. He relies on his abilities, thinking they will get him out of every problem. Unfortunately, he found a problem where that didn't work." She looked up and saw the confused way Rsiran was looking at her. "Neelish sellswords have a particular type of training that hardens their minds. Once, such training was essential to keep their people and their soldiers safe. Now, it serves simply as tradition. Still, it serves a purpose."

"What purpose?"

"It makes them valuable around men like Brusus."

Men like Brusus. Rsiran eyed his friend, wondering what Della meant. "What is Pushing?"

Della ran her hands along Brusus's chest again, as if smoothing the skin. All traces of the blackened skin were now gone, leaving pale, unmarked flesh. He didn't move, but his breathing was steady and regular. His face looked slack and waxy, and his hair seemed to have gone a deeper grey in the last hour.

She stood slowly, using her arms to push up from where she knelt beside Brusus. The effort of healing appeared to have weakened her, similar to what he felt after Sliding. Had this been how she had felt after healing him? Was this why she had been unable to fully heal his neck? Was she a Healer rather than simply a healer?

"Pushing is rare. Very few can manage and fewer learn to control it." She sighed. A debate seemed to rage behind her eyes as she considered her answer. She frowned at Rsiran, the corners of her mouth tightening. "It is where a powerful Reader can influence a thought, making someone do something they didn't know they wanted to do."

"But Brusus isn't powerful..."

She laughed. The sound was weak and thready. She limped to the small wooden chair in front of the fire and slumped down into it. "That is what he chooses to project."

"Brusus has been Pushing *me*?" Is that why he had been helping him, why he left the mines?

"Do not take affront, Rsiran. He Pushes everyone. He has been doing it so long that he no longer has to think about what he does. Only in moments of great stress does he slip."

Like when he fought with the sellsword, Rsiran realized, remembering how his eyes flared a deep green that seemed almost impossible given all that he knew of Brusus. Now, it seemed he knew very little of Brusus.

Like Brusus knew very little about him.

Della smiled. "You have a quick mind, Rsiran."

Rsiran started thinking about all that he knew about Brusus. "I thought he was Sighted." All those times he had thought he felt a Reader creeping through his mind, he had suspected Jessa. What if it had been Brusus all along?

"He is Sighted."

"But you said he was a Reader."

She looked at him, a hint of disappointment written on her eyes.

"And a Pusher," Rsiran realized. "But to have such abilities would take one with Elvraeth blood."

"Yes, it would."

Rsiran jerked his head around at the sound of Brusus's voice. He had opened his eyes. They were a deep green and looked much the shade of Della's. His face looked weathered and some of the waxy look had gone from it.

"Brusus?" Rsiran said.

Brusus tried to smile but failed, his head flopping slowly to the side instead.

"You're Elvraeth?" Why would one of the Elvraeth live in Lower Town? Why would he want to break into a warehouse that he had every right to access?

"No," he said. His eyes fluttered shut.

"But—"

"Della?" Brusus croaked.

Della sighed and pointed for Rsiran to come toward her and sit. He glanced at Brusus who seemed to have fallen back into a deep sleep, his breathing steady, and his chest rising and falling slowly. He had only awoken to manage those few words.

Rsiran sat on the soft carpet next to her chair and looked up at her. Sitting as he did reminded him of when he was a child, sitting by his mother's knee as she knitted and told stories. It was a time before he had changed. Or they had changed. A happier time.

"I would not share this without his permission. As I will not share your secret without your permission. He trusts you." The words hung between them. "I would guess that he Read you—in some ways, he is more skilled than I—but it is clear even without Reading that you care for him." She waited for Rsiran to nod before continuing, turning to stare at the dancing flames in the fire. "Brusus has Elvraeth blood but is not Elvraeth."

Rsiran shook his head. "I don't understand."

She smiled bitterly. "Pray that you never understand fully." Her voice had changed, losing some of the thready quality and becoming a bit stronger, her tone edged with anger or regret. "Though I suspect you will understand better than most. Brusus shares the same bloodline, the same lineage, as any who live up in the palace. Were he to want to, he could trace his bloodline all the way back to the first Elvraeth." She sighed, and her eyes slipped closed, as if what she said next was difficult to say. "Had he been born a century earlier, he would have lived there as well, would never have known anything about Lower Town or the harbors, would know only life within the walls. Had he been born to any other, he would have been spared his fate."

"What fate?"

"Brusus is the child of an Elvraeth Forgotten."

"Forgotten?" Rsiran repeated the word, looking from Della to Brusus. The Forgotten were those banished from Elaeavn, stricken by the Elvraeth council from all records so that they simply ceased to exist. Only the most corrupt, the most impossible to reform, were Forgotten. Usually the threat alone was enough for reform. He had never heard of the Elvraeth subjecting one of their own to it. "The Elvraeth banish their own?"

Della opened her eyes. The flames reflected there. "The practice began within the palace. It was a means of punishment and control, but over time, as with much within its walls, it twisted into something political and corrupt." She looked over at him. "Few outside the palace understand the politicking that takes place there. For such a beautiful place, many within its walls can be ugly." She shook her head. "All are family, but I think that makes it worse. Most are more cruel to family than they would be to friends."

Della sighed. "Or perhaps it only seems that way. Living here in Lower Town, I have seen many ugly things as well, but almost as much beauty." She smiled at him. "Think of how you were taken in, how Brusus and his friends helped you, *saved* you when you were injured and near death. Such a thing would not happen within the palace. No, sometimes I wonder if it is best he never lived up in the clouds. Living so high leaves you far to fall. Many Elvraeth have been Forgotten over the years."

Jessa had said the same to him. "I don't understand how... why?"

"The reason is often fear. Fear of losing power. Fear of disruption of alliances. Fear of the council. Most often, one's own family is responsible for the banishment."

Rsiran remembered what Brusus had told him of the Elvraeth. He had wondered at the time how Brusus had known so much about them, had been impressed by the ease with which he discussed them. Had he only known!

"There are really five families that live within the palace," Della went on. "Each claims the surname Elvraeth, each claiming to be descendants of the first. Those five families each have a seat on the council." She shook her head. "There are exceptions, but most within the

Elvraeth are no better than school children. They fight. They scream. They form friendships. Some lose out. Fewer are banished, Forgotten. Stricken from their families and sent away from the palace, away from the city."

"And Brusus?"

As Della looked over at Brusus, some of the anger seeped from her eyes. "Brusus was but an infant when his mother was banished. Her crime was one of curiosity, a dangerous trait among the Elvraeth. Earlier attempts at reform had failed, and she was deemed too risky for her house. So she was Forgotten. Her name was stricken from all records of the Elvraeth as if she never existed. Her parents turned their backs on her for their own protection. Her husband was taken from her and betrothed to another. Her child—Brusus—was sent from the palace with her. There could be no traces that she ever existed."

There was something about the way she spoke, some hint of long-repressed anger and sadness, that combined with the way she looked at Brusus, left Rsiran with a sudden question. "Were you banished, Della?" he asked. "Are you Brusus's mother?"

She smiled a sad smile and shook her head. "The Forgotten must leave Elaeavn, Rsiran. His mother left the city and cannot return. Doing so risks worse than banishment."

Rsiran did not know what punishment was worse than banishment, but did not ask. "Then how did Brusus stay in the city?"

Della took a deep breath. "Some secrets are not mine to share, even if he grants permission. Know that he was well cared for. But, as his mother was banished, he will never be Elvraeth though he carries their bloodline."

Rsiran turned and watched the fire for a moment, thoughts turning over in his head. Brusus had abilities greater than he seemed. Regardless of whether his mother was Forgotten, he was of the Elvraeth. Even

Della with her impressive healing abilities, her ability to Read, must have more of that bloodline in her than she admitted. "How many are there like him?"

Della looked over at him. "How many?"

Rsiran nodded. "You said that there are many Forgotten among the Elvraeth. Where do they go? How many are there like Brusus?"

Della sighed again. "Not many like Brusus. It is rare that one so young is sent from the palace. Most Forgotten are banished as an example, a way of coercing the rest of the family. Few have children of their own. As to your other question, I cannot say where the other Forgotten have gone. They must leave Elaeavn. After they have gone, most leave no trail. Likely, they fade into their new home, into obscurity. That is the punishment the Elvraeth fear most."

Rsiran looked back to where Brusus rested, his breathing more steady and the color already returning to his cheeks. When he awoke, Brusus would know about his ability. There was no other way to explain how he managed to get him to the healer before the poison took his life.

In spite of the fact that something good had come of his ability, he still felt unsettled. Exposed somehow.

A cool shiver ran across his skin, and he huddled closer to the fire.

CHAPTER 25

DUSK HAD FALLEN BY THE TIME RSIRAN finally left Della's home. He stood outside her green-painted door. She lived on a small side street well away from the heavy traffic running up and down Sjahl Street, the sounds of the nearby market heard only as an occasional shout rising over a muted din. Even the waves crashing on the shore barely a dozen streets below were little more than a soft splashing, more soothing than anything. A crispness hung about the air, whether it was something real or a residual effect from the incense burning within Della's home, Rsiran didn't know.

In the time he had visited, so much had suddenly changed. No longer was he alone, left to suffer for something he could not control. He had thought that few could really understand what he went through, the pain of being pushed away, banished to the mines. But that was nothing compared to what Brusus had experienced.

Now more than ever before, Rsiran wanted to help Brusus. If whatever job he did for the Elvraeth failed, there was only one way Rsiran *could* help.

Rsiran looked around the street and saw no one. He Slid.

He emerged in the old smithy. The air stank of his forging the night before, the bitter scent of lorcith clinging to it. How had he missed the smell before? Brusus must have known and said nothing. He shook his head, wishing he would simply have been honest with him. Now Brusus lay sleeping, motionless after nearly dying in an attack that Rsiran could have prevented by simply Sliding them away before the sellsword had a chance to attack.

He sighed. The past could not be changed. The only thing he had control over was what he did from here.

As he looked around the smithy, a small breeze blew through the crumbled roof. Two of the lanterns still flickered with light, leaving shadows dancing across the floor. He glanced over at the forge, considering. Plenty of coal remained, more than enough to fire up the forge again and work the lorcith he had already collected. Between the blade he'd made last night and what remained hidden, he suspected they could sell his work for a nice profit. Then he would be back where he had been… needing to mine additional lorcith before he could do any more work.

The urge to do *more* was strong. Much of the evening had been spent resting, sitting by the fire with Della, watching Brusus until she had sent him away to rest. Rather than resting, he felt energized.

Rsiran changed into the dirty greys from the mine. And then, without thinking about it too much more, he grabbed the pick and the small hammer and Slid.

Rsiran was cautious with this Slide, emerging in the wide opening before the mine's branching tunnels split off. A wave of weakness washed over him, but less than he had felt during other Slides. Darkness engulfed him completely, and he backed against the wall until he felt the cool stone through his shirt. Then he stood motionless.

There was a soft fluttering of air thick with the bitter scent of lorcith that pulled on his shirt. Somewhere to his left, muted voices echoed from the sleeping quarters. Likely it was still early enough that they were eating and only now preparing to settle in for the evening. No other sounds came.

The lack of the steady tapping was both disconcerting and reassuring.

Standing and listening did nothing but waste time. Now that he was within the mine, he could Slide with more accuracy.

Gathering himself, he Slid into the deepest mine, emerging as close as he felt safe to the blunted end of the tunnel. Another wave of weakness hit him, and he staggered. His hand slammed into the stone, and he bit back a small scream. The hammer dropped from his grip and skittered across the ground, too loud in the silence of the tunnels.

Rsiran held himself up, leaning on the stone for a few moments until the fatigue eased. He was still aware of it, felt as if he were heavier, but the overwhelming need to sit and rest had passed.

Slowly his eyes adjusted to the darkness. Not for the first time, he wished for Sight.

His hand throbbed, and he opened and closed his fist, working some of the pain away. Careless of him to drop the hammer. What if whoever mined at night had heard him? Rsiran suspected that they were Sighted. His only advantage was the ability to Slide.

Searching with his foot, his boot pushed against the hammer and he leaned down and picked it up. His hand brushed the floor of the tunnel and seemed to hum, almost as if pulsing in time with the throbbing he felt from slamming into the stone.

The sensation was distinct and unmistakable. Lorcith.

He had never considered that the ore might be beneath him. Always he had mined along the walls, once nearly overhead, but had not thought to listen for lorcith beneath him. How many others had neglected mining below them as well?

He ran his hands along the stone, feeling for lorcith. His palms practically sang with the music. All around him were deposits, nuggets both massive and small.

There was no need for another massive nugget. The one he worked last night would be too large to effectively forge. Maybe with another smith working alongside him, he might be able to manage forging something larger, but as it was, he needed smaller—more manageable—deposits. Something better for making knives, whatever it took to pay Brusus's debt.

Rsiran stopped when he felt a fist-sized nugget in the ground. The sensation was a tingling, almost a vibration, that shot up his arm. Lorcith called in his mind like a song, demanding its release.

The sense was more potent than it had ever been, a louder sensation that seemed to resonate within him. Did focusing on it make it easier for him to locate the lorcith?

Tucking the hammer into his pants, he grabbed the pick and took a deep breath. Then he swung.

The strike rang out loudly. A small spark flickered briefly where the pick struck the stone. Rsiran waited, listening carefully for the sounds of anyone moving within the tunnels, but—other than his heavy breathing—he heard nothing.

He struck at the stone again. Again he waited, listening.

At first, he paused to listen every few strikes. After a while, he fell into a rhythm: picking away at the rock for a few beats and then pausing for a handful of heartbeats. He made slow work but managed to free the nugget of lorcith and tucked it into a pocket.

Rsiran sat on the floor for a few moments running his hand across the stone, feeling for another smaller sized lump. He found what he sought near where the floor sloped up toward the wall. Larger collections were all around, each easily larger than any he had mined before. Larger than any he had ever seen his father purchase. Part of him wished he had time to mine one of them. What would such a massive lump of lorcith direct him to forge it into?

After resting another moment, Rsiran stood and started again, striking at the smaller nugget buried near the corner of the wall, still pausing to listen.

It was during one of these pauses that he felt a change to the breathing of the cave.

Dry wind blew against his skin, the bitter spice of lorcith mingling with dusty stone chipped away by countless miners over the years. Rsiran felt something different—almost like an interruption in the expected flow—and the air suddenly smelled of sweat and blood.

No longer was he alone.

He stiffened but heard nothing.

Rsiran sniffed the air softly, carefully. There was no mistaking the odor.

He saw nothing in the mines other than shades of black. That meant nothing to him. Someone could be standing right in front of him, and he wouldn't know it…

There was a sudden gust of air, as if something moved quickly toward his face.

Rsiran didn't hesitate. He Slid two steps away.

He emerged from the Slide as something thumped against the wall. Whoever attacked him grunted softly as if staggering into unexpected nothingness.

His attacker was Sighted but Rsiran had the advantage of Sliding.

Mixed with his fear, hot anger boiled up. Whoever attacked him was likely the same as before. Maybe even the same person who had nearly killed him. Were it not for his ability to Slide, he would have died within the mine weeks ago.

That memory burned within him. All Rsiran had wanted was to serve out his time, collect enough lorcith to impress his father so that he could return to Elaeavn. If not redeemed then at least forgiven. The attacks had taken that away from him, had driven him to be something—someone—else. And he should be thankful for the push, but at the moment all he felt was rage.

Rsiran jumped forward toward where he had heard the attacker stumble. His fingers brushed the edge of rough fabric and he grabbed tightly. Then he Slid.

Emerging in the clearing before the mouth of Ilphaesn, clear moonlight spilling down seeming as bright as the sun to eyes adjusted to darkness, he tore his attacker with him. The connection prolonged the Slide, seemed to stretch it out like hot metal pulled apart, but Rsiran did not let go.

Then his attacker appeared in the clearing. With an angry push, Rsiran shoved him away.

Rsiran staggered. After so many Slides in one day, he should be nearly spent. Anger seemed to feed his focus.

When he turned to see his attacker, Rsiran nearly staggered again.

It was the boy.

"You?" he asked.

The boy backed away. The advantage of his Sight suddenly stolen from him, he shrunk toward the safety of the mines. He clutched a large burlap sack tightly in his fist, and he shook it, as if considering swinging it toward Rsiran. His other hand clutched his mining pick in a trembling grip.

"How did you…" The boy looked around, his eyes widened, as if suddenly realizing where he was. His body shook, tremors racking him, and he took another step back toward the closed mouth of the mines. Iron bars blocked the entrance, and he slammed up against them, as if hoping to squeeze between and reenter.

"You attacked me? But you tried to *help* me!"

The boy shook his head. Green eyes darted from side to side. "Not help. You can hear the metal. I know you can," he said accusingly. "But you take too much. Always too much." His head swiveled as he looked for some way to escape. "I tried to warn you. Take nothing but small rocks. Leave the larger alone, but you didn't listen."

Rsiran took an angry step forward, stopping when the boy raised the pick up in front of him. "Why do you care how much I take? There is more than enough lorcith in the mines!"

The boy shook his head. "Not for them. They will not have it."

"Who? Who will not have it?"

The boy turned his head, his eyes wild and darting. He tilted his head toward the village near the base of Ilphaesn and then looked toward Elaeavn.

Rsiran glanced over his shoulder. From where they stood, Elaeavn spread out beneath them, clearly visible in the moonlight. None of the illusion could be seen near Ilphaesn; rather than creating the effect of the sheer rock walls, buildings looked as they were. Even the palace did not appear to float from where they stood.

Soft shuffling came from behind him and he whipped his head around.

The boy had the pick raised and ran toward him. His burlap sack lay on the ground near the mouth of the cave entrance. Rsiran Slid toward the sack. The boy skidded across the ground where Rsiran had been.

Picking up the sack, it fell open to reveal lumps of lorcith filling it. "Why do you collect the lorcith?"

The boy caught himself and turned, holding the pick threateningly in front of him. Here, under the moonlight where Rsiran could see him, he did not feel as frightened as he did deep within the mines. At least here he could Slide away.

"That is mine!"

Rsiran hefted the bag, surprised by its weight. How much had the boy harvested during the night? Where did he put all that he collected?

"What's this for?"

"They cannot have it!" he shouted. Then he lunged again.

Rsiran Slid away, moving only a few steps with the Slide. Short distances were not as taxing as longer travel.

"Why do you care what they have?"

The boy leaned on his pick, his breathing heavy. "They do not understand it like I do. They want to force it to become something it is not." His eyes darkened.

"The smiths? Is that who you don't want to have the metal?" Rsiran knew how his father felt about lorcith, the way he spoke about learning to ignore the call of the ore, that a smith must learn to exert his will upon it, craft it into something of the smith's choosing, not what the lorcith would choose.

The boy shook his head. With his long hair and the pout to his face, he seemed ragged and wild.

"Why don't you use what you have to buy your freedom?"

"Freedom? I have more freedom in the mines than I do in Elaeavn. At least the days are mine here."

"But why attack me? I did nothing to you!"

The boy sneered. "You help *them*. You bring the metal to *them*."

"I did nothing but try to earn my way out of the mines. I can't help it that I hear the lorcith. You must understand how difficult it is to ignore."

He snorted. "Difficult? Not difficult. You bargain with it, tell it you'll come back. That is the trade you need to make."

"Is that why you go back at night?"

He shook his head. "Not just me."

Rsiran frowned. "What do you mean?"

The boy's face changed, his eyes alighting with a strange energy. "You don't know?" he said, watching Rsiran's face. Then he giggled in a high-pitched sort of sound. "He doesn't know." He shook his head. "Lucky for you I found you first. If it was the other…"

"What other?" Rsiran asked. Could there have been another working the mines at night? As implausible as this boy wandering alone in the dark, making bargains with the lorcith during the day to return later, he had heard the tapping while talking with the boy those first nights in the mines. And he didn't think the boy had been the one to attack him. He had seemed genuinely concerned. "Who else mines the lorcith at night?"

The boy skittered away from Rsiran. "I want to go back." He hopped on his feet, dancing around a bit as if cold.

"Back? Into the mine?"

The boy nodded.

"You could be free," Rsiran suggested. He wouldn't take him back to Elaeavn, but he could return on his own if he wanted to.

The boy's eyes narrowed. "What freedom? Freedom to run every time I see a constable? Freedom to hide along streets? Freedom to dig for scraps?" He shook his head. "Here I am free to work. Free to eat. I know where my freedom lies. I choose to stay."

"There are other freedoms to be found in the city." Like the freedoms he had found with his new friends. Surely they would take the boy in as well? "I won't take you back into the mine."

The boy's eyes widened, fear etched into them and tightening his face. "If I am outside in the morning, the Towners won't let me return!"

"Then sneak in once the gate is first opened."

The boy shook his head. "There are always two Towners stationed outside the entrance."

Rsiran thought back to when he was first brought into the caves. Had there been more than one person watching the entrance? He didn't think so, but he had been so focused on what was happening that he didn't really remember.

"There must be another entrance."

The boy's eyes widened, and he shook his head. "No other way into the mines. Not that connects to the prison mines."

Rsiran wondered if that meant there was another mine elsewhere along the mountain. If so, he could Slide there to mine additional lorcith.

"Please put me back inside. They find me here, and they would think I escaped. Send me back to Elaeavn. I would face the council then!"

The boy feared being Forgotten more than he feared working in the mines. And how long had Rsiran lived thinking his life was horrible?

"Drop the pick," he said.

The boy shook his head. "You know I can't."

Rsiran understood his fear. Those who lost their tools—the pick and the hammer—faced the potential for punishment. Usually, it was little more than a fine, extra lorcith tacked onto their sentence. But sometimes, worse punishment was exacted.

"Then I can't return you." For what the boy had done to him, he probably shouldn't anyway, but leaving him at the entrance to the mine seemed excessively cruel.

The boy dropped the pick to the ground. His body shook.

"Kick it over here."

The boy kicked the pick across the ground with a spray of dust. "Can I have my sack?" He suddenly sounded very young.

Rsiran shook his head. "No." If it held as much lorcith as he suspected, Rsiran knew he wouldn't have to spend time in the mine to collect enough to help Brusus.

The boy's face turned sullen, but he didn't say anything more. Rsiran set the sack on the ground and the pick on top of it. "What else do you have?"

The boy shook his head, his eyes wild.

"You *poisoned* me! I want to know what it is!"

The boy shook his head more violently. Lanky hair fell in front of his face. "That wasn't me!" He took a step backward.

For a moment, Rsiran thought that the boy might start running. Partly, he wished that he would. Living in the mines as he wanted to do was no way to live. But then the boy stopped and hunched over, waiting.

After stepping up to the boy, Rsiran grabbed his wrist and Slid inside the entrance of the mine.

After they emerged, the boy jerked his arm free and backed away. Darkness enveloped them, lit by the orange light from the sleeping quarter. The scent of the bitter lorcith was stronger within. The boy slipped backward, watching Rsiran as he went.

"I'm sorry," he said softly. "I didn't have a choice."

There was pain in his voice that Rsiran understood. "I could help you."

The boy shook his head. "Leave. Please don't come back."

Rsiran watched the boy slip around the wall and back into the sleeping chamber. Then he Slid back outside the entrance, grabbed the sack and the pick, and Slid back to the smithy in Elaeavn.

CHAPTER 26

RSIRAN CRUMBLED TO THE GROUND in the smithy after he emerged from his Slide. Darkness threatened to press around him, and spots of light shimmered in front of his eyes. A wave of nausea pushed through him, and he leaned over, thinking he might vomit.

He had pushed himself too hard.

Still, he felt a sense of exhilaration at what he had managed. Not only finding out who had attacked him but in using his ability to Slide to defend himself. He couldn't help but smile as he remembered how he had pulled the boy out of the mine, taking away his advantage.

"Where did you come from?"

Rsiran rolled over. Jessa crouched near one of the posts supporting the ceiling. For some reason, he wasn't surprised to see her, even considering the locked door she must have come through. Her hair was pushed back from her face, and worry etched in her eyes. A gold flower was tucked into a thin white shirt. Dust and dirt smeared one sleeve. Surprisingly, she wore a skirt that bunched up around her knees.

"Jessa?" His tongue felt thick and his mouth dry as worry about Brusus came to mind. "Brusus?"

She shook her head. "He hasn't woken up yet. From what I understand, it might be a while. Della said you saved him." There was a note of accusation in her voice mixed with the question in her eyes.

Rsiran rolled onto his back and stared up at the ceiling. Still not awake. Could he have acted sooner? Had Brusus known of his ability, they could have Slid from the warehouse, avoided the guards altogether. Then maybe Brusus wouldn't be lying at the healer's house, not waking up.

"It was a Neelish blade that cut him," Jessa said.

Rsiran nodded. "I think so."

"He showed you the warehouse?"

"Yes."

"Did he show you what was inside?"

"Yes."

Jessa breathed out softly. "I see."

Rsiran turned his head to look over at her. He couldn't read the mixture of emotions on her face. "You said there was no rebellion."

"There isn't!"

"Then what's he doing? Working for one of the Elvraeth against the Elvraeth?"

Jessa laughed bitterly. "Then you didn't pay attention."

"I heard what he said."

"Maybe, but you didn't pay attention to Brusus. For him, it's always about the money. That's why he took the job, not because of some fighting between the Elvraeth." She took a deep breath and shook her head. "He should be dead, you know."

"That's what Della said," Rsiran answered.

"How did you get him to her in time?" She looked over to the door. "How did you get back into the smithy?"

Rsiran watched her and sighed. He wouldn't lie anymore—not to Jessa after all that she had done for him. After she had saved him. Would admitting to her what he could do—what he was—drive her away? The healer had told him that he needed to trust. It had to start somewhere. It felt fitting that it should be with Jessa. "I Slid."

Jessa shook her head. "I don't understand."

His strength was starting to come back, and he pushed up onto his elbows to look over at her. "That's my ability. I can Slide."

"I don't know what that is, Rsiran."

At least she didn't run. Rsiran wasn't sure he would be able to stand it if Jessa abandoned him too. "You're Sighted?" The nausea finally passed, and he managed to sit all the way up. With a little more time and maybe some water, he might be able to function.

"You know I am."

He hadn't, at least not at first, but that was when he thought Brusus had no ability. "And Haern is a Seer."

She nodded.

"And Brusus...." He caught himself. How much did Jessa know about Brusus? And was it his place to say anything about Brusus's past if Jessa didn't know?

"I know about Brusus," she said.

Rsiran sighed and nodded. "Well... I don't have any of those abilities. I can Slide."

"How did that help you save Brusus? How did that help you get into here?"

He had only tried to explain Sliding once before. The first time he Slid, he hadn't even known what he had done. Rsiran had gone to his father for answers—answers his father did not have. His father had left and when he returned, anger Rsiran had never before seen twisted his face. That anger never again left him.

Instead of trying to explain and failing, he stood. Closing his eyes, he gathered what remained of his strength, and then Slid toward Jessa.

The distance between them was barely ten steps, but the effort nearly dropped him. He emerged from the Slide shaking, his legs trembling, and he sank to his knees.

Jessa's eyes widened. "Does Brusus know?"

Rsiran swallowed. His mouth was dry, and he tasted sickness in his throat. "He does now."

"But not before?"

Rsiran shook his head and shifted from his knees to sit on the ground. "Not before. Only Della knew."

"You've been hiding your ability?"

He nodded.

"Why? Why hide this?"

"If you understood what this means..."

"That you can move without walking? That walls won't stop you? That this is how you planned to help Brusus without telling anyone?" She became increasingly angry as she ran through the list. Her face flushed, and she twisted one of her hands in her hair.

Rsiran sighed and shrugged. "I had to hide what I can do. I have always had to hide. My father said it is a dark ability, marking me cursed by the Great Watcher. Only thieves and criminals can Slide." Now, after what Brusus had shown him in the warehouse—and his sneaking into the mines—was he anything else?

She reached over and punched him in the shoulder. "Careful who you're talking about."

Rsiran tried to laugh but his throat wouldn't let him.

"Is that why you were hurt? Was it your father?"

"Not my father." He looked over and met Jessa's eyes. "My father wanted to teach me a lesson, wanted to teach me what he expected of me so I could be the apprentice he demanded."

"What was the lesson?" She shifted closer to him and placed her hand on his arm. The anger was gone from her face, and now all he saw was concern. He liked the warmth of her hand resting on his arm.

"I was sent to work in the Ilphaesn mines."

Her hand stiffened. "By the council? Is that why you left your family?"

"Not the council. At least those sent by the council have a way of earning their freedom." He swallowed hard. "My father sent me."

She sucked in a breath. "So that's your access to lorcith."

He nodded.

"But how were you injured?"

"I was attacked by someone who didn't want me to mine the lorcith." And poisoned, though Rsiran wondered how. The boy didn't seem capable of poisoning him, though he hadn't expected him to be the one mining at night. There was another, but why? Who did the boy work with?

"Wasn't that why you were there?"

Rsiran shrugged. Did he tell her how he could hear lorcith too?

"So when I found you?"

"I had Slid back to the city."

"Is it hard to do?"

The question caught Rsiran off guard, and he laughed. "When I'm tired or hurt. Otherwise, it's as easy as seeing a place and stepping there."

"You have to see where you're going?"

"Not entirely. Knowing where I'm going makes it easier." He grew more relaxed explaining his ability to Jessa, as if it were something

227

normal. Maybe it was the way she questioned him or the lack of judgment in her questions.

"Are there limits?"

She edged a little closer, and her body pressed next to his. One hand smoothed her skirt, pushing the end of the fabric flat. Rsiran didn't move, enjoying how she felt up against him. After so long spent wanting nothing more than to be by himself, separating himself from others, it felt strange to *want* to be close to someone.

"Seeing where I'm Sliding is helpful, but not necessary. For accuracy, I have to be able to see where I want to emerge from the Slide or have been there before. Otherwise I could end up anywhere."

"Doesn't sound like much of a limitation."

"Can you see in the dark?" he asked.

She frowned at him. "Yes."

"What else can you see?"

She shrugged. "Pretty much everything. I don't really notice it anymore."

"So not much limitation for your Sight."

She pushed on his shoulder but didn't move away. "Only the darkest rooms. There, all I see are shades of grey."

"Must be nice to never live in darkness." How useful would Sight have been when he had been working the mines? Would he have ended up like the boy—ended up wandering the mines alone every night, unafraid of the darkness, preferring to work the mines to returning to the city? How must the boy feel to be threatened by Rsiran? And with her Sight, could Jessa help him mine lorcith in Ilphaesn? Then he wouldn't have to fear being caught alone.

"I could say the same to you. Never feeling trapped, always knowing you can escape wherever you might be. Never worried about doors or locks keeping you from entering."

Rsiran looked over to the door. "I don't think any lock keeps you out."

She shrugged. "I didn't say that *I* worried about those things, only that it must be nice!"

He laughed and leaned against her. They sat that way for a few moments, neither of them speaking, simply resting their bodies against each other. Rsiran listened to her steady breathing, smelled the sweet scent of the golden flower she wore tucked into her shirt and the mint on her breath, and felt the strength in her hand as she held onto his arm. In that moment, he was thankful his father had sent him away, otherwise he might never have known Jessa.

After a while, she sat forward. "Why was Brusus attacked?"

Rsiran sighed, regretting that the moment had passed. "We were outside the warehouse when the sellsword approached. Brusus tried to talk his way past, but the man seemed to know we had been in the warehouse. Brusus tried to get past him..."

"Had he watched you in the warehouse?" Jessa asked.

Rsiran shook his head. "I don't know. He came out of the shadows after we left. He wanted to report Brusus, probably to the constables."

"They would not. Neelish sellswords are privately hired. Most that patrol the warehouses there are hired by the Elvraeth. Some have contracts with the local merchants."

Rsiran remembered the attack vividly. Now that he considered what happened, it was nothing like he would have expected from the constables. Constables were tasked with policing and reporting. The sellsword had seemed more interested in simply eliminating Brusus.

"Brusus said he was hired for a job."

Jessa nodded. "One of the Elvraeth hired him. Used the warehouse to draw Brusus in. Made a big show of being offended by everything there."

"You were there?"

She smiled ruefully. "I wasn't supposed to be. I trailed Brusus when he left to meet with him. Thought I could tag along behind him without him noticing…"

"But he did."

If Brusus had Elvraeth blood, his abilities would allow him to detect Jessa easily. Whatever allowed him to Push thoughts onto others would likely let him Read them as easily. But if that was the case, how had Brusus not known he could Slide? Or had he always known?

Jessa laughed. "He did. Always seems to know. Might not have strong abilities, but he's crafty."

Rsiran stiffened briefly, suddenly realizing that despite his earlier assumption, Jessa didn't know about Brusus. How many of them did? He couldn't be the only one aside from Della, could he?

"What happens if Brusus doesn't complete the job?" he asked, needing to know if he should begin forging more lorcith for Brusus. It was the only thing Rsiran could do to help.

"I don't know. You know he's already plenty in debt. That's why he wants the knives. And with the Elvraeth, I think he figures lorcith might tempt him. As to what he was to do? I'm not sure what was expected of him."

Rsiran glanced over at the sack of lorcith. How much time did Brusus have?

"Did he show you the crates? The one with the strange cylinders?" Jessa asked.

"He did. I don't know what kind of metal they are made from. I think Brusus was hoping I would."

Her face fell. "At least one is of gold. He refuses to sell it. Wants to know what they make first. He thinks they form some type of device."

"I don't know what could be made from the cylinders themselves."

"They're not all cylinders." Jessa said it hesitantly. "I'm not sure even Brusus knows, but I snuck into the warehouse a few times without him and went through those boxes. The ones to the front are all cylinders. Toward the back they are different. Not even sure what to make of those."

What had he gotten himself into? What was Brusus working on that they didn't know about? The longer he sat next to Jessa, the more his energy returned. The overwhelming sense of fatigue and the need to sit and try to sleep was fading. Even the nausea, the thick bile taste at the back of his throat, was fading. His throat was still dry and he could use a drink, but he didn't think he would fall over if he stood.

Reluctantly, he stood, separating himself from Jessa.

"Where are you going?" she asked.

He pointed to the brown burlap sack crumpled on the ground. Lifting it, he was suddenly very aware of how heavy the sack was. How had the boy carried it silently through the mines? How many nights had he spent mining what Rsiran now held? How had Rsiran managed to Slide while carrying this much lorcith, especially as weakened as he had been near the end?

He carried it over to Jessa and dropped it on the floor between them. "I took this from the boy who attacked me."

"A *boy* attacked you?" She didn't even try to hide the laugh hidden in the question.

"He was Sighted, and it's dark in the mines!"

Jessa shook her head. "I didn't think the council sentenced anyone younger than sixteen to serve in the mines."

Della had said something like that as well. "He couldn't have been any older than twelve."

"Maybe he only looked young."

"Maybe," he agreed, opening the sack.

Inside, as he had hoped, were lumps of lorcith. He took them out one at a time, holding each carefully before setting it aside. Jessa's eyes widened after he had taken out a dozen. There were still probably two-dozen more in the sack.

"You can forge all of this?"

He shrugged. "Not tonight, but give me a few nights, and I can make some progress." As long as the lorcith didn't resist him, he figured he could probably make three or four knives each night. Whether that was what the lorcith wanted to guide him to make was another matter.

Jessa punched him on the shoulder. "How much did Brusus get for the knife you made?"

"Two talens."

Jessa's mouth twitched as she did the math in her head. A smile spread across her lips. "Too bad you don't have anything bigger. Didn't he say a longer blade would fetch more? Maybe you could try dagger length next."

Speaking so easily about Sliding and his forging felt freeing to him. Jessa hadn't been surprised or alarmed by his abilities, only curious. Her simple acceptance meant so much to him that he decided to trust her with everything.

"Here," he started, and hurried over to where he had hidden the blade he forged last night and looked behind the bellows. He would show Jessa what he made, and together they would work to find a way to sell it so that they could help Brusus.

Only the blade was gone.

In spite of his fatigue, his mind was suddenly alert and a cold sweat burst over his flesh. He had been careful to hide the sword, not wanting anyone else to find it before he was ready to reveal his newest creation. Partly, he hadn't been convinced that he even wanted to sell the blade.

"Was anyone else here before you?" he asked.

"I don't think so. After hearing about Brusus, I came after dark to look for you. When you weren't here but the lanterns were lit, I waited for you to return. Why? Is something wrong?"

"Was the door locked?"

"I had to sneak my way past it, if that's what you're asking," Jessa said defensively.

The blade had been here when he left with Brusus. Rsiran wished he would have checked to see if it was still there before Sliding to the mine but had not. He had been so focused on what he had to do, on what had happened to Brusus.

With another surge of panic, Rsiran checked the other side of the forge. The large lump of lorcith was still hidden among the debris. He turned back to Jessa. "It's missing."

Jessa stood and came over to him. "What's missing? Something you need to get the forge working?"

He swallowed and shook his head. Had he been wrong to trust Brusus? Had he been wrong about Jessa?

"I Slid to Ilphaesn last night."

Jessa visibly tensed.

"I decided to see if I could manage what I promised Brusus and mine the lorcith in the dark. I returned with a large lump, nearly as big as I'd ever seen. And then I decided to try and forge it."

"What did you make?"

"A sword."

She caught her breath. Most knew the penalties for possessing a sword. Only the constables were allowed anything longer than forearm length. The steel blade Brusus carried would get him hauled before the council. A lorcith blade?

"Was that a good idea?"

233

Rsiran shook his head. At the time, he hadn't really had much to say about what he created. The lorcith guided his forging. That was one secret he didn't share with Jessa. "Brusus thought a longer blade would be more valuable. I wanted to help, so I…"

He kicked along the ground where the blade had been. The lower beam of the bellows had been pushed away from the wall, leaving enough space for the blade to hide, but now that space hid nothing but dust.

"There are other ways of helping that don't put you in danger," Jessa said.

"Like sneaking into warehouses?"

She stared at him. "I could only get in trouble if I get caught. And I'm an excellent sneak."

"Who else knows about this place?" Other than Jessa and Brusus, he could only think of Shael. "Would Shael break in to take it?"

Jessa shook her head. "Shael has an agreement with Brusus. He might be a thief, but he's an honorable one. He would never take from Brusus."

"What if Brusus hadn't paid him?"

Jessa breathed out slowly. "Then he might come looking for something of value," she said. "We all have different debts, Rsiran." She took a step back, widening her stance defensively. "Don't look at me like that. Even I have debts. You live in Lower Town long enough, and you acquire debt, but you also earn favors. That's how life works. Almost better than real currency most of the time."

"Anyone else who might know of this place?"

She shook her head. "Firell and Haern know of it, but neither knows where it is. And Firell has been out with his ship since we last saw him. Haern… well Haern has a funny way of looking at things, but I couldn't see him trying to break into the smithy. He and Brusus have known each other too long for that."

"He hasn't known *me* that long."

Jessa frowned at him. "You have to trust some of us, Rsiran. Otherwise you're going to live your life jumping around, looking for harm that isn't there."

He sighed. Part of him wanted to see it complete, wanted to see the hilt attached and see what the sword looked like when whole. But he knew what a sword like that meant if he were caught.

Rsiran looked at the burlap bag containing the lorcith. "I have to start again. Brusus needs me."

"But not tonight."

Rsiran looked at the sack of unforged lorcith. How long would it take him to work through all of it? Working at a pace like last night, letting the lorcith guide him, he doubted it would be much more than a week. And then what? Return to the mine? Find the boy and take what he collected again? How long would he keep forging the blades for Brusus?

He wanted to help, but maybe there was another way. Stepping around the forge, he rested a hand on the smooth cold anvil and closed his eyes. But all he knew was hammering metal, and Brusus had seemed so *eager* when suggesting they could sell his knives. Considering what Brusus had done, could he back out now?

"Leave it for tonight." Jessa took his hand in hers and lead him away from the forge. "You look tired. Besides, we need to check on Brusus."

Rsiran sighed. He was tired but didn't think visiting Brusus would change that. It would only lead to more questions.

CHAPTER 27

THEY LEFT THE SMITHY after Rsiran had hidden the lumps of lorcith, mixing them into the bin of coals. Though the other lump of lorcith had not been disturbed, he didn't want to risk losing the rest, not until he knew what had happened to the blade. He held out hope there was an innocent answer.

Jessa led him out into the street. He locked the door carefully behind him and pocketed the key. She smiled at him and shook her head. Clearly, keys weren't necessary for everyone. She started off with a confident stride, moving quickly along the dark street.

The night was dark, clouds hung over the moon, and no stars shone overhead. It was almost as if they were hidden from the Great Watcher himself. The street running in front of the smith smelled foul, the mixture of sewage and rot filling his nose forcing him to breathe through his mouth. Even then, he could still taste it. He was thankful that Jessa hurried.

She never let go of his hand as she led him down the street. When they reached the end and lanterns suddenly lit their way, Rsiran smiled as Jessa still didn't release her grip. Her fingers felt small and warm inside his, but there was strength in the way she held him.

"I could probably Slide us there," he suggested after they had been walking for a while.

She pulled him onto a side street, one he was unfamiliar with, and she slipped quickly along, light from the lanterns of the main thoroughfare fading behind them. "And miss the night?" she asked. "Besides, I have something I want to do along the way."

Rsiran realized they were moving down toward the water, sinking deeper into Lower Town. The path Jessa took was unfamiliar, but he recognized the sound of the waves growing louder, he recognized the salt spray that mixed in the air, and he could feel the ground sloping beneath his boots.

They passed small buildings tucked against each other. Few were painted; most simply left the beige stone alone, their slightly pitched roofs likely looking the same. The effect was to blend from a distance, to make the city disappear into the cliff face, so Elaeavn could disappear when seen from afar. Only, Rsiran knew, the effect didn't work when viewed from above. How many of those ancient planners had mined Ilphaesn? How many had stood atop Krali Rock?

"Where are we going?"

Jessa raised a finger to her lips as they stepped around the next corner. Rsiran suddenly recognized where they were and the long squat buildings stretching out alongside the street. He had been along a street exactly like this only hours before, had watched Brusus nearly die on a similar one. And now Jessa brought him back?

She stopped along one of the long low buildings. Was this the same warehouse or different than the one he had visited earlier? The door was different—taller, made of faded wood—either elm or sjihn harvested from the Aisl long ago, and he did not need to duck under the sloping roof overhead.

Jessa stepped up to the door and unrolled a pack, looking like Brusus had done earlier. Choosing a slender rod, she worked it in the lock. In much less time than it had taken Brusus, the lock clicked and she pushed the door open.

Then she disappeared into the darkness.

Rsiran glanced up the street. Had he heard the sound of boots along the cobbles or was it simply his imagination? They should not be here. Not after what happened earlier. He didn't have the strength needed to get them both away if another sellsword found them.

The wind gusted, blowing between the buildings as if trying to sweep him away.

He shivered, stepped through the door, and pulled it closed.

Jessa grabbed his arm and tugged him forward. He dragged his feet along the ground as quietly as possible, trying to remain silent but afraid of taking a misstep and falling. If he had Jessa's Sight, he would move as confidently as she did. As in the mines, his ability felt useless.

"Why are we here?"

He felt Jessa turn but couldn't see her. With the door closed, the warehouse was nearly as dark as the mines had been. Worse—at least he knew the mines, could find his way by feel. And there was always the strange sensation of the lorcith that guided him.

"For Brusus." They took another few steps and then Jessa pulled on his arm, guiding him to the left. "You really are like a babe in the dark, aren't you?"

Had he been able to see her, he might have jerked away. "At least I don't need to pick locks to get inside."

She snorted a soft laugh. "You saw how much that slowed me." She dragged him a few more steps and then pulled him to the right.

"Besides, you're too tired. Otherwise I might have tried letting you use that ability of yours with me." She pressed against him. "I admit I'm curious what it feels like to Slide."

"Not much different from walking. You take a step and you go from one place to the next. Only thing you notice is the sound of wind rushing through your ears." The first time he Slid a long distance, the sensation of the blast of wind and noise had surprised him. Now he rarely noticed it.

"I'd still like to try it."

Rsiran felt her push against him again and smiled. He wondered what she would think of Sliding to the top of Krali Rock or to the heart of the Aisl Forest. Would she be scared as he had been the first time? Considering Jessa, he doubted it.

He squeezed her hand. "What can we do for Brusus here?"

She pulled away from him. As he followed her, he was forced to push between two rough wooden crates pressing on both sides. Then he understood where she took him; what she intended.

"We don't know how long until he wakes. I don't know how long the Elvraeth that hired him gave for the job, but Brusus seemed more irritable than usual lately, so I suspect that he was expected to finish it soon. Might be why he wanted you to get working on the knives," she said, glancing back at him. She stopped and patted one of the crates. "This crate must have something to do with what the Elvraeth asked of him."

Rsiran could see nothing in the darkness. "This is the crate with the strange cylinders?"

"It is."

She let go of his hand and shuffled around in the darkness. Of course, to her there was no darkness. There was a soft *click*, and he realized she had picked the lock of one of the boxes.

"What do you think they do?"

"I don't know. Maybe try to assemble this. See what was sent to the Elvraeth."

"You will not find assembly easy."

Rsiran jumped at the strange voice. Had he known where Jessa was standing, he would have grabbed her hand and tried to Slide. She kicked something as she stood, but he could not feel where she was. Without her, he stood frozen in place. Fear coursed through him.

His imagination provided more details than he wanted. In his mind, a slender sword sliced through the air before it plunged into his chest. He saw Jessa, bleeding, with him unable to do anything, weakness stealing his ability to Slide.

His heart hammered.

"Josun?" Jessa said.

"Brusus's girl," the other said. "And quite strongly Sighted. Even here you see well. And your friend?"

"Can see nothing," Jessa said.

From the sound of her voice, Rsiran knew roughly where she stood. He considered jumping for her, grabbing her hand, and Sliding. The fear that raced through him would give enough strength to make the Slide. The only thing that held him back was the casual way Jessa spoke, as if she recognized this man.

"Can't have that now." A pale blue light flickered on. It glowed steadily, nothing like the flickering oil lamps, and reminded Rsiran of the orange lantern from the sleeping quarters in Ilphaesn.

A tall man, eyes a deep green and hair the deep silvery color of lorcith, stood before him. He wore a long, heavily embroidered cloak over a blue shirt that seemed woven of a fabric Rsiran had never seen. Deeply tanned leather boots reflected some of the blue lantern light. A slender blade hung at his side. With a jolt,

Rsiran realized he could *feel* something from the sword and knew it was lorcith made.

He was looking at one of the Elvraeth.

Rsiran had only caught glimpses of the Elvraeth before. The rare times his father had been commissioned to do work for them, it had always been ordered and arranged through their servants, never by the Elvraeth themselves.

This must be who had hired Brusus.

"Done staring, young man?" the Elvraeth asked.

"My Lord," Rsiran answered.

With a flash of teeth, the Elvraeth smiled. "Not lord. None of us are lords, young man. Your friend here, at least, has the right of it." He glanced at Jessa. "I am Josun T'so Elvraeth. Here, in this place," he said, sweeping his hands around the shadowed warehouse, "I am Josun."

He waited, watching Rsiran for a few moments. The smile on his face didn't change. Rsiran had the distinct sense of something crawling in his mind, like spiders along his skin, as the Elvraeth tried to Read him. With a sudden effort, he pressed the barriers in his mind more firmly into place. Around Brusus and the others, he had been careful to leave them up, never knowing who was a Reader. With the Elvraeth, he wasn't sure he was strong enough to avoid being Read.

"Here is where you tell me your name."

Rsiran let out a soft breath. "Rsiran Lareth," he answered slowly.

Josun tipped his head. The sense of crawling along Rsiran's mind intensified for a moment before fading. Were the Elvraeth truly more gifted Readers? Could he climb over the barriers he built in his mind? And if he had, would he know that Rsiran could Slide? Would he care?

"There is a Lareth who is a smith," the Elvraeth commented.

Rsiran nodded, wondering how he would know. "He is my father."

"Are you not apprenticed to him? Such is the custom, is it not?"

Rsiran knew he would not be able to fool the Elvraeth. "Once," he admitted.

"But no longer."

He shook his head. "We had a disagreement about the direction of my training."

The Elvraeth's smile widened. "Must have been quite the disagreement. From what I understand, apprenticeships within the smith guild are quite difficult to acquire. While it is a shame you gave yours up, I am sure Brusus has found you useful."

"Why is that?" Rsiran struggled to keep up with the speed of this man's thoughts.

"There are many uses for smiths, young Rsiran. Especially one with master smith bloodlines."

The comment hardened the blood in his veins like steel tempered by water. Did the Elvraeth know he could hear lorcith? His gaze pulled toward the slender blade Josun wore, feeling the strange sensation of being aware of where it was, almost as if he were back in the mines and the lorcith guiding his steps.

With his ability to Read, how much did the Elvraeth already know about him?

"Why are you here, Josun?" Jessa asked.

Rsiran was thankful for the change in topic and had wondered the same thing. Brusus had not hidden the fact that one of the Elvraeth had hired him, but why would he be here tonight? Why at the same time they were?

The Elvraeth turned to Jessa. Deep green eyes flared. "I could ask the same of you." His tone hardened and the smile on his face faded.

Rsiran found his heart racing again, fear slicking his palms.

"You hired Brusus," Jessa answered with a shrug. "We're here for him."

The Elvraeth took a slight step forward. The pale blue light seemed to blink. Even his movement seemed graceful, as if he simply flickered forward from one place to the next. "I hired Brusus."

"If you don't want the job completed, we'll leave," Jessa suggested.

The Elvraeth sniffed and a wolfish smile returned. "I did not say you could leave."

Rsiran looked over at Jessa. For the first time since he had met her, a worried look spread across her face. She tried to hide it, but her eyes tightened and the muscles under her cheek tensed.

The Elvraeth saw the same things as Rsiran. "You can relax, young sneak. I will not be reporting to the constables, or I would have to explain my presence here as well." He shook his head. "No… I think you can both be as useful as Brusus."

Rsiran realized Jessa had been taking small steps toward him, and he made an effort to move closer toward her as well. His mouth was dry, and he stank of sweat. The initial surge of fear he had felt at seeing the Elvraeth had faded, and now fatigue threatened to knock him down again. He didn't know if he would be able to Slide them from the warehouse if needed. But for Jessa, he would try.

"How?" she asked. "We don't even know what you hired Brusus for."

The Elvraeth's smile widened. "I only asked Brusus to perform a simple demonstration."

Jessa's eyes narrowed.

"Yes—a demonstration. The rest of this," he said, nodding toward the warehouse, "was my demonstration to him. What he chose to do with that knowledge is up to him and had very little to do with what you see around you."

"None of this matters to you?" Rsiran's tongue was finally unstuck with surprise.

The Elvraeth turned and looked at him. "Matters? Of course it matters. Did Brusus not tell you *why* I requested the demonstration? Why I have grown tired of the waste I see every day within the palace? Can you not see it for yourself?"

"I know what Brusus told me," Rsiran said cautiously, careful to not reveal too much to the Elvraeth.

Josun only laughed. It was a bitter sound. "What did Brusus tell you? Did he tell you that that for centuries, my family has received gifts? That for centuries, these gifts lay unclaimed? No one has ever bothered to even open most of these crates. For some reason, doing so violates the order of the council."

Rsiran nodded, suddenly fearing the heat in the Elvraeth's words. "He showed me one of the crates he opened."

The Elvraeth took a step toward the crate. There was something odd about the way he moved that Rsiran could not quite place. He tipped the lantern toward the box Jessa had opened and picked up one of the strange metal cylinders.

"Ah… this." He tilted the cylinder. "From a nation that no longer even exists." His eyes scanned the faded harsh lettering. "A gift that none ever understood, let alone bothered to try and assemble, the letter that accompanied long since destroyed. There is much that can be learned from other cultures, but the *council* disagrees." He spat the last few words. One of his hands ran along the strangely layered wood as he spoke. "And you think Brusus intends to assemble what lies within this crate." His mouth turned in a tight smile. "Such was possible once. Now… now this is no more than a curiosity left to lie dormant and die like the people who made it."

The Elvraeth stepped away from the crate and pointed toward the nearest stack. His long brown cloak hung limp, barely moving as he stepped. Somehow, Rsiran *felt* the movement by the pull from the sword.

"Now consider the same curiosities in each of these. Multiply that by *thousands*. Then you may begin to understand what is wasted here."

Rsiran swallowed. The enormity of what surrounded him felt overwhelming. "But you didn't want Brusus to open any of these crates?"

The Elvraeth shook his head. "I knew he would, else I would not have shown them to him. I needed him to see what was here, needed him to *want*."

He turned toward Rsiran and met his eyes. Standing arrogantly as he did in the midst of the warehouse, Rsiran could look nowhere else. He had the vague feeling of danger, like he had felt in the darkness within the mines of Ilphaesn.

"What is it that you need done, Josun?" Jessa asked.

Rsiran finally noticed the casual way she had been ignoring his title.

"Nothing that I *need* done, only what I have asked of Brusus. And since you seem so interested in helping him, I will accept your offer. Perhaps with your help, I will not have to wait quite as long for results."

He spoke the last with a knowing tilt to his lips. Did the Elvraeth know what had happened to Brusus earlier? Did he know of the attack or of the way Rsiran had Slid them to safety? Was he Reading him now, learning every secret he tried to hide? He didn't feel any pressure on the barriers in his mind, but that didn't mean that one of the Elvraeth couldn't simply step around them.

Maybe, he realized, he had learned of the attack a different way. Didn't Jessa say the Elvraeth hired the sellswords? Surely such an attack would have been reported, especially one with an unusual outcome.

"What's the demonstration?" Jessa asked. "I was with Brusus when he met you here the first time. You never told him what you wanted done."

The Elvraeth tilted his head as he studied her. "Is that what he said? Perhaps it is because with Brusus, I have learned I do not have to be explicit."

"I am not Brusus."

He snorted a small laugh. "Too true." His eyes narrowed. "Then I will humor you. What I need done is a demonstration for my family."

Rsiran stiffened. Meeting one of the Elvraeth was intimidating enough. How would he react to meeting more of them?

The Elvraeth looked at Jessa with an intense stare. "I would like the family to see what others see when they look up at the palace. I would like them to feel what others feel when standing before the council. That is the demonstration that I request."

Jessa shook her head. "I don't understand."

"Don't you?" the Elvraeth asked. "You see all of this waste around you?" She nodded. "You live in Lower Town where children sleep along the streets or work the docks to help their parents, and do not see the problem with what you see around you?"

"I see it," Jessa said. She barely moved. Something the Elvraeth had said triggered an emotion within her. "I still do not know what you would like us to do."

A dark smile spread across the Elvraeth's face. "For once—and only for a moment—I would like my family to know what it is like to feel weak, to feel what much of Elaeavn feels every day, to understand limitations."

"How?" Rsiran asked.

He hesitated saying anything, but a tingle of fear began growing in his belly. What Josun wanted would draw the attention of the rest of the Elvraeth family—would draw the attention of the council. They risked true punishment; more than simply getting sent to the mines, Rsiran recognized the real risk of banishment or worse.

But if they didn't, what would Josun Elvraeth do to Brusus? Would he use the knowledge of him entering the warehouse to have *him* banished? After everything Brusus had done to help him, Rsiran couldn't run that risk.

The Elvraeth tipped his head toward Rsiran. "Does your asking mean that you accept the challenge, young Lareth?"

There was a sense of finality to the question. Rsiran glanced at Jessa, uncertain what to say. She nodded to him. The Elvraeth watched only Rsiran.

Rsiran's mind went to Brusus lying on the bed at Della's house. He could have prevented the injury altogether had he dared act, had he only dared reveal his ability. Now, Brusus did not awaken, and Della did not know how long it would be until he did come out of the stupor. If not him now, then would it fall on Jessa? Could Rsiran let her risk herself for whatever the Elvraeth had in mind? "What if I don't? If I can't?"

The Elvraeth's face twisted into a sad expression that did not quite reach his deep green eyes. He turned, his hand resting atop the lorcith sword. In that moment, Rsiran knew the blade as his, stolen from the smithy and now set with a jeweled hilt. The sword seemed to draw him, as if pulling his attention.

How would the Elvraeth have gotten his sword?

How would he have even known of it?

"It would be unfortunate if the rest of the Elvraeth learn of Brusus's plans for you, young Lareth." He smiled but it didn't reach his eyes. "They feel *quite* differently about the ancient ore than your friend. And to think he broke into this warehouse in order to smuggle away Elvraeth property?" He shook his head, a look of mock surprise coming to his face. His mouth hardened and he leaned toward Rsiran. "So if you cannot do this job, then I pray to the Great Watcher that Brusus is up to the task."

Rsiran swallowed. Josun knew. He heard it in his tone and saw it in the way the Elvraeth looked at Rsiran. More than anything, it was probably the reason he had found them tonight. Worse, he possessed one of Rsiran's own forgings, shaped into a forbidden blade.

Now he had something on both Rsiran and Brusus.

And it was probably enough to get them exiled.

Rsiran could not take that risk. Already they had helped him much more than he helped them. It was time for him to repay that debt, whatever the risk.

"I will do what I must," he finally answered.

The Elvraeth smiled at him again.

Rsiran could not shake the fear rolling through him.

CHAPTER 28

THEY SAT AT A CORNER TABLE IN THE WRETCHED BARTH. A steaming mug of ale set in front of Rsiran went ignored. A few others sat at tables around them, but otherwise the tavern was hushed. They took the opportunity to talk quietly, the sounds of the bandolist playing near the back of the tavern drowning out their voices. The serving woman, Lianna, somehow seemed to know they wanted to be left alone, and after serving the ale, had given them a wide buffer.

Jessa sniffed the pale flower tucked into her shirt and looked up at him, eyes wrinkled with fear. Rsiran had never seen her scared. "I don't know how we are to do this. Breaking into the palace? *Poisoning* members of the council?" She shook her head, her eyes darting around as she spoke as if fearful who might be listening. "If Brusus was to do this, I don't know what he planned. Maybe you were right about a rebellion."

Rsiran didn't know. Worse, what the Elvraeth asked of them was nearly impossible. How had Brusus—even with his Elvraeth blood— expected to break into the palace?

"If we don't, then Brusus is in danger." He eyed the leather pouch sitting on the table. Neither wanted to touch it. Inside was a mystery powder. What the Elvraeth meant as a demonstration was little more than a poisoning. Had Brusus known—or suspected? Was that why he delayed what Josun asked of him? "What else could he want?"

"What all the Elvraeth want," Jessa said. "Power. Probably the council."

Rsiran stared at the pouch, unable to take his eyes off it. "What if this is about more than power? And why should we care if Josun sits on the council?"

"We're all in danger," she said. "All of us who helped him. Including you."

Rsiran nodded. Possibly him most of all. "I know."

The threat was clear. Perform the 'demonstration' or Brusus would be accused of selling lorcith-forged weapons. Selling weapons generally ran the risk of sentencing to the mines. Selling lorcith-forged weapons ran the risk of banishment.

"What he asks..."

"Requires me." Only someone able to Slide would be able to perform the demonstration. If he had any doubts that the Elvraeth knew what had happened in the alley next to the warehouse earlier, that alone erased it.

And doing this task would take him fully down the path his father promised his ability meant for him. For Brusus's sake, could he do anything else?

Jessa narrowed her eyes at him. "You will not do this yourself. You are barely more Sighted than a child! *All* of the Elvraeth are Sighted. You think they won't notice you carrying around a lantern as you stumble through the palace?"

What he intended was not ideal, but after living within the mines for as long as he had, no longer was he afraid of the dark. "I don't intend to stumble."

She snorted. "You're no sneak."

"And you cannot Slide."

Jessa shook her head. "What is the use of such an ability if you're seen, Rsiran? Even if you escape, they'll know your face. You will still face sentencing."

Rsiran suppressed a shiver. Not for the first time this evening, he wished Brusus were with them. He had such a sense of confidence, a sense of assurance, that he would know what to do. And maybe there was nothing that they should do. Perhaps if Brusus were with them he would warn them off?

"I won't be caught." He tried to sound more confident than he felt. If what the Elvraeth told them was true, he would have to Slide more times in one night than he had ever managed before. He ran the risk of over extending himself. He could imagine getting trapped in the palace, too weakened to Slide to safety…

Not only would he have failed, but Brusus—all of them—would be in danger.

Jessa scooted closer and set a hand on his arm. "Rsiran—I don't think we should do this. This… this is bigger than simply selling Elvraeth property. This is… damn, I don't even *know* what this is."

Rebellion, he didn't say. And if they did it, they had chosen a side—or had one chosen for them. "I don't think *we* should. *I* will do it."

She punched his shoulder. "Do you really think Josun will punish Brusus if we don't go through with it?"

"He knows about us," Rsiran said. "About *everything.*"

Jessa frowned. "What do you mean?"

Rsiran closed his eyes. He hadn't figured out how, but Josun knew. "He knows about Brusus. He knows how I saved him. And he knows of my sword. I can't simply do nothing."

"And doing what he wants will fix what he knows?"

Rsiran sighed and opened his eyes. "No. But it buys me time."

Jessa peered around the tavern, head tilted slightly forward so she could breathe in the fragrance of her flower. "I'll talk to Haern."

"Is that wise? Should we be including *more* people in this?"

"Brusus would include him."

"Are you sure? Brusus didn't seem to have included Haern in the warehouse."

Jessa looked offended by the suggestion. "They have known each other for as long as I've been in Elaeavn. I think he would trust Haern."

"Then talk to him. See what he thinks."

She reached for the pouch on the table, and Rsiran caught her hand. As Jessa looked up at him, her eyes flashed with a hint of anger before softening.

"Why don't I keep this safe? I'll hide it at the smithy, keep it buried in the coals."

She narrowed her eyes. "Safe? Like that sword you crafted?"

Rsiran felt his heart skip. The sword was part of the reason he was forced to do what Josun wanted. Had he only managed to do what his father asked—had he only managed to ignore the song of the lorcith— the Elvraeth might not have quite as much on him.

He still wanted to know how the blade had gone missing. How had the Elvraeth even learned of the sword in the first place?

"Where do you suggest?" he asked.

She sat for a moment, chewing her lip as she thought. Her head tilted down so that she could sniff the flower, and a few strands of her hair fell into her face. She ignored them, and Rsiran fought the urge to reach over and brush them away.

Finally, she sighed. "Perhaps they are safer at the smithy." She pulled her hand away from the pouch and placed it on his arm. "Promise me you will wait for me to do anything."

Rsiran considered his answer before nodding.

"Promise me, Rsiran!"

"I promise."

He hated that he already knew he would not keep the vow.

CHAPTER 29

RSIRAN STOOD OVER THE FORGE. The coals glowed hot, sending faint tendrils of smoke out into the smithy and up through the wide stone chimney. Sweat dripped on his brow, staining the grey shirt from the mines that he wore. The clothes Brusus had given him lay folded near the back of the smith for now. The air stank with the bitter smell of a mixture of his sweat, and the heated lorcith he gripped with the tongs borrowed from his father.

When the lorcith was ready, when it glowed a faint orange bright enough to see, indicating it was workable, he hurried to the anvil, set the heated lump atop the surface, and began hammering. As usual, he felt the lorcith drawing on him, pulling on his mind and guiding each strike. The shape emerged quickly.

Another knife.

In less than an hour, he had managed to shape the knife to his and the lorcith's satisfaction. As it cooled, he set it alongside the others. Already there were half a dozen, and he had only been working this one night. Anything to take his mind off what the Elvraeth asked of him.

He could not shake the question of how Josun knew of the sword. Rsiran had only forged it the night before, and in that time, he had learned of the blade and taken it. Now he used it as leverage against them. Had he Read him? But that would mean Josun had been around him before, but when?

Sighing, he picked up one of the knives and twisted it in his hand. The deep silver of the lorcith gleamed with a dull light, the metal seeming to slide as he twisted it. The effect was the result of how he had folded it during the forging, the lorcith itself guiding his hands. This time, he recognized what was happening, recognized the technique from when he had forged the missing sword blade. The recognition made the work go more quickly, almost as if the lorcith strove to teach him.

Already he had learned more from simply working with the lorcith than he had ever learned from his father.

The realization angered him. From his father, he learned what he could not do. An apprentice smith must not attempt forging without his master's permission. A smith cannot forge a weapon for killing unless directed by the Elvraeth. And worst of all, a smith must not listen to the guidance of the lorcith.

Only it was with this guidance that Rsiran truly came to understand what he was doing and what he was capable of creating.

Each of the knives was different. Some were folded like the sword, the metal having that strange quality where it appeared to slide across itself. Others looked more like traditionally forged lorcith, the deep silver a solid color without any signs of the bizarre shimmering. A few had an interesting embossing, as if the metal had wanted to leave the hammer imprint along the surface. Each was beautiful in its own way, and each carried his small mark near the base of the blade.

But he suspected that mark would be the real leverage Josun would use against him.

Rsiran shook his head and turned back to the knives. Had he a grinding stone, he would have sharpened them. As it was, they lay forged and formed, but not quite ready for use. Perhaps that was best.

The brown burlap sack containing the rest of the lorcith lay next to the bellows, the top bunched and pressed down so that the ore inside was easily accessible. He was tempted to grab another lump and get back to crafting, but the effort of his work throughout the night had already begun draining his energy. There was more he needed to do before the night was over.

Looking over to the table, he had dragged from the far side of the smith, its once stained surface now faded and chipped, he considered the small leather pouch sitting among the dust. Handprints marred either side of the table where he had gripped it, creating a ring around the pouch. Made of a supple leather and died a deep brown, the pouch was otherwise unremarkable. A single braided black drawstring pulled it closed.

Rsiran had almost refused when he realized the target of the demonstration. Not the entirety of the Elvraeth as he had indicated at first, but the council itself. Josun wanted the council to feel weakened. He wanted them poisoned.

There was only one reason Rsiran could think of—the rebellion he'd overheard. And Jessa thought Josun wanted to sit on the council himself. Why should Rsiran care about Elvraeth politics? What did he care who ruled on the council? Why did he care *which* of the Elvraeth ruled? What difference did it mean for him?

He had never expected to be pulled into the lives of the Elvraeth. Now that he was, he wanted nothing more than to be free of them. Even if he succeeded in what Josun asked, would he really be free?

No. And that was the problem.

But what could he do? How could he keep his new friends safe? Nothing but do what Josun asked.

He sighed. The leather pouch held a small quantity of poison. Nothing too toxic, he was promised, nothing fatal. Josun did not want any of his family injured, only weakened enough that they would realize what had happened. All Rsiran and Jessa needed to do was mix a small amount of powder into a pitcher and make sure it reached the Elvraeth council. Rsiran hadn't worked out how Josun would take a place on the council, but suspected that was another layer he had yet to discovered. Were Brusus well enough, he could ask him.

Rsiran suspected the task would be easy enough. He could Slide into the palace, deliver the powder, and Slide out. If he was fast enough, he would not even be seen. And that was what the Elvraeth planned. If he didn't act, Jessa would try to sneak her way into the palace. He needed to move before she ended up doing something foolish and got caught.

They would go together, Sliding into the palace, doing what Josun wanted done, and then Sliding back out. Only Rsiran wasn't certain he wanted Jessa involved at all.

Her Sight would help. In the palace, all of the Elvraeth would have some ability of Sight so he did not expect there to be much light. But the thought of her risking capture and banishment nauseated him.

As he stared at the pouch, he realized he was simply wasting time. If he was going to do something before Jessa tried on her own—and likely without him—he would have to do it soon.

Not tonight, though. Jessa had not yet returned, and he had spent too much time at the forge to have the energy needed to Slide into the palace.

But not to Della's place.

After changing back into the cleaner clothes, he pocketed a pair of the forged knives. Then he Slid to the healer's home.

Emerging from the Slide did not seem to take as much energy out of him as it usually did. The usual fire in her hearth had burned down. Incense and medicine hung heavy in the air, covering a faint sickly odor. Della lay asleep in the chair next to the fire, a thickly knitted blanket wrapped around her shoulders. He looked around and saw Brusus lying on the cot. His chest rose and fell slowly, and his eyes were closed.

"He has not woken again."

Rsiran turned and saw Della still staring at the fire. She had noticed his arrival, as if sensing him. "When will he?"

She shook her head. "Not sure yet. The blade was tipped in clohth powder. Rare here but common enough in Neelan. It took me a little while to determine what they used on the blade. Only when I knew what it was could I work to counteract it. Unfortunately, I might not have been fast enough."

"But you stopped the bleeding."

She turned her head to look up at him. Her face was drawn and tired. "But maybe not in time. Only the Great Watcher knows what will happen now. He has a strong body, and thankfully, you got him here quickly."

Rsiran closed his eyes, feeling the same sense of angst he had felt all day. "I could have Slid us both away from the warehouse before he attacked."

Della nodded. "Aye." She turned her tired eyes toward Brusus. "But you did what you could at the time. You are not a Seer, Rsiran. You could not have known the sellsword would attack." She shook her head. "We all have secrets. Brusus has his own that he keeps for his own reasons. His reasons are much the same as yours, you know." Her deep green eyes seemed to flare, and her brow furrowed. "Each of us must decide in time what we can and cannot do. Each of us must learn what it is that motivates us. Only then can we be free to do what we must. Only then can we be free from fear." She smiled sadly as if Reading his thoughts. "Yes, fear. Fear of who we are. Fear of what we might become. Fear of what others might think. Fear of acting."

Not for the first time, Rsiran wondered how much she knew. "I'm more afraid of *not* acting."

Della smiled. "That is a choice as well. When you know what you value, you will know what you must do. Do not do what you think others want from you. That is a path I know all too well. That is a path to sadness and disappointment."

Rsiran didn't say anything. Up until recently, he had always done what was expected of him. He had been the supportive brother to a sister more skilled than he, had worked diligently in the smithy learning how to care for the forge and the rest of the smithy, had fought against the only ability he possessed, had willingly gone to work in the mines of Ilphaesn, and nearly died. All because it was what others wanted from him. He no longer knew what it was that he wanted.

But, he decided, that wasn't entirely true.

He wanted to be accepted and cared about. Why was that too much to ask of his family? He hadn't gotten in so deep that he couldn't return to his home. If he returned, showed his father that he could be contrite, and promised to abandon and ignore the ability to Slide, he might have the chance at redemption.

And then he would always know what he had sacrificed.

Rsiran sighed. Not for the first time, he wished his family would simply have accepted him as he was, accepted that he was gifted with a different ability. Without his ability, he would have died within the mines. Brusus would have died on the street outside the warehouse.

"I need to help Brusus," he whispered.

Della looked up at him and frowned. "You have already helped him, Rsiran. Anything more puts you and your friends at risk."

"Doing nothing might put him in as much risk."

Della stood and hobbled over to him. Over the last few weeks, she had grown increasingly weak. How much of that was his fault? The effort of Sliding weakened him; the longer the Slide the more fatigued he felt. How could her strange healing be so different?

"I am sorry," he told her.

She laid a gnarled hand on his shoulder. There was still much strength in her grip. She smiled at him, and some of the age melted from her face. "Only apologize for your own mistakes."

"See that he gets these." He pulled the unsharpened knives from his pocket and set them onto one of the side tables.

Della picked up one of the knives and held it out, twisting it so it caught the remnants of firelight. Even from where Rsiran stood, the metal seemed to slide.

"They are beautifully made. I have not seen work like this in many years. Back before..." She trailed off and turned to him. "You must be careful in making these. There are those among the Elvraeth who fear such weapons. Especially like this."

"Why?"

"The Elvraeth are powerful but even their power has limits." She waggled the knife in the air. "There are blades that can limit even their power."

"I don't understand."

She shook her head. "Pray to the Great Watcher that you never have to." She nodded at the knives. "These are beautiful. And dangerous." Her eyes turned to Brusus. "Do you know who he planned to sell them to?"

Rsiran knew very little about Brusus's plans for the knives, only that he had a buyer willing to pay. "I don't know." Possibly Shael, but he didn't really know. "Will you get them to him when he awakens?"

She nodded. "I will. But Rsiran, you are free to visit him anytime. I have not closed my home to such things."

Rsiran didn't see how she could close her home to his Sliding. "There is something I must do, and I wanted him to see that I haven't been idle while he was sick."

Della laughed. "I doubt he would ever think that." She moved past him to Brusus. She hummed softly as she looked under a dressing on his chest. A sense of energy built in the air as she hummed, and the sound was soft but haunting and beautiful.

Rsiran sighed and then Slid away from her home.

He emerged in the alley next to the Wretched Barth. A pair of black cats peered at him in the darkness of the alley, and one yowled softly as he passed. Why had he Slid here?

At this time of night, the tavern would be mostly quiet. Any activity from earlier in the evening would have died out as the tavern goers went off to their homes or to rented beds. Rsiran stood on the street, the flickering lantern giving him enough light to see through the shadows of the overcast sky. He stared at the building where he was first introduced to Brusus and his friends. The sounds of the harbor were quiet with only the steady washing of waves against the shore. Something pulled on him, like the call of lorcith, but he did not know why.

"You seem distracted, Rsiran."

He turned. Haern watched him from the shadows of a nearby building. He wore a deep green shirt with simple embroidery—something much fancier than Rsiran usually saw him in—and simple brown leather pants. Grey hair hung loose around his head, and his eyes had a deep green hue.

"Haern? What are you doing here?"

Haern's mouth tightened. It was about as much of a smile as he had ever seen from him. "If I weren't a Seer, I might ask the same of you."

"You came to find me?"

Haern nodded and stepped away from the shadows. Light from the lantern reflected off well-polished boots. "I know what you are, Rsiran."

Rsiran blinked slowly. He would have to get used to others knowing about his ability. Already Della, Brusus, and Jessa knew. And now Haern. "Did Jessa tell you?" He couldn't fault her for sharing with Haern but wished she had spoken to him about it first. Of those he had diced with, he knew the least about Haern.

But Haern shook his head. "Didn't need to."

"Then how do you know?"

Haern's mouth twitched. "I've worn the grey myself. I can't say how many would recognize the dress, but as someone who has lived in those mines, worked the caverns of Ilphaesn, I can tell you I'll never forget." He stepped forward again. "Did you escape?"

Rsiran shook his head but caught himself. That wasn't entirely true. "When were you sentenced?"

Haern's face clouded, almost as if drawing in the shadows around him. "I was young. Foolish. And I made a claim that I should not have made." He shrugged. "It is so long ago that I don't really remember the details. I remember the clothes. I remember the bitter way the mine smelled. I remembered hating the dark." Haern shivered. "And when you came to the Barth wearing the greys, I recognized them. Why didn't you change into something else?"

Rsiran glanced down at his attire, different now that Brusus had given him nicer clothes to wear. But the greys from Ilphaesn did not bother him. And they suited him.

"I don't mind the greys." The color reminded Rsiran of the lorcith mined within Ilphaesn. Most wouldn't understand.

Haern cocked his head and looked at him strangely. "Most could not wait to change into something else after earning their release. Myself included. Most I know felt it was too much of a reminder of where they had come from—a place to which none wanted to return."

"I didn't think the mines were so bad. Just the miners."

Haern did smile then, the scar on his face twisting strangely. "Then why did you run?"

"I didn't run."

Haern looked at him and the expression on his face changed. If anything, it hardened. "What do you mean?"

Rsiran shook his head. The look on Haern's face should have warned him, but he was tired of hiding what he was. Too many already knew anyway. "You're the Seer."

The green of Haern's eyes flashed deeper, and his face went slack as he focused on Rsiran. Rsiran felt a soft sense in his mind, like a puff of air, and then it was gone. Haern's face never changed.

"Why are you here?" Rsiran asked.

"There was something that I Saw."

Rsiran was thankful that he didn't have to hear Haern tell him what he thought of Sliding.

"A viewing of something that might be. I knew you would be here, but not more than that."

"What did you see?"

Haern took a step toward him. "What happened to Brusus?"

Rsiran stiffened. "You don't know?"

Haern shook his head. "I haven't seen him for days."

"He was injured. Badly. He's at Della's home."

Haern stopped moving. He was only an arm's length away from Rsiran. "How was he injured?"

Rsiran hesitated. Haern was acting strangely, even for him. Usually he was quiet and reserved, something Rsiran expected once he learned that Haern was a Seer, but this was stranger still.

"A Neelish sellsword."

"Why would the sellsword attack Brusus?" Then he sucked in a quick breath of air. "He wasn't still foolish enough to take that job from Josun, was he?"

Rsiran's heart thumped in his chest. With each jolt, nervous energy pounded through him. He nodded. "We were outside the warehouse earlier today."

Haern took a step back and his eyes fell closed. "That fool!" His eyes opened, and the green Rsiran saw there was intense and deep. "I warned him against taking the job, even before he met with that man. Too much risk involved and very little reward for Brusus."

"What risk?"

Haern eyed him suspiciously. "You went into the warehouse?"

Rsiran nodded.

"You understand there is a reason the Elvraeth simply store those crates there?"

Rsiran shook his head. "Brusus said that—"

Haern cut him off. "There are items there we are not meant to see. Brusus will try to tell you otherwise—try to convince you the valuables have been neglected—but that is not for us to decide."

"I met Josun too." He didn't tell Haern what Josun demanded of him.

"Josun will say whatever he must to accomplish his goals. And they are *his* goals, no matter what he tells you. Few of the Elvraeth are to be trusted, but that one least of all."

The heat to his words startled Rsiran. "You know him?"

Haern nodded slowly. "As much as one can know one of the Elvraeth."

The way that he said it made Rsiran realize that Haern didn't know Brusus's secret. Other than him and Della, it seemed no one did.

"An earlier job. A trial, I suspect. I met him. Saw what I could of him, but there is darkness along every path with him, and only darkness. Where there is that much darkness, nothing green can grow. Even then, I warned Brusus, but he wouldn't listen. And now he has pulled you into it with him."

"And Jessa," Rsiran answered softly.

Haern closed his eyes. "Damn that foolish man!"

Haern started down the street, and then paused, motioning for Rsiran to follow. For a moment, he considered simply Sliding away, worried about Haern's strange behavior, but decided he needed to see what Haern would say.

"What does he want from you?" Haern asked as they walked down the street.

As the street widened, the wind gusted, pulling on Rsiran's clothing and tossing his hair into his eyes. He shoved it back as waves crashed against the shore loudly, forcing them to walk closer together to be heard. Haern smelled clean with a faint hint of perfume. One of his hands gripped his stomach through his shirt as they walked. Rsiran could not shake the familiar sensation of lorcith.

Rsiran worried about answering but decided to tell Haern what he knew. Brusus obviously trusted many of his secrets to Haern. And Jessa trusted him. More than anything, that swayed him. "Brusus was hired to perform some sort of demonstration."

"And now that he has been injured?"

Rsiran nodded. "The Elvraeth has asked that we complete the demonstration."

Haern stopped and placed a hand on Rsiran's arm. Rsiran felt the soft sensation like a breath of air in his mind again, and then it was gone.

"You know that you cannot do this thing."

"Why not? Jessa thought that between the two of us…"

"The two of you will be caught." Haern sighed. "I see Jessa, exiled. Forgotten. You… you are less clear. You have always been difficult for me to See, Rsiran." He shook his head. "Do not do this thing. Keep Jessa safe. She will not do well if exiled."

Rsiran did not know how to answer. The Elvraeth had made it clear that the demonstration must be done. With Brusus now injured, it fell on him and Jessa. And if Haern Saw true, Jessa could not be allowed to be a part of it or she would be caught. Exiled and Forgotten.

He would not let that happen to her.

They walked a little farther along the street, and the waves grew louder. As they reached the harbor road, the air felt damp, moist from the salt spray coming from the sea. No one else was out at this time of night, and no one moved along the road. The only movement was the water and the ships moored out in the harbor sliding on dark waves like shifting shadows. Even the gulls were quiet.

As they neared the rocky shores of the bay, Rsiran felt Haern's hand on his arm again and stiffened.

"I See that my words will not change your mind."

"You have told me that if we do this thing for Brusus, if we perform this demonstration for the Elvraeth Josun," he went on, careful not to mention what the demonstration was, "that we will be caught."

Haern fixed him with hard, unblinking eyes. "Jessa will be caught. I See her future only too well." He shook his head once. "As I said, I cannot See you clearly." He looked at Rsiran with an accusation on his face.

"Don't worry about Jessa. I will make sure she doesn't get involved. And I have no intention of getting caught."

Haern shook his head. "Unfortunately, I'm unwilling to simply take your word. I wasn't certain what to make of you at first. Usually, my ability helps with that. Rare that I find someone that I cannot See." Haern sighed. "I'm sorry it has come to this."

His other hand shifted, and Rsiran saw a faint silvery glimmer and suddenly understood the pulling he had been feeling. Haern had a lorcith-forged knife.

The pulling on him was familiar, and now that he saw it, he understood why. It was one of his.

"I'm uncomfortable with my vision failing me. If I can't See you, I can't account for you—"

"What are you doing, Haern?" Rsiran jerked his arm, trying to tear it away.

Haern held him in a tight grip, squeezing his arm painfully. He pulled the knife up and slashed it toward Rsiran. Rsiran tried again to pry his arm away, but Haern held him.

He *felt* the movement of the lorcith knife, *felt* it slashing toward him.

There was nothing left to do. Rsiran attempted to Slide.

But failed. He had never failed.

The look on Haern's face explained all that he needed. Somehow Haern held him in place.

The knife arced toward him.

Rsiran tried to Slide again, even to step away. But the way Haern held him kept him from stepping into the Slide.

If he didn't do something now, Haern would kill him.

In his panic, the pulling of the lorcith thrummed deeply inside him. All he wanted was to push it away.

And suddenly, the knife flew out of Haern's hand, spinning wildly into the sky before splashing into the water.

Haern's eyes widened. In that moment, Rsiran wrenched free.

He took a step and Slid.

Before he disappeared, he swore he saw a satisfied look on Haern's face.

CHAPTER 30

RSIRAN EMERGED IN THE SMITHY. The lanterns flickered, and steady wind gusted through the hole in the ceiling. The scents of lorcith and hot coals were still heavy on the air.

His heart hammered. Haern had attacked him.

Could he have been wrong to trust Brusus and his friends? Never before had he any reason to doubt them. Haern had always seemed friendly and willing to help, even lending him coin so that he could dice with them.

Why then had he attacked him?

Rsiran knew the answer but didn't understand. For some reason, Haern couldn't See him, and this made him nervous. And what he could See made him fear for Jessa.

If they performed the demonstration—the poisoning—for Josun, she would be captured and exiled. Forgotten. Haern could not See what would happen to him, but Rsiran harbored no illusions he would escape the same fate.

Regardless of Haern's reasoning, he was a Seer. The visions from Seers were always reliable and should be trusted. And in this case, feared. For that reason, Rsiran could almost understand why Haern had attacked. Wouldn't he do the same thing to protect Jessa if he could? Perhaps Haern had Seen it as the only way to prevent her involvement.

That still did not explain why he had tried to kill him.

Rsiran's mind raced, and he found that he was working near the forge, layering coals, as a way to calm his thoughts. Since meeting Brusus, he had always felt safe, always felt welcomed, and now that seemed to have been taken from him.

Suddenly he felt as if he had nowhere to go.

He set one of the smaller lumps of lorcith atop the coals and it quickly glowed a soft orange. The heat increased the bitter scent of the ore, and he breathed it in. He felt jittery, as if his entire body quivered with anxiety, and wished very much that Brusus were awake.

For a moment, he considered Sliding to speak to Della again. Her advice always seemed to make sense, but he remembered how tired she appeared. The strain of healing had worn her down, aged her dramatically in only a few weeks. He would not add to that.

Jessa would not be any help. She would chafe at the idea something might happen to her. Possibly she wouldn't even believe that Haern had attacked him.

And he feared doing nothing. Doing nothing put everyone who had helped him at risk.

Before he realized what he was doing, Rsiran managed to forge three more small blades.

Each was identical and different from any he had made before. Soft curves along the blade seemed almost to melt into the handle. They were weighted nicely and balanced finely on his palm. The metal of each was heavily folded so it created the appearance of movement, as if oozing across the blade. Near the bottom of the blade, barely visible through the deep silver sheen, was his mark. Rsiran would not give these to Brusus to sell.

He felt an overwhelming and unexplainable urge to sharpen them, as if the blades demanded that last bit of finishing before they would be satisfied and let him go.

As he was too anxious and alert to sleep, he decided to comply with their demand. Such a simple request and one he knew he could quickly accomplish, if only he had sharpening stones. And he knew where he could find some.

He Slid to his father's shop.

Emerging left him only slightly weakened. Either he grew accustomed to the energy drain from Sliding or he grew stronger with his ability.

Even darkened, the shop was as he remembered. The air smelled of steel and iron and copper. Very little scent of lorcith hung in the air. That which did seemed faded and aged, as if his father had not worked with the metal in weeks. Moonlight filtered through the dusty window. The forge was cold and dirtier than he had ever seen it, coals from the day left to sit atop it. A hammer was left leaning against the anvil. Even along the wall, tools simply rested where they should have been hung. Water in the quenching bath smelled stagnant and stained from several days of use. The bins where his father usually stored the rods of iron or steel were nearly empty.

Something had changed.

Once, Rsiran would have cared. Now, he struggled to find the necessary emotion for a man who felt he needed to punish his child for having an ability he didn't understand.

The grinding wheel should be atop one of the long benches near the back of the shop, but a collection of paper and discarded work cluttered around it. Rsiran shuffled several pieces out of the way, each in various stages of completion. Some were bowls, others simple dinnerware, a few looked to be oblong rods that reminded him of the strange metallic cylinders within the warehouse. None were made of lorcith. It was as if his father had simply abandoned the metal.

When he reached the wheel, it was damaged. One of the partially completed projects had been simply tossed on top of it, cracking the wheel. Rsiran couldn't help but feel a little curious. Such casual disregard for his tools was unlike his father.

The knives in his pocket pulled on him, as if begging to be sharpened. He would need to find an alternative to the wheel. Along the wall, only slightly buried by the projects on the bench, were a pair of sanding stones. Rsiran grabbed them. They would work better than nothing.

"You look well."

Rsiran turned slowly, his heart suddenly hammering loudly. By now, he should be accustomed to people creeping up on him as he snuck around in the dark, but he still startled. The reassurance that he could simply Slide away eased his fear somewhat.

His father leaned against the door to his private office in the back. Rsiran had not heard him open it, but had probably missed it while moving around discarded projects. A trace of short whiskers dotted his normally clean-shaven face. Lines pulled along the corners of his eyes, as if he hadn't been sleeping. His clothes were wrinkled and stained. Even where Rsiran stood, he smelled the stink of ale on his breath.

"Father."

"Come to steal from me again?" He heaved himself away from the wall with a grunt.

Rsiran tensed. Always he had intended to return the borrowed tongs and the hammer. Once he had forgotten, it had simply been easier to keep using them. "I borrowed from you. I intended to return what I borrowed before now."

A sneer spread across his father's face. "Borrow, you say? Can you simply borrow lump metal and think to return it?"

Rsiran shook his head. "I did not..."

"You think to lie to me now, Rsiran? After I know what you have become? What I told you that *ability* would turn you into?"

Seeing the anger in his father's eyes, Rsiran prepared to Slide. He would not risk getting trapped again. He was lucky to have escaped from Haern as it was and still did not fully understand what had happened.

"You think my ability has turned me into a thief? It was my ability that saved my life when I was nearly killed in the mines. Where you sent me!"

His father's eyes narrowed. "I assigned you to learn. As an apprentice. You needed to learn to master the call of the lorcith. As I had to learn. You know so little, but think yourself worldly. And now... now you will never learn what you need."

"You sentenced me like a criminal!" Rsiran practically shouted the last. "A criminal who had done nothing more than discover that I finally possessed an ability of my own. Finally, I had my own gift from the Great Watcher. Only you saw it as a reason for shame." It felt freeing to finally tell his father how he felt. "You *made* me feel it is a reason for shame."

"It *is* a dark ability!" his father roared. "Look what it has made of you! A thief, sneaking here in the night, stealing from your family!"

"Family? Does family punish each other like you punished me? Shouldn't family care if someone nearly dies?" He took a deep breath to calm himself. "I have found a different family. One that accepts who I am. One that cares what happens to me."

His father took a step toward him, and Rsiran pulled one of the unsharpened knives from his pocket. He held it in front of him. As with Haern, he was aware of the lorcith. It seemed to hum in his hand, pulling on him.

"Don't," he whispered.

His father stopped and shook his head. "You make my point rather well." He tipped his head toward the bins of metal. "Take what you want and go. Return to your new *family*. You will see there is not much more lorcith for you to steal."

Rsiran shook his head. "I didn't come for lorcith."

"Taken enough, then?" his father accused. Rsiran still held out the knife and his father hadn't moved.

Rsiran struggled with what his father was saying. He thought Rsiran stole lorcith from him, which meant that *someone* was stealing from him. "Why would I need to steal lorcith from you, Father? I have access to much more than the small nuggets you purchase. You made certain of that."

Rsiran felt a small sense of satisfaction in the way his father's eyes widened, if only slightly.

"Then why have you come?"

The sanding stones weighed heavily in his pocket, pulling at him with a renewed sense of guilt. "I… I wanted to see the shop." With everything that had been happening to him, even a small amount of familiarity was welcome. Only, the shop had changed much since he last stopped.

His father snorted. "This? Kept it up well, haven't I?"

"What happened?" Part of him knew the answer already. Smelled the answer as it wafted off his father.

His father's face contorted. "Do not pretend you care about what happens to your family. You made that clear when you ran from your

274

commitment, using that vile ability of yours to run away." He shook his head. "Now you're another Lower Town thief, sneaking into my shop in the middle of the night." He turned his back on Rsiran. "Go. Run back to your thieving friends."

He started toward his office, staggering slightly as he walked. As he reached the door, he paused. "I have been lenient in the past, not knowing for sure if it was you. Now that I know, I will report you to the constables."

Rsiran watched as he disappeared behind the door. He should feel angry, should be upset by his father's reaction, but he could not muster the necessary emotion. All he felt was empty.

Taking one last look around, he Slid back to the hidden smithy.

CHAPTER 31

R SIRAN STAYED AWAKE INTO MUCH OF THE NIGHT, slowly running the grinding stones along the knives, honing them to a
sharp edge. Only the knives that he had folded again and again until
the lorcith seemed to move even when cooled were honed. The others
didn't seem to need it; didn't demand they be sharpened like these did.
By the time he was done, he had finished nearly a half dozen knives,
pocketing a few. He slipped two into the waist of his pants.

Then Rsiran slept most of the day.

When he awoke, fading light filtered through the hole in the ceiling. A soft breeze gusted in, carrying the stench of sewage and rot in
the air. Noise from the streets drifted in as well, distant yelling heard
as a steady murmur, almost like a burbling stream. Occasionally, he
heard a louder yell, likely from somewhere along this street, that was
urgent or pained. He ignored it all as much as he could.

He rubbed the sleep from his eyes and sat up. The lanterns had
burned low, and the oil was nearly gone. Much longer, and he would

have awoken in darkness. After his time in the mines, he still did not enjoy the dark.

If they were to proceed as planned, Jessa would find him tonight. With Haern's warning, he did not dare risk her Sliding with him to the palace. He would have to do this himself.

Rsiran knew that should frighten him. If Josun didn't know Rsiran could Slide, then there was no way he could be successful. Even if he did succeed, there was no guarantee they would be left alone. Always, Josun would know about the lorcith-forged weapons, and always, Brusus would be left looking over his shoulder, fearing the constables might be after him. Always, Jessa would be at risk.

He sighed. Doing this thing for the Elvraeth did not guarantee safety for anyone, especially if this started—or continued—a rebellion.

But he had a different idea, one that might at least see his friends safe. All it required was for him to reach the council and turn himself—and Josun—in.

What other choice did he have if he wanted to keep Brusus safe? What other choice did he have to avoid Jessa's banishment? Rsiran might end up exiled—Forgotten—but couldn't he simply Slide back to Elaeavn?

He took the small leather pouch off the faded low table and pulled it open. Before he did anything, he wanted to see what was inside. A fine white powder filled the bottom, and he held it carefully, not knowing what would happen if he spilled it on his hand. It had a sickly sweet aroma. Something about it was familiar, but he could not place why. Smaller grained than sand, it looked more like flour. What was this powder that would poison the council? If it would make the Elvraeth sick, there was no telling what it would do to him. Possibly kill him.

He should have shown Della. Likely she would know what it was, but if she knew what he had in mind, she would *definitely* try to stop him.

On impulse, he slipped out one of the knives and dipped it into the powder. It clung to the lorcith, staining the blade a chalky white. The sickly aroma faded when mixed with the bitter scent of the lorcith, disappearing completely.

Rsiran wiped the blade on the ground. It only seemed to smear the powder along the metal. Hoping the substance wouldn't harm his skin, he tucked the blade back into his waistband.

After carefully drawing the strings tight, he tucked the pouch into his pocket, making sure to keep it from the knives. Of course, it would serve him right if he managed to make it into the palace only to have the powder spill out into his pocket.

A sudden knocking on the door startled him.

Rsiran turned toward the door and waited. If it was Jessa, he suspected she would simply pick the lock. Anyone else would knock again.

There was not another knock.

He listened for the sound of her working the pick into the lock but didn't hear anything. If he stood around too long, she would get into the smithy. And he didn't know if he could leave her then.

Rsiran heard a soft scraping behind him. Rather than looking, he Slid.

He emerged on the top of Krali Rock overlooking the city. The first time he had Slid here had been an accident. At that time, he had not even known that he could Slide. He had simply awoken atop the rock. He remembered well the fear that had gripped him that first time, not knowing what had happened, not sure how to get back down, only that he should not have been able to get to the top of the rock. The climb down had terrified him, but not as much as the look on his father's face after Rsiran told him what had happened.

From below, Krali looked like a tall finger of rock rising above the city. Standing atop Krali was different. The surface was flat and scuffed, and held scrapings from someone else having been here. Wind buffeted him, blowing his shirt and pants against his body and threatening to throw him off the rock. Almost as if he was not meant to be there.

From where he stood, the orange sun faded as it dipped toward the horizon, leaving the clouds on either side of it looking pink tinged. The water looked like a flat sheet of glass, the ships floating within the harbor little more than pieces set atop it. Below him, the city stretched out, none of the illusion visible from Krali Rock.

If he squinted, he could almost make out familiar buildings. The Wretched Barth smashed between other buildings. The warehouse, a long low rectangle, its slightly sloped roof slipping toward the other warehouses on either side. Della's home where Brusus lay unconscious, relying on whatever healing Della could muster to bring him back from near death. The street where Rsiran had first walked with Jessa, sniffing at the flower on her shirt as she talked. His old home, where Alyse would be getting ready for bed, already having forgotten about him. His father's shop, fading as it was into disrepair.

And then there was the palace.

Standing atop Krali and looking down at the palace provided a unique viewpoint. The five slender towers, each made of the same ivory stone as the rest of the city, created a sort of ring, leaving a grassy clearing in the middle. Brusus claimed that each tower housed a different Elvraeth family and each struggled with the others for more power within the family.

From here, the palace did not look like it floated at all. Rather, it seemed to flow out of the cliff, as if grown rather than chipped away. For the first time, he noticed a small squat building, different than any others within Elaeavn, in the middle of the clearing. Made of a darker rock, it almost looked to be entirely of lorcith, only Rsiran had never seen so much lorcith in one place.

He took a deep breath. The wind gusted and swirled around him, making him unsteady. He shifted his weight to maintain balance.

Standing where he was, looking down on a view that so few had ever seen, he felt almost like he had a purpose, as if the Great Watcher did have a reason for him after all.

Except the Great Watcher would not approve of what he was about to do. Already, he had done things that shamed him before the Great Watcher. Stealing lorcith from Ilphaesn? Forging weapons out of the metal? And now, worst of all, asked to attack his chosen few? Where Rsiran went now, he did in violation of the Great Watcher.

Yet he had been left with no real choice. If he did nothing, Brusus and the others would suffer. Rsiran could prevent that from happening.

The wind gusted again, and he took a small step back. Behind him, he felt something brush against his back and he turned.

And nearly fell from Krali Rock.

Jessa stood behind him. One hand balled into his shirt, her fist twisted into the fabric, and her knuckles white. She stared at him with wide green eyes. The lavender flower tucked into her shirt stood fast against the wind, almost as if holding her in place.

"How did you…" he asked.

"Grabbed your shirt. Saw you starting your Slide. You sort of flicker right before you do it. Not sure I would see it if I weren't Sighted. I realized that you were going to do the job without me so I grabbed on." She spoke quickly as she glanced down, and her body stiffened slightly. "Wasn't expecting this."

Rsiran took her hand from his shirt and twined his fingers into hers. He felt a mixture of emotions seeing her. Partly he was glad she was here. Doing what he intended would not be easy alone. But what Haern had told him stuck with him. If she went into the palace, she ran the risk of capture and banishment.

"You can't come with me."

She squeezed his hand painfully. "I can't stay here."

"I'll get you back to the smithy. But I must do the job myself."

Jessa pulled him toward her. There was barely enough room for the two of them to stand atop Krali Rock without falling. "Is that what Haern told you? Is that what he Saw?"

Rsiran nodded. "You cannot come."

"You aren't going by yourself, Rsiran. You may have this ability, but are you actually thinking of Sliding into the palace and doing this? For Josun? If what you think is true… if he wants to start some sort of—"

"Not for Josun," he said. "If you come, Haern saw that you would be captured."

"And you?"

"What?"

Jessa pulled on his hand. Rsiran teetered atop the stone, wind gusting against his face as if threatening to push him down.

"What of you?" she demanded. "What did Haern see of you?"

"Nothing."

She glared at him. "Nothing? Haern saw nothing of you? He saw me captured and exiled while you…"

"I think my Sliding makes his visions difficult."

"I think you're not telling me everything."

"Talk to Haern! Ask him what he saw! Ask him why he tried to kill me!" His voice rose to a yell. The sound carried off into the wind, disappearing toward the Aisl Forest where it faded.

Jessa looked at him. At first her head twitched slowly and then she shook it faster and faster. "Haern wouldn't do that."

"No? He brought me down to the harbor. Stood me among the rocks. Held me in place." Rsiran still didn't know how he had managed to do that. Always he had been able to Slide. "Tried to cut me with one of my own knives!"

Her face changed as he recounted what had happened. When he mentioned the harbor, her eyes had flickered wider for a moment.

"How did you escape?" The question was hard to hear over the sound of the wind.

"How did I…"

"Escape," she repeated. "How did you get away from Haern?"

"The knife fell out of his hand."

But that wasn't quite right. The knife had flown from his hand as if twisted away. Almost as if Rsiran's desire to push it away had made it happen.

Jessa frowned. "Fell from his hand? From Haern?"

He nodded. There was no way else to explain what had happened, was there?

"Rsiran, I know you haven't known us for long. You know Haern as a Seer only. And he is. Partly that is why Brusus always valued his opinions, trusting the visions he Sees. But Haern wasn't always who he is today."

"What was he?"

She blinked slowly and shook her head. "Something he's struggled to hide. To forget. But he can't change who he was, only who he is."

"Jessa?"

"Haern was an assassin. Raised out of Elaeavn, he worked in Asador and Cort and Thyr, taking jobs where he claimed his visions led him."

"Jobs?"

"He was an assassin," she repeated. "But he abandoned that years ago, returning to Elaeavn for the first time as an adult."

Rsiran hadn't heard of anyone *choosing* to live outside of Elaeavn. Doing so usually meant that they were one of the Forgotten. But if Haern returned, that meant he was not, unless he violated his exile. And the penalty of doing that meant certain death.

As he looked down on Elaeavn, the city seemed so much bigger than he had ever realized. Had he truly been so sheltered from everything living with his parents? Had his world ever really been so small? "Why?"

Jessa glanced away as she shook her head. "Brusus claims Haern Saw something once, a vision that prompted him to return. He hasn't taken a job like that since. He's changed now. Different from the man he once was." There was something else she didn't share, and she sounded so intent, as if trying to convince herself. "So, Rsiran, Haern would never do anything like that. There must have been a reason."

"There was a reason. He was protecting you the only way he Saw how."

"I can't believe that about Haern."

"Do you trust his visions?"

She nodded.

"Then trust what he saw about you. Know you can't come with me."

She pulled on his hand and motioned out toward the city, toward the palace. "A Seer's vision is not fixed, Rsiran. It can be changed. Like your future isn't fixed. Everything depends on the choices you make. The Great Watcher doesn't set a destiny for us." She turned him toward her. "Think of the choices you've made since we first met. How different would you be had you made only one different decision?"

One different decision? Had he not gone against his father the first time he might never have been sent to the mine. Had he chosen to stay in the mine rather than Slide away, he might have been dead, or healed by some unskilled healer from the village outside Ilphaesn. Had he not returned to Elaeavn and been found by Jessa...

He looked at her. "I can't risk you getting captured."

"That isn't your choice to make. I make my own decisions as you make yours."

Rsiran realized that by trying to decide for her, he was doing exactly what his father had done to him—treating her as if he *knew* what would happen.

He was not the Great Watcher.

Rsiran sighed. Up here, above the city with the wind gusting in his face, the air was cool and tasted of salt. The city looked clean and small. Everything seemed possible.

"I don't intend to do what Josun intended," he admitted to Jessa.

She tilted her head. Rsiran noticed how she paused to sniff at the flower in her shirt, and he bit back a smile as he wondered how she smelled anything with the wind blowing as it did.

"What do you intend to do?"

He had intended to do whatever it would take to keep his new friends safe, even if that meant turning himself in, turning Josun in, to the Elvraeth. But maybe he didn't have to sacrifice himself. Maybe there was another way.

"Something else. Something where he can't force us to help him again," he said, a plan forming in his mind.

Jessa waited, and then nodded as he told her his plan.

CHAPTER 32

RSIRAN GRIPPED JESSA'S HAND TIGHTLY AS THEY SLID. He had fixated on an open area outside the walls. He was aware of the warmth of her skin, the slight moisture on her palm, and the extra effort the Slide took.

They emerged on the outside the palace. He had not dared attempt a Slide from atop Krali Rock into the palace, preferring to see where he was Sliding before risking that. Rsiran was not certain he could do it anyway. Sliding to someplace new required some knowledge of where he would emerge. As he had never been here, the only place he could safely emerge would be the clearing near the dark stone building. That would leave them exposed and visible, especially to the Elvraeth where all were likely to be Sighted.

He looked up at the tall stone wall that circled the towers rising high overhead. Jessa squeezed his hand. A small alcove atop the narrow wall looked like an ideal place to emerge from the next Slide.

Once they emerged, Rsiran caught himself from teetering forward. Already the effort of the Sliding wore on him. How many more Slides could he manage? Alone, he suspected he could try a couple. With Jessa along?

Yet he would do as many as needed to keep her safe, even if it meant he could no longer stand. Even if it meant he was captured. *She* would be safe.

Moonlight filtered through the remnants of clouds and glimmered off the pale stone. A soft breeze gusted in from the sea, nothing like the heavy wind that buffeted them atop Krali. The wall circled the outer aspect of the palace more for camouflage than protection.

This close, he felt a renewed sense of anxiety.

What was he thinking, attempting to enter the palace? Looking from a distance the idea had seemed reasonable, but now that he was close enough to see the stone towers rising over his head and could almost feel a sense of energy around him, he did not know if he could go through with it.

"Rsiran?" Jessa whispered. "You don't have to do this."

He looked over at her. She crouched next to him on the wall, none of the anxiety he felt showing on her face. She had looked more scared simply standing atop Krali than she did here on the low wall. "This is the only way, Jessa. With what Josun wants…" He didn't know how to finish. "I… I don't know how else to keep you safe."

Somewhere in the darkness a cat yowled. Rsiran waited but another did not follow. He shivered. Bad luck.

She smiled. "Not alone. I'll help make sure you get where you need to go," she said and squeezed his hand. "You shouldn't linger here for long, though. I don't know much about the Elvraeth security. Few have ever tried to break into the palace."

"None are foolish enough."

But that wasn't true. Somehow, the boy had snuck into the palace, or so he had claimed. Sitting atop the wall, Rsiran wondered if that truly happened. He thought of him in the mines, remaining behind trapped in all that darkness by choice, and decided that he no longer mattered. Rsiran was free from that.

Jessa shrugged. "None have ever had the need."

Rsiran shifted on his feet and crouched low against the wall. Even crouching as he did, he felt exposed. The dark pants and shirt he wore left him outlined on the wall, visible to anyone inside who dared look out.

The wall positioned him so he could see much of the inner portion. The wide clearing stretched in front of him. The dark squat building near the middle looked more rounded on top up close than it had from afar. Even here he could not tell if it was made of lorcith. The rest of the palace was made of the same brown ivory stone as those of Elaeavn. The towers seemed to rise from the ground, as if grown. Windows worked into each tower, marking the various floors. Most were covered with silvery bars that crisscrossed the opening, as if to keep the Elvraeth from escaping.

There was a symmetry to the windows along the sides of the towers and the main portions of the palace, almost a pattern, but he could not quite place what it was.

A figure moved along the ground opposite them. He wore a dark cloak, either deep green or black, that barely moved as he walked. Pants were of the same dark color. A long sword shifted from beneath his cloak occasionally. He gripped a crossbow in his hand.

They had to hurry before this guard saw them. And if there was one, how could they be certain there weren't others?

Jessa pointed, and he nodded. "My Sight isn't that bad."

She grunted, as if telling him she couldn't be sure.

As Rsiran looked around for the place to Slide, he felt the presence of lorcith. It was a different sense than he had felt within the mines, less an awareness and sense of the ore calling than a presence designed to push them away.

At first, he thought it might be from the dark building, but as he shifted his focus, he realized that was not the case. The pressure seemed to come from everywhere around him.

Several moments passed before he realized it was the bars on the window that he felt.

Rsiran took a deep breath. Jessa was right; they shouldn't sit atop the wall much longer. Choosing one of the towers, he focused on the upper portion, imagining what the floor would look like inside the window. That should be far enough to get them into the palace but not so far that he overshot. If he was wrong—if the Slide took them inside a wall or worse, simply Sliding over the tower— then they might not survive. Rsiran was careful to maintain his focus.

Then he pressed into the Slide.

And was pushed back.

The sense was like a soft pressure against his whole body. Since he had learned how to Slide, always he had been able to navigate the space between the planes that allowed him to take a single step and travel. The only time he had failed was when Haern had held him in place. This felt different.

Rather than held in place, he simply couldn't step forward. Before they even tried, they would fail.

But the pressure was not completely unfamiliar. Something about it reminded him of the sense he had from the lorcith.

"Tell me what you see of the windows," he said, looking at the bars covering the windows.

She glanced at him and frowned. "You want to sneak in through one of the windows? I thought you were going to Slide into the palace."

"I'm not sure I can." The sensation, the pressure, was strange, but the longer he stood atop the wall, the more certain he became that it was the lorcith itself, as if the metal itself worked to exclude him.

"I don't understand. You got us here. You took me to the top of Krali. I can see the palace…"

"I'm not sure I understand either," he admitted. "I feel like there is something pushing against me, blocking me. I think it has to do with the windows."

Never before had lorcith prevented him from Sliding. He had even Slid huge nuggets from the mines. He had Slid with forged lorcith. He had forged lorcith with him *now*. But somehow it held him back.

And if he couldn't Slide into the palace, Josun would make certain they suffered.

Jessa looked toward the towers. "They're windows. Probably large enough for us to crawl through if we can make it across the clearing without being seen. The bars might make it difficult, but we could probably pry them off."

"What about the bars? What do you see there?"

She shrugged. "They are thick and silver. They look twisted, like a braided rope. Where they meet in the middle there is a small circle. I think something is engraved or printed on the circle, but I can't make it out." She sounded surprised by that fact.

"How are they attached to the stone?"

Jessa squinted, her brow furrowed in concentration. One hand went to touch the flower on her shirt, almost stroking the petals. "Can't tell that, either. Maybe they come out of the stone, almost like they are buried into the wall itself." She looked over at him. "That might make them a little hard to pry off."

Another of the dark-cloaked patrols moved across the inside of grounds. The guard patrolled on this side of the wall. Was it the same person or another?

He pulled Jessa back a step. Much closer, and they would have to Slide away.

"I don't know how I'm going to get inside."

Jessa smiled. "I told you that you would need me."

"If I can't get through the windows, then how will I get inside?"

She pointed toward the dark stone building in the center of the clearing. "The door."

Rsiran looked but didn't see any sign of a door on the dark stone. And starting from there meant they would have to somehow sneak through the entire palace to reach the council. Once inside the palace, he wasn't entirely sure how to find his way. He hoped the lorcith would guide him, but what if it didn't?

"Are you sure?"

Jessa sniffed softly. "I'll pretend you didn't say that," she said. "Center of the building. Can you get us down there?"

"Us?"

"If you have to sneak through the palace, you're taking me." Her tone allowed no argument.

Rsiran decided he could Slide her to safety once he knew where they were going.

The guard was drawing closer to where they crouched. Rsiran scanned the yard but didn't see any others. He focused on the area in front of the building. Pressing forward with his Slide, he didn't meet any resistance like he had earlier. Squeezing Jessa's hand, he took a small step and emerged outside the building.

The effort of the Slide made him lean forward as a wave of dizziness threatened to overcome him. Jessa pulled on his arm to keep him upright. As he stood, he noticed she had been right. A door was cut into the face of the building, barely more than a simple line around the frame marking its border. A silvery handle, clearly of lorcith and folded like his knives to make it look like the metal was liquid, was at waist high.

"Are you sure this connects to the towers?" he whispered.

Jessa shook her head. "Not sure about anything here."

She went to work, ducking down in front of the door. The folded leather lockpick set was already out, and she pulled out a slender rod and stuffed it into the lock.

Rsiran looked across the courtyard. Soft grass grew all around, green even in the light of the moon. The five towers loomed high overhead. Blue light glowed behind a few of the windows. He saw no sign of the guard who had been patrolling near them, but they needed to hurry. The demonstration would be over before they started if they got caught in the open.

Up close, the dark building behind him was not the same color as lorcith as he first thought. Rsiran set a hand on it and found the surface cool and smooth. A faint humming pulsated in the wall, as if coming from a great distance. The sense was familiar and reminded him of the way lorcith seemed to call on him when he had been in the mines, but different.

His breath caught. Not stone at all, but a form of lorcith, an alloy. But Rsiran did not think that possible.

Jessa stepped back and bumped into him. "Can't open it. There seems to be something in the lock."

Rsiran slipped past her and looked at the lock. Oblong and thin, more like a slit than any lock he had seen. A simple round hoop sat above it. On an impulse, he pulled one of his forged knives out of his pocket, the folds flowing and sliding in the light of the moon, and pushed it into the slit.

At first, there was resistance, but then the knife pushed past it, as if stabbing through a barrier, and he felt a soft click. The door opened.

Jessa glared at him. "How did you do that?" she whispered, moving past him and into the doorway.

Rsiran shrugged. "Guess you're not the only sneak."

She elbowed him in the side as she hurried into the building.

Before following her through the door, he pulled the knife out of the slit and stuffed it back into his pocket. Rsiran saw a shadow move and pulled the door closed behind him. It shut with a soft *click*.

"This better be part of the palace," he suggested as darkness surrounded him.

Not for the first time, he was thankful Jessa was with him. Without her Sight, he was not sure that he would even be inside already. Now that he was, he would need her Sight to guide him. Hopefully Haern's vision wasn't accurate.

The darkness around him was complete, somehow seeming even darker than what he had experienced in the mines. There seemed to be a distant sound, like a humming or a buzzing, and he felt a soft thrumming through the soles of his boots that vibrated through him.

Jessa grabbed his hand, and he gripped her tightly.

She led him forward. "Stairs."

The sudden sound almost made him jump. With her warning, he dragged his feet forward, feeling his way along the smooth floor. Everything about it reminded him of being in the mines. Even the sense of lorcith around him was like the mines.

"How will we find where we're going?" Jessa asked after they had taken several dozen steps.

"I'll feel it," He hadn't told her that part yet.

"What do you mean?"

He pulled on her hand as they walked and pulled her closer so he could feel her next to him. She smelled like the flower on her shirt, sweet and perfumed but with a hint of spice. Even scared as he was, Rsiran couldn't help but smile.

"Lorcith is different from other metals."

"You've said that."

He shook his head, wishing he could see her face as she could see his. Always he felt so limited with his ability. "It is different for me," he told her. "I can… feel lorcith. That is how I did so well in the mines. That is why I was attacked."

"You can *feel* it?"

"I don't know why."

"I've never heard of such an ability."

They had stopped walking. The air around them was still, nothing like the steady breathing in the mines, and almost heavy, as if damp. A hint of the bitterness of lorcith hung in the air, but Rsiran didn't know if that was from the knives he carried or the palace. Somewhere far ahead came a faint blue glow, so dim that it was almost imagined.

"I think my father has it too. Maybe all the master smiths." Rsiran shrugged. If only his father had told him more about *that* gift rather than chastising him for his ability to Slide.

Jessa grunted. "Must be why it is so hard to get an apprenticeship with the guild."

"Probably why my father stuck with me as long as he did," Rsiran realized. But if that was true, why had he wanted him to suppress it?

It was an ability that Rsiran did not fear. Other than nearly getting him killed in the mines, the ability to feel the lorcith, to hear its call, had guided his hands, helped with his forgings.

"Do you feel it now?"

Rsiran tried to feel for the lorcith sword the Elvraeth Josun had stolen from him. Only now was he starting to understand why he had felt it that night in the warehouse, the same reason he felt the knife when Haern had attacked him. The same reason he felt the knives in his pockets and tucked into his pants. He could feel lorcith he'd forged more strongly than any other. Perhaps something more, but he was almost afraid to test that.

"Not yet."

Jessa sighed softly. "This won't work if it's not here. You might have to do what he asked after all. Deal with Josun later."

"You think poisoning the council would be easier? You think helping a rebellion better?" he whispered.

Jessa led him forward, toward the soft blue glow. Only as it became brighter did she answer. "Easier than losing you." Rsiran felt her shiver.

"You could always leave," he suggested.

"What—sneak back out the door? Try to get across the lawn without one of the guards seeing me and firing at me? Climbing that wall to escape back into Elaeavn, only to sit and worry about what was happening to you? No. I stay with you."

"Thank—"

He cut off as she jerked him back against the wall and clapped a hand across his mouth.

Down the passageway, there was movement, shadows sliding in front of the faint blue light. As he watched, one of the shadows moved closer.

"Rsiran—" Jessa whispered so softly that he almost didn't hear it.

Hopefully whoever was coming toward them was not a Listener. Of course, if they were Elvraeth, they probably were.

Jessa kept a hand on his mouth and backed him down the hall.

He could see nothing, forced to trust whatever Jessa saw. His heart hammered. A Listener would know they were there simply by the sound of his breathing, the sound of his heartbeat. Someone Sighted wouldn't even need that.

And they were in the Elvraeth palace. Everyone here had abilities stronger than his.

Rsiran felt completely out of his league. Why had he thought he could simply Slide into the palace?

Something loomed closer. Next to him, Jessa's breathing quickened. Her hand slicked with sweat. She pushed him more urgently, unmindful of the noise.

Rsiran heard footsteps clearly now, padding softly but quickly along the stone of the corridor. They had been seen.

Haern was right. They would be captured. Exiled. Forgotten.

Shame came over him. Had he really thought he could break into the palace? Had he really thought he could out maneuver one of the Elvraeth?

Another thought hit him, one that should not bother him but still did.

Now his father would know that he was right. Would likely revel in the fact that he had been right to sentence him to the mines. Now he would not have to ever worry about remembering his son.

At best, Rsiran would be Forgotten. But there were other punishments, those he couldn't Slide from. What if he were sentenced to death?

But not Jessa. He would not let that happen to Jessa. He would prove Haern wrong in that.

They needed to move. Even unable to see anything, he knew they needed to move.

There was only one thing he could do, but he had to be able to Slide.

Here, trapped in this building made of some strange lorcith alloy, he didn't know if he could manage, but Rsiran knew he had to try.

Pressing his eyes closed, he focused, straining for lorcith, searching for one of his forgings. Footsteps came closer. Jessa squeezed his hand painfully. It had to be now.

Fear coursing through him seemed to give him strength.

There was a distant sense, but one still within the palace, like a pinprick in his mind.

Rsiran latched on, uncertain what he felt but daring to risk it.

Then he stepped into a Slide.

CHAPTER 33

THE SLIDE WAS MORE DIFFICULT than any he had ever attempted. It felt like his skin tore as he pushed through a space too small. He held the distant sense firm in his mind. As he Slid, it became sharper, almost painful. Rather than the sense of rapid movement he was accustomed to feeling, he felt an oozing that reminded him of the folded metal knives. There was no sound of wind whipping through his ears. Only a heavy muted feeling.

And then it was over.

He staggered forward, caught only by Jessa still gripping his hand tightly. Had she felt the Slide the same way he had, felt the slow oozing, the pain of it as it almost tore the flesh of his body, or had it felt no different to her?

He took a few ragged breaths and finally opened his eyes.

He expected darkness, but instead saw a soft blue light. The light was similar to the orange glow deep within the mines that he had grown to hate, the never-ending persistence of the lantern, the unchanging lighting giving him no sense of night or day.

He looked over to Jessa. Her mouth was open as if to scream, but she shut it when she saw him looking.

"Are you okay?" he asked. His voice was hoarse. Fatigue unlike any he had ever felt swept through him, as if he had spent a full day hammering at the forge with the heavy mallet. Even if they managed to secure the sword and leave the poison behind as planned, he was not sure he could get them back out.

They would be trapped.

She shook her head. "They will know we're here," she answered.

"Maybe. But not who is here. Not yet, at least." Rsiran didn't know how much longer that would be the case. And even if they found him, could he explain to the council? Would they believe?

She closed her eyes and nodded. "We must hurry."

He nodded, afraid to tell her it probably wouldn't matter.

The room was unlike any he had ever seen. Well appointed, a plush carpet lined the floor, a luxury not found in most of the homes in Elaeavn. A blue lantern, the shape more ornate than the one in the mines, sat atop a table. Rsiran was not surprised to see that it was made of lorcith. Had he more time, he suspected he could even determine the smith who made it.

Next to the lantern, a small ledger lay open, tight lettering written upon the page in what appeared to be code. Or, Rsiran wondered, it might be a language unique to the Elvraeth. A small carafe of wine stood on the table next to the ledger. On either side of a large hearth sat a pair of chairs. A smokeless flame burned in the hearth, giving unnecessary warmth to the room. A tapestry that appeared to be some sort of map, *Elaeavn* marked along the bottom corner, hung opposite the fireplace.

Rsiran was shocked to see this wasn't even sleeping quarters, but some sort of sitting room. A pair of large wooden doors along the far wall likely opened into the sleeping quarters. This room alone was nearly as large as his parents' house.

Jessa flipped through the ledger and then slipped it into her pocket. She shot him a hard look. "If we make it out."

"What if we're caught?" Stealing would only add to their punishment.

"They have more than enough reason to banish us already."

She said the words with a strength he found surprising. Not that he would underestimate Jessa.

"Where is it?" she whispered.

Rsiran looked around. He *felt* the presence of the sword nearby. Now that they were in these rooms—likely the rooms of the Elvraeth Josun—he knew the sword was near. He'd thought that the Slide would carry him to it, using it as an anchor of sorts. That it hadn't meant he had nearly lost control of the Slide. He had risked not only himself, but Jessa.

He shivered at the thought.

"I'm not sure. Maybe through there?" He pointed toward the door.

Jessa approached the entry carefully and tried the handle. If any would be locked, it would be the door leading into this room. She twisted and pulled it open.

If Rsiran thought the sitting room ornate, the room on the other side was more impressive still. A massive bed took up most of the far wall. Nearly a dozen pillows stretched across the end of it. Luxurious linens in greens and blues covered the bed. Several tapestries hung along the wall, each made in different styles and only one seeming as if it was from Elaeavn. That tapestry caught Rsiran's eye.

It looked to be a depiction of the Great Watcher sitting in the heavens, staring down at a sea of green. Within that sea of green, several bluish dots glowed. Rsiran felt a sense of movement around the dots, almost like bodies writhing between the green and blue. The effect was nauseating, and he tore his eyes away.

Along the back of the room was a tall chest. Another lantern sat atop the chest, the light glowing with a softer blue. A basin rested near the chest, clear water pooled inside it. A small faucet jutted out of the wall near the basin. Rsiran was not surprised that the Elvraeth had somehow piped water up to their rooms. Such as thing was incredibly expensive. For the Elvraeth, it seemed no cost was spared.

Resting near the basin was the long sword.

Rsiran felt it pull at him. The hilt atop the sword was new, jeweled as he had seen in the warehouse. He wondered if Josun had put an edge on the blade as well.

"There," he said, and turned to Jessa.

Rsiran froze.

Josun stood next to Jessa, his hand over her mouth, her eyes wide and angry. A knife pushed up against her ribs, the tip poking through the fabric of her shirt. The flower that had been tucked into her shirt had fallen to the ground. Lavender petals spread across the ground, crushed under his boot.

"I see you have completed your demonstration," Josun said.

All hint of friendliness had faded from his voice. In its place was a sense of violence, of barely controlled rage. His hand shifted, and the knife pushed deeper into Jessa's side. Blood staining her shirt spread out in a dark smear.

"You stole my sword," Rsiran said. Josun's words sunk in. "Wait… what did you say?"

A wicked smile spread across his face. "The demonstration is complete."

A sinking feeling settled into Rsiran. "No. We didn't do your poisoning. We didn't come to help with your rebellion. I came for my sword…"

A confused expression twisted Josun's face. "Rebellion? Ah, so little you know, Lareth." He pressed the tip of the knife into Jessa's ribs and she stiffened. "And perhaps I'm mistaken. Perhaps the council was not poisoned tonight." He smiled again. "But if you did not, then I must wonder who else did? Who else carries whistle dust with them?"

"Whistle dust?" That must be the powder he had tucked into his pocket.

"Quite impressive how you managed to reach each member of the council in the same night. Only a master thief would manage that feat. Or another with a different ability." He offered Rsiran a wolfish smile with a flash of teeth. "So maybe this will be a *quiet* rebellion as another council forms."

Rsiran pulled the pouch out of his pocket. "We haven't done anything to the council. We came to collect the sword. Nothing more."

Jessa stood stiffly, terror in her eyes.

Rsiran wondered if he could Slide fast enough to help her. If it was anything like the last time he tried to Slide, he didn't think it likely. Then he had been helped by his awareness of the sword, not fully knowing what it was that aided him.

"I'm not certain others will view it in the same light. Seers have a hard time with visions involving Sliding. All they will have seen is that someone Slid into the council chambers, and poisoned those within. Once they find you, they will not care to look for any other possibilities." His wolfish smile widened. "It is unfortunate that I must dispose of her. She really *is* a skilled sneak." He leered at Jessa. "Perhaps she could be useful in other ways."

Jessa started to struggle, but the knife pressed against her again, and blood stained her shirt.

Rsiran shook his head, unable to believe what was happening. Why was he using them? What had they done to him?

"You?" Josun asked. "You think this is about you?"

Rsiran realized that he could Read him, even with his barriers in place. The thought made him shiver. "They're your family."

Josun tilted his head in acknowledgment. "Among the Elvraeth, everyone is family. Blood means little." He leaned forward. "But... you were more right than you realized. This is but a beginning."

The words seemed designed to pierce Rsiran. Josun was Reading him again.

Steeling his barriers, he strained to block Josun from his mind. Darkness clouded over Josun's face, and Rsiran hoped he was successful. If only he had Brusus's ability. If only he could Push Josun.

"Is that why you wanted Brusus?"

The grin changed and he nodded. "Brusus made an excellent pawn. So much about using him was perfect. Child of a Forgotten. Skills and bloodline so that he could reach the palace." He paused. "But then I met you."

Rsiran took a quick breath, suddenly understanding when Josun would have learned of the sword. "You were there when Brusus brought me to the warehouse."

Josun laughed. "So easy to Read. And with a gift that I could use much more easily than Brusus's."

"You sent the sellsword."

Josun shrugged. "I had to motivate you. And now here you are. I had not expected your sneak whore to lead you back to the warehouse. I thought I would have to do more work to draw you in." He pushed harder on the knife pressing into Jessa's flesh. "And now that I have her... Perhaps the Great Watcher indeed smiles on me."

As he spoke, he flickered forward toward the sword resting along the wall near the basin, moving in a blur, as if simply disappearing and reappearing.

Josun could Slide.

Rsiran suddenly understood the smooth way he moved in the warehouse. Josun Slid constantly. Openly. Something Rsiran had never dared.

Josun's smile widened when he emerged from the Slide. He wore no signs of fatigue, none of the weakness that Rsiran felt whenever he Slid.

"For a long time, I didn't think I would meet another with this ability. Even the first of my family found Sliding rare. And dangerous. Seers couldn't pierce the haze Sliding creates." His dark smile twisted. "That was why they wanted to eradicate it. First, by claiming it a dark ability. And when that didn't work, through breeding. They never eliminated it completely." He smiled widely. "And now? Here I am. Still able to Slide. And then I found you. Such a useful skill for many reasons."

Jessa struggled a moment, and Josun tightened his grip on her. The tip of the knife pressed into her side, and she gasped. Blood dripped onto the floor, no longer content to simply stain her shirt. Torn lavender flower petals clung to her boots, stuck with mud and blood.

Rsiran took a step forward, and Josun shook his head. "I think it best that you stay where you are. The tchalit should be here soon, seeing as I signaled for them."

"Why are you doing this?" Rsiran asked.

Josun tilted his head as if debating whether to answer. "Perhaps Brusus would have sent a better message. Child of a Forgotten avenging another Forgotten, but you created more opportunity, Lareth, more deniability. And with my other plans, I couldn't have someone else Sliding through the city."

Jessa started to struggle to remain upright, sagging against Josun. He held her up with a look of disgust on his face. Rsiran would have to do something soon if he wanted to save her. He began thinking of how he could Slide to her and then out of the palace again. It would only work if he *could* Slide. Inside the palace he was not certain he could.

Josun smiled at him, as if Reading him. "I do not think you are skilled enough to save her." Josun shook his head. "I must admit it fascinates me that even in spite of the council's attempt to eradicate Sliding, it still surfaces. Perhaps that is proof that the Great Watcher truly intends for us to have the ability." He laughed, as if he had made a joke. "Now. How should we finish off your friend? Now that I think about it, she will pose more questions. I can always find another whore." He shoved on the knife. "I could claim self-defense. Tell the tchalit that she attacked me. Or whistle dust? I believe you have enough in that pouch for what I would need. Really, though, it takes only a little once it reaches the blood."

Josun tilted his head as if considering the options. "Perhaps the whistle dust is best. Deflects any attention from me. We could simply claim that you intended to leave her to take the blame. No one will mourn the loss of another Lower Town whore."

Jessa stiffened again at the comment.

Rsiran resisted the urge to throw himself at Josun. "She is not a whore."

Josun frowned. "Oh? Did she not seduce you into attacking the council? Did she not convince you that the demonstration must be done to save Brusus? Had you only known what she would lead you into. Ah, well, perhaps that is not entirely true. It was *you* after all who brought her here. I must admit to curiosity about that. I knew you would be able to breach the palace, but did not expect you to make it so far. And to think I had taken such care to direct the tchalit toward where you would need to enter. Tell me—how did you reach my quarters?"

Jessa's eyes faded, the color draining from them and her face turning a soft pale as she wilted in Josun's grip. How much longer did she have?

He needed to reach her, but anything he did, Josun would anticipate. Rsiran needed to block Josun from Reading him.

With sudden inspiration, he created an image of lorcith in his mind, using that image to reinforce the barriers in his mind. There was a sense of pressure and then release.

"Interesting," Josun said softly.

Rsiran knew then that he could not Read him. Maybe he would have enough time to act. Enough time to save Jessa. Perhaps even escape.

"It was the sword."

With the barriers in his mind now strong, he felt the sword pulling on him, felt the knives in his pocket, felt a distant awareness of the lorcith all around him.

"Ah, that. I must admit it is skillfully made. A shame it will disappear with the girl."

"It's mine. You stole it."

"Stole? How can I steal what was already mine?"

"Yours?" Rsiran readied himself for what he needed to do, readied himself to Slide to Jessa, hoping that it worked.

"With lorcith taken from the mines of Ilphaesn. The mines are owned by the family."

"The sword is mine," Rsiran repeated.

He felt anger growing inside him. Josun wanted to use them. Planned on killing Jessa. And would leave Rsiran with the blame. What did it matter what else he did now? If he could not save Jessa, then everything else meant nothing.

"I think it adds nicely to my collection."

Rage swelled through Rsiran. The lorcith blade thrummed against his awareness, pulling at him. In response, he *pulled* back.

He didn't know who was more surprised when the sword flew toward him. Rsiran caught it by the hilt.

Josun recovered quickly. "Interesting. An ability I have not witnessed. Could it be new? Had we more time, I would try to study you, but as you are about to be taken into custody…"

The Elvraeth tilted his head, as if listening. A moment later, a soft pounding came from the outer chamber. The guards—tchalit he called them—had arrived.

Rsiran had to act now.

He Slid toward Josun, sword outstretched, his other hand reaching toward Jessa. The Slide happened smoothly, none of the grating he felt when he had Slid Jessa into the room. The only thing he felt was fatigue.

Josun seemed to have anticipated his move and Slid away, emerging near the door, still holding Jessa. "Once they reach this room, you will find it much more difficult to Slide."

Rsiran's heart fluttered. Josun was right. He wasn't skilled enough at Sliding to save Jessa that way. He needed something else.

The lorcith thrummed against him, almost calling to him. Could he *push* as he had *pulled* the sword? Was that what happened with Haern?

Jessa nearly fell from Josun's grip, and he pressed the knife deeper. Rsiran had to try.

Feeling one of the knives tucked into his pocket, he focused on the blade, focused on the lorcith. All he needed was a moment. Long enough to startle Josun so that he could rescue Jessa and attempt to get away. The knife seemed to answer, as if understanding.

And then he *pushed* on it.

The blade tore through his pants and whistled through the air. When Josun saw the knife coming at him it was too late. Though he tried to Slide away, he failed. The knife sank into his thigh. Blood bloomed around the blade.

He dropped Jessa to grab at the dagger.

The door slammed open. Rsiran recognized the man who entered, the thin man from the mines, the scar on his head drawing Rsiran's eyes.

Why would he be here? And with Josun...

There was no time for answers, not if he wanted to save Jessa.

Sliding to her, he emerged only long enough to snatch her hand. Then he Slid.

Rsiran focused on a distant sense, using the awareness of lorcith outside of the palace as an anchor, the same as he had done when Sliding to the sword in the first place. He didn't know what it was he felt, only that the awareness was there, distant and faint, but enough to hold onto, to pull himself along as he Slid.

Something held onto him, as if he were pushing out through an opening too small to fit. He nearly screamed at the pressure. He held tightly to Jessa, afraid to let go, not certain what would happen to her if he lost his grip. Would she be lost in some place between?

The effort was intense, more than he had ever exerted in a single Slide.

For a moment, he feared he could not do it, that he would be stuck within, left to whatever fate Josun intended, Jessa bleeding from the knife wound to her side.

The thought of watching her die gave him strength.

He pressed into the Slide with every ounce of energy he could muster, pushing with every bit of anger and rage, of frustration at what his father had done to him, every bit of hope and friendship and—possibly—love that he felt from Jessa.

He would not let Haern's vision come true. He would not fail her.

And then something popped.

Rsiran emerged, Jessa's hand held tightly.

Fatigue overwhelmed him, and he stumbled. His vision was dark, blackened by the effort that his Slide had taken. He smelled something smoky and familiar. The muffled sound of voices came as if from a great distance. Jessa's hand cradled his.

He went down. Blackness overcame him.

He did not know if the effort of the Slide had been too much, if he had pushed too hard.

Rsiran didn't care. As long as he saved Jessa, it didn't matter.

CHAPTER 34

WHEN HE FINALLY CAME BACK AROUND, Haern looked down at him. His scar seemed to gleam.

"Haern?"

Haern leaned over him. His face was tight and clean, and his breath smelled of tobanash. His blue shirt was buttoned to the collar and was tucked into brown pants made of some loose fitting material. Rsiran searched quickly for a weapon, instinctively sensing for lorcith. He felt a collection of his knives somewhere nearby and the sword somewhere else, but nothing on Haern.

Now completely awake, he looked around. He lay on a small mat on the ground in Della's main room. A fire burned in the hearth nearby. Incense gave off a spicy scent and helped clear his head. Light filtered through windows at the front of the house, and shifting shadows played across the walls.

The sudden fear he felt at seeing Haern cleared his mind completely. Glancing around, he saw a foldout cot set near the fireplace.

Jessa's dark hair splayed off the side. At first he wasn't certain she still lived, but her chest rose and fell steadily. He heaved a sigh of relief and sagged back onto the cot.

"You ignored my advice," Haern said.

Rsiran made a point of looking at him. "You tried to kill me." Had he more energy, the anger he felt at seeing Haern would simmer over into his words.

Surprisingly, Haern smiled. "Did I?"

"Didn't you?"

Rsiran remembered the experience clearly, remembered the way the knife slashed toward him, almost as if in slow motion, his awareness of the lorcith in the blade he forged surging, the sudden urge to *push* the knife away from him… and the way the knife suddenly flung away.

Haern only shrugged. "I seem to have a different recollection. I could See only glimpses of you, but what I saw gave me enough to know which way you needed to be pushed." He said the last with a smile.

"So you weren't trying to kill me?" Rsiran asked, incredulous. The malice on Haern's face had seemed so real.

"Your dying would have shifted my vision for Jessa," he said unapologetically. "She would have failed to enter the palace and return to help Brusus. The possibility of her success was minimal without help." Haern narrowed eyes that suddenly flared a deep green. "I could not See what would happen when she returned to Brusus. Perhaps Brusus would have failed or she would have helped him succeed. Either way, they would have been farther along whatever pathway the Elvraeth had set them upon. I Saw nothing but darkness in that direction."

Rsiran was not sure he followed what Haern was saying. "You wanted me to try to break into the palace on my own? That's why you tried to kill me?"

Haern smiled. "Much like with Josun, I See very little of you, Rsir-an. Something of your ability masks you. But I Saw that without any prompting, you might not learn of your other talent, the one I Saw to be essential to your success." He watched Rsiran's face. "On your own, you would have been captured. Possibly killed as well. And then Bru-sus and Jessa would have been left alone for a while. I suspect eventual-ly Josun would have turned his attention back to Brusus." He frowned. "There is something about Brusus that he wants."

"You knew Jessa would not stay behind. You knew she would force me to include her."

Rsiran wondered how clear Haern's visions were. How much did he know about what would happen? Did they have any choice in what they did?

"I knew you needed to try to leave her behind. Beyond that…" He shrugged. "I could not See. Only," he paused and looked from Rsiran to Jessa, "that it was one of the few paths where the possibility of suc-cess existed."

Rsiran shook his head and closed his eyes. "I still don't understand."

"In time you will."

"Is Jessa…"

"She will be fine. The knife penetrated deeply, but the wound was not tainted. Della healed her. Rest is all she needs now."

Rsiran rolled over to look at her again. From where he lay on the floor, all he could see clearly was her hair and the outline of her body in the flickering light of the fire. The near paralyzing fear he had felt at the possibility of losing her had surprised him. Had Josun counted on that?

"What of Josun?" Rsiran asked.

A different voice answered. "About that."

Rsiran turned. Brusus stood in the doorway, a large binding wrapped around his shirtless torso. Blood stained the bandages. His face was haggard and drawn. Lines wrinkled his forehead that had not been there before. Streaks of thicker white shot through his otherwise dark hair. He held the sword Rsiran had taken back from Josun.

He leaned against the doorway and looked relaxed, but the strain on his face told Rsiran all he needed to know about Brusus's strength.

"You were foolish to attempt what you did," Brusus said.

Rsiran nodded. Only a complete fool would try to break into the palace. "I didn't think I had any other choice."

Brusus snorted. "Haven't I shown you anything? There is always another choice." He took a deep breath and started to sigh, but a fit of coughing interrupted him. After it passed, he shook his head. "Took nearly dying for me to see what Josun wanted. Had I only trusted Haern, I might have known sooner."

"Known what?" Rsiran asked.

"I told you there were layers to him," Brusus said. "To Josun, partly this was a game. A game he played where you were one of the pieces. Where *I* was one of the pieces." He shook his head. "As far as Josun is concerned, the Elvraeth struggle for position, for power. Most of his life has been spent trying to position himself higher within the family."

Rsiran frowned and opened his mouth to comment on Brusus's birth, but held back the comment when Brusus shot him a look. "He's not the only one, Brusus," Rsiran said, thinking of the man from the mines. Others were involved in Josun's rebellion. And they knew of him, and what he could do. They would come for him. "There are others in this rebellion."

"Perhaps," Brusus said. "But you—and I—were but a piece," Brusus said. "A distraction. Perhaps bait. All intended as part of his larger plan."

Rsiran considered arguing with Brusus, that Josun hadn't known of Rsiran until he had gone to the warehouse. But was that even true?

If Josun spoke in layers, what prevented even that from being the truth? And saying something would only risk revealing what he knew of Brusus, and he wasn't sure Brusus wanted the rest of the group to know that secret.

"He wanted to blame me for what he planned. He knew I could Slide."

Haern and Brusus looked at each other. Brusus had a worried look on his face.

"Did he say what he planned?" Brusus asked.

Rsiran shook his head. He licked dry lips, wishing for water. "He wanted me to poison members of the council. I thought he wanted power, but that wasn't all."

Brusus closed his eyes for a moment. "His demonstration. Power for him, but revenge might be a more accurate term. His sister was exiled. I only learned about it after..." Brusus sighed. "I've been more a fool than I realized."

Exiled—Forgotten—just like Brusus's mother.

"Brusus," Rsiran started, fearing what he needed to say next. "He will come after us again. The Elvraeth will come for us."

"No. He will not. *They* will not."

Rsiran turned back. "What do you mean?"

It was Haern who answered. "From what I can See, Josun is dead."

"Dead?" The knife had only been a distraction, a way to get Jessa away from him. And it had only been his leg.

"I can tell from your face that you didn't know," Brusus said.

"He was alive when we... I... Slid us away."

"And it was Josun who hurt Jessa?" Haern asked. He made no effort to hide the heat in his voice.

Rsiran nodded. "I pushed one of the knives at him. Hit his leg."

Brusus looked down at Rsiran's pants. "Explains how your pants were damaged. Della fretted over a possible injury, fearing poisoning, especially with that..."

Rsiran didn't hear the rest, checking his pocket. A long slice had been torn in his pants where the knife had been pushed out through the fabric. When he brought his hand back it was coated in a white powder. The whistle dust Josun had given him. Had the knife been stained with it?

He wiped it on his pants, afraid of what it might do to him.

"You know what that is?" Brusus asked.

Rsiran nodded. "I was to have mixed it into the council's drinks, but that wasn't what he really wanted to do with it."

Brusus and Haern shared another knowing look. "Painful. Possibly fatal," Haern suggested.

"Whistle dust is a brutal poison and a horrible way to die." Della came out from behind Brusus and pressed a hand on his dressings before nodding to herself. She appeared even older than the last time, weak and frail.

Rsiran hated that he had contributed to her change.

"Don't you go fretting about me, young man," she said. "Without you, I think this one might have gotten in deeper than what even he could manage." Della pointed to Brusus.

Not for the first time, Della seemed to have Read his thoughts.

"Whistle dust in liquid is caustic," she went on. "Throat damage, vomiting, general achiness. A slow death. In the bloodstream, the effect is different. Painful burning. Excessive bleeding. Immediate death."

Rsiran rubbed his hand on his pants again, not wanting to be touching the whistle dust any longer than he needed to. "His sister was really exiled?" he asked.

Brusus frowned. "Several months ago. I haven't managed to learn why."

"Does it matter?" Della asked him. "Now that he's gone, does any of it matter?"

Brusus looked over to her with a strange expression on his face.

Haern watched him, eyes flaring green, and then shook his head once. "Let it go, Brusus. All I See is darkness."

Once, Rsiran wouldn't have been able to believe the Elvraeth exiled their own family. But had his father done anything so different? Hadn't he exiled Rsiran from his family?

The only difference was that he didn't want revenge.

"But if one of the Elvraeth is dead?" Rsiran had worried about getting caught with the sword. Was it known that he Slid to the palace and killed Josun? And what of the rest of the rebellion? If the thin man from the mine had been involved, there was more to it than even Brusus realized.

But maybe with Josun dying, it didn't matter.

"I haven't heard anything from the palace," Brusus said.

"And you would have?" Rsiran asked, hope seeping into his voice.

"Yes."

Rsiran stared up at the ceiling. The tchalit hadn't seen him. And if Josun were dead, maybe the thin man wouldn't come after him. Doing so would only reveal what Josun intended. Maybe they really *were* safe.

"You don't understand the Elvraeth, Rsiran." Della set her hand on his shoulder. "This would not be the first time something like this happened. This might have gone deeper than most, but…" She closed her eyes, and took a few short breaths. "Be reassured Brusus has heard nothing."

Brusus watched Della and sighed deeply. Then he pulled his cloak around his shoulders and walked out of Della's house.

Haern watched him leave and finally shrugged, pushing himself up to follow Brusus.

"Thank you, Rsiran," Della said when they were gone.

He shook his head. "For what?"

She met his eyes. "For simply being. Without you, I fear what would have happened to Brusus. What still might happen if he gets the opportunity. It eats at him what could have been, if not for something he had no control over. We must keep him safe from himself. And his past."

As she tottered past, she squeezed his shoulder. Warmth spread out from where she touched him. Then she left, disappearing into the back room.

Rsiran managed to stand. He felt weak but better than he expected. Stranger too. Everyone knew about his abilities now. There was no hiding what he was, what he could do. And no one seemed upset that he could Slide or that he listened to the call of the lorcith.

He walked over to Jessa and crouched next to her cot, resting with his hand twined in hers, feeling the warmth of the fire spread over him.

Epilogue

Rsiran sat at the small table in the back of the Wretched Barth. Soft flute music drifted from the front of the tavern, the melody strangely familiar. The scent of roasted fish came from the kitchen and mingled with the warm ale in front of him on the rough wooden table. His latest forging, a long handled spoon with intricate work along the handle, rested in front of him.

"What am I supposed to do with this?" Brusus asked. His pale green eyes stared at the spoon, drifting to Rsiran's mark, as his finger rubbed the carvings. Dark hair slicked back from his face, more grey than it had been, but a vibrancy had returned to his cheeks.

"I thought you would sell it," Rsiran suggested.

Haern laughed, the long scar on his face twitching. Setting down the dice cup, he picked up the spoon and twirled it in his fingers. Seeing the way he twisted the utensil made Rsiran remembered how well he handled the knife. Haern's eyes flared deeper green for a moment, and then he smiled. "I See someone enjoying this, Brusus. Seems to me there is value in that."

With that, he dipped the spoon into the bowl of stew in front of him.

"Bah!" Brusus winced as he reached past Haern and grabbed the dice. "You know I can't sell spoons. And you wouldn't let me sell that sword."

Rsiran smiled. The sword was well hidden this time. Safe. The smithy locked so that only Jessa could enter. Other than someone Sliding in, the building was inaccessible.

"Certainly not this spoon," Haern said, in between bites.

Rsiran still wasn't sure how he felt about Haern. The man *had* tried to kill him, regardless of what he had Seen. But because of what Haern had done, Rsiran had learned something else about himself. And Jessa lived.

Brusus grabbed at the spoon, and Haern held it overhead, away from him, splashing stew across the table.

"Damn, Haern!" Jessa said, returning to the table with a fresh mug of ale.

Today, she had a pale blue flower tucked into her shirt, the color so much like the lanterns in the palace. Rsiran didn't think that anyone else saw how she sniffed the flower as she sat. After all these weeks, she showed no signs of the night they'd broken into the palace. The wound had healed fully, not poisoned like Brusus's injury. And his had finally healed fully.

Jessa grabbed the spoon from Haern's hand and slammed it on the table. "Now I'm definitely going to take your money."

Rsiran smiled. After everything he had been through, it felt good to be sitting in the Barth with the only real family he had ever known. Jessa looked at Rsiran, her eyes smiling. Her hand slipped under the table and rested on his knee. He closed his fingers over hers and squeezed gently.

He still didn't know what would happen to him, or whether there really was more to the rebellion than Josun. Rsiran hadn't shared his concern about the man he had seen before Sliding from the palace, and so far, there had been no reason to. The Elvraeth had not come looking for someone who had Slid into the palace. Perhaps Della was right—that Elvraeth infighting made it not unusual for such an attack. And though his father had promised to turn him in to the constables, he doubted they would even know where to look. The missing lorcith in his father's shop—and the fact that the boy had been mining it at night—and whatever Josun had really planned should bother him, but right now he didn't let it. That was for later. Perhaps one day he would Slide to Ilphaesn, steal the boy from the mines. Rsiran could show him other ways to listen to the music of the lorcith.

Right now, he didn't care if the rest of Elaeavn came crashing down around him. He had nearly lost Jessa, lost Brusus, and nearly lost his own life. It was time to start enjoying the gifts he had been given. Including his ability, which it turned out, wasn't so dark after all. How could it be, when it had saved everyone who mattered?

DK HOLMBERG is a full time writer living in rural Minnesota with his wife, two kids, two dogs, two cats, and thankfully no other animals. Somehow he manages to find time for writing.

To see other books and read more, please go to www.dkholmberg.com

Follow me on twitter: @dkholmberg

Word-of-mouth is crucial for any author to succeed and how books are discovered. If you enjoyed the book, please consider leaving a review online at your favorite bookseller or Goodreads, even if it's only a line or two; it would make all the difference and would be very much appreciated.

OTHERS AVAILABLE BY DK HOLMBERG

The Dark Ability

The Dark Ability
The Heartstone Blade
The Tower of Venass
Blood of the Watcher

The Cloud Warrior Saga

Chased by Fire
Bound by Fire
Changed by Fire
Fortress of Fire
Forged in Fire
Serpent of Fire
Servant of Fire

The Painter Mage

Shifted Agony
Arcane Mark
Painter for Hire
Stolen Compass

The Lost Garden

Keeper of the Forest
The Desolate Bond
Keeper of Light

Made in the USA
Middletown, DE
12 June 2016